Praise for the Violet Brewster Mystery Series

'An entertaining and engaging cosy mystery set against a beautiful backdrop'
Clare Chase

'A thoroughly enjoyable and suspenseful story'
Daily Mail

'Jane Bettany delivers cosy with a dash of sass – thoroughly enjoyable and utterly irresistible'
Peter Boland

'A murder mystery with a blossoming romance . . . what more could one ask for? Delicious!'
Katie Gayle

'Completely compelling from the get-go, I didn't want to put it down! Brilliant cosy mystery at its most charming best.'
Jonathan Whitelaw

'A perfect cosy mystery with an engaging cast of characters and a beautifully drawn setting'
Roz Watkins

'Violet Brewster is everything you could want in an amateur sleuth: empathetic, determined, and ruthless in her quest for truth . . . A must read!'
Charlotte Baker

'A book to put to the top of your "must read now" pile!'
C.L. Peache

JANE BETTANY is the author of the DI Isabel Blood crime novels, set in the fictional Derbyshire town of Bainbridge, and the cosy crime series featuring amateur sleuth Violet Brewster, which is also set in Derbyshire.

Jane's debut novel – *In Cold Blood* – won the 2019 Gransnet and HQ writing competition, which was for women writers over the age of 40 who had written a novel with a protagonist in the same age range.

Before turning to novel writing, Jane had been writing short stories and non-fiction articles for over twenty years, many of which have appeared in women's magazines, literary magazines, newspapers and online.

Jane has an MA in Creative Writing and lives in Derby.

Also by Jane Bettany

The Violet Brewster Mystery Series
Murder in Merrywell
Murder at the Book Festival
Murder at Maple Grange

The Detective Isabel Blood Series
In Cold Blood
Without a Trace
Last Seen Alive

Murder on Bluebell Hill

JANE BETTANY

ONE PLACE. MANY STORIES

HQ
An imprint of HarperCollins*Publisher*s Ltd
1 London Bridge Street
London SE1 9GF

www.harpercollins.co.uk

HarperCollins*Publishers*
Macken House, 39/40 Mayor Street Upper,
Dublin 1 D01 C9W8
This edition 2025

1
First published in Great Britain by HQ,
an imprint of HarperCollinsPublishers Ltd 2025

ISBN: 9780008714802

Printed and bound in the UK using 100% Renewable
Electricity by CPI Group (UK) Ltd

MIX
Paper | Supporting
responsible forestry
FSC™ C007454

For more information visit: www.harpercollins.co.uk/green

For my dad
Alan McCaig
(1933–1977)
Remembered with love and gratitude

Chapter 1

'I'm not enjoying this,' Fiona Nash said, as she spread another layer of clotted cream onto the half-eaten scone she held in her left hand. 'It's very dry, verging on stale. At least a day old, if not two.'

Violet Brewster watched her friend take another bite. 'It can't be that bad, Fi, otherwise you wouldn't be eating it.'

Fiona shrugged. 'Just doing my duty,' she said. 'Checking out the opposition.'

It was Sunday afternoon, and they were sitting in *The Cuckoo's Boot* – the newly opened tearoom at Bluebell Hill Garden Centre. It was a bright and airy space, furnished with on-trend mismatched tables and chairs, and adorned with several large and vigorous-looking house plants. Violet tilted her head, admiring the high ceiling, subtle décor and relaxed ambience of the place.

'It's just a café, Violet,' Fiona said. 'No need to look quite so overawed.'

Violet reset her expression to neutral, reminding herself that she wasn't there to have fun. The new tearoom would be a direct competitor to Fiona's own café in Merrywell's popular shopping village. Violet's mission today was to help scrutinise the rival venue and assess its potential impact on the Nash family business, *Books, Bakes and Cakes* (known locally as the BBC).

Fiona was eating her scone in the Cornish fashion, the clotted cream atop a generous layer of strawberry jam. Violet had chosen the Devon method, putting the jam on last.

'My scone tastes fine,' she said, licking away a smudge of cream that had found its way onto her top lip. 'Not as good as one of yours, obviously . . . but not bad.'

Fiona gave an exasperated sigh and reached for the teapot. 'This isn't up to much, either,' she said, as she began to pour. 'Too weak.'

'Try stirring the pot,' said Violet, thinking her friend was being overly critical.

Dabbing the corners of her mouth with a napkin, Violet leaned back to observe the customers in the crowded tearoom. There were several familiar faces from the village, including council leader Judith Talbot, and her long-suffering husband, Andrew; Violet's next-door neighbour, Toby Naylor; and avid dog lover Lisa Wenham, who was sitting in the corner looking slightly out of place, her scruffy waxed coat draped on the back of her chair and a shopping bag wedged between her feet. At the table by the window were Nigel and Sandra Slingsby, who were slowly devouring the contents of a three-tier cake stand.

'Nigel and Sandra are over there,' Violet said, smiling at the couple and giving them a friendly wave.

Fiona glanced briefly in their direction. 'Traitors,' she muttered, as she removed the teapot lid and squeezed the teabags between two spoons. 'I expected a few people from the village to be here, but not Nigel and Sandra. They're two of my most loyal customers – at least, I thought they were.'

'I'm sure they're only here to satisfy their curiosity,' Violet said. 'They're checking the place out, just like we are.'

'They could have done that with a cup of coffee,' Fiona said. 'But I see they've ordered a full afternoon tea.'

Violet smiled. 'Now, now, Fiona. Don't be grumpy. It's a free country. People can eat whatever they want, *wherever* they want. Having said that, I don't for one minute think the Slingsbys are going to shift their allegiance. They'll be back at your place before you know it. *Books, Bakes and Cakes* is a minute's walk from their house, whereas the garden centre's a good mile south of the village. They'll have had to get their car out to come here.'

Fiona topped up her tea, which looked a much better colour following her ministrations with the teabags. 'Fair point, but you can't deny this tearoom will syphon off business from my café. People are fickle. When a fancy new venue opens up, customers have a tendency to jump ship.'

'The locals are bound to be intrigued – but just you wait and see – they'll visit this place once or twice, and then hotfoot it back to the BBC.' Violet smiled. 'Let's face it, your baked goods are irresistible.'

'And freshly made *every* day,' Fiona said, prodding the half-eaten scone on the plate in front of her. 'Seriously though, I can't afford to lose trade, even temporarily. Times are tough. Profit margins are being squeezed. The last thing I need is a mass exodus from the café.'

Violet gave a sympathetic nod. 'That's one of the drawbacks of running your own business,' she said. 'There's always someone waiting in the wings, hoping to steal your customers. In my opinion, the smartest way to deal with that threat is to outshine the competition – and you do that consistently, Fi. Everyone knows your bakery and café are the best for miles around.'

Fiona preened, basking in the compliment. 'Thanks, I appreciate the sentiment – although it won't stop me worrying. I'm sure Clayton Spenbeck would feel the same if I started selling plants.'

'Talk of the devil,' Violet said, as she peered over Fiona's left shoulder. 'Clayton's just walked through the door.'

She watched as the garden centre owner positioned himself in front of the tearoom counter and began a furtive conversation with the tall, dark-haired woman who was standing behind it. Clayton's prominent front teeth, the white streak in his thick head of brown hair, and his quick, darting movements put Violet

3

in mind of a startled chipmunk.

'He hasn't seen me, has he?' Fiona said, keeping her head down.

'It doesn't look like it, but so what if he has? You're not doing anything wrong.'

'I know, but still . . . it's awkward. He'll guess why I'm here.'

'Even if he does, Clayton's far too polite to say anything. He seems like a nice bloke.'

'I used to think so, until he started poaching my customers. I don't understand why he's done it. It's not as if he needs the extra business this tearoom will bring. The garden centre on its own must be making a small fortune. Why does he have to be greedy?'

'To be fair to the man, we have no idea what his financial circumstances are,' Violet said. 'For all we know, his business could be struggling. This isn't the only garden centre in Derbyshire that's opened a café to attract more customers. Maybe Clayton's trying to keep pace with *his* competitors.'

Fiona crinkled her nose. 'Eleven years ago, when Eric and I first moved to Merrywell, this was a small but very well-respected nursery, specialising in hanging baskets and bedding plants. Dennis Spenbeck was in charge back then – Clayton's dad. Dennis had a genuine passion for horticulture, and his plant knowledge was second to none. *He* was never interested in diversifying. He was content to keep things simple.'

'Yes, well . . . the world's changed a lot in the last decade,' said Violet. 'And Clayton's obviously ambitious.'

'It's not Clayton who's ambitious – it's his wife,' Fiona said. 'Hilary will be behind all this – you mark my words. When Dennis died two years ago, she couldn't wait to turn the nursery into a fully-fledged garden centre. I suspect the Spenbecks sell more patio furniture and scented candles these days than they do plants.'

'They're only doing what similar businesses are doing.'

'I accept that,' Fiona said. 'And my gripe isn't with them expanding the garden centre. What I object to is them moseying in on the café trade.'

Over at the front counter, Clayton Spenbeck was surveying his new domain. When he spotted Violet, he raised a hand and set off in her direction.

'Uh-oh,' Violet said. 'Don't look now, but Clayton's heading this way.'

'Ladies,' he said, smiling nervously as he approached. 'Violet. Fiona. How lovely to see you both.'

Fiona forced a lukewarm smile.

'Hi, Clayton,' Violet said. 'How are you?'

'Very well,' he replied. 'Very well indeed. The last few months have been hectic, of course . . . what with getting things ready for the spring season and setting up the tearoom.'

'You've obviously been working hard,' Violet said. 'I love what you've done with this place. It looks great. And *The Cuckoo's Boot* . . . what a fabulous name!'

'Hilary chose it,' he said. 'Apparently, cuckoo's boot is another name for bluebell, so she thought it was rather apt.'

Fiona folded her arms and said nothing.

'Actually, Violet,' Clayton said, 'I'm glad I've bumped into you. Hilary and I want to produce a short, promotional film for the tearoom . . . something we can put on our website and social media channels. Is that something you'd be interested in helping us with?'

Violet smiled instinctively, buoyed by the prospect of a new commission for her videography business, *The Memory Box*.

'Definitely,' she replied. Then, noticing the disgruntled expression on Fiona's face, added: 'I mean . . . possibly. It sounds interesting, certainly. Perhaps we could arrange to meet?'

'Perfect,' Clayton said. 'I don't suppose you're free in the morning?'

'Erm . . . let me check,' Violet said, conscious that Fiona was now pouting sullenly.

As Violet opened up the calendar app on her phone, Clayton turned to address a young male waiter who was delivering two cappuccinos to the next table. 'Tuck your shirt in, Simon, lad,' he said. 'You're letting the side down.'

The young man in question rolled his eyes and pushed back his floppy blond fringe. 'Why do I have to wear this thing anyway?' he said. 'It's way too formal. Why can't I just wear a T-shirt?'

'Because we want our staff to look smart,' said Clayton. 'That's why we provide uniforms. If you want to keep your job, you'll have to comply with the dress code. If you don't like the rules, I know plenty of others who'd be more than willing to take your place.'

The young waiter snickered defiantly, but nevertheless tucked the errant shirt tail back into the waistband of his trousers.

'If that's how they speak to their staff, they're going to have a fast turnover of workers,' Fiona whispered.

Violet shot her a look, shushing her with a frown. 'You're in luck, Clayton,' she said, as she consulted her online diary. 'I'm free all morning tomorrow. What time would you like to meet?'

'Would you be able to come here early, before we open up?' Clayton said, turning his back to the waiter. 'Say, eight o'clock? Hilary and I will walk you through the site and explain what we have in mind.'

'OK,' Violet replied. 'I'll see you at eight.'

'Great. If you drive round to the loading area, I'll leave the back gate open and you can let yourself in.' He fished around in his pocket and handed over a business card. 'That's my phone number. Call me when you arrive and I'll come and find you.'

'Thanks,' Violet said. 'I'll see you tomorrow then.'

As Clayton drifted away to greet his other customers, Fiona maintained an uncharacteristic silence.

'You're very quiet, Fi,' Violet said, as she sipped her tea.

'What's that old adage? *If you can't say something nice, you're better off saying nothing at all.*'

Violet curled her toes, feeling instantly remorseful. Fiona's peeved tone suggested Clayton wasn't the only one getting the silent treatment.

'I take it you don't approve of me making a promotional film for the Spenbecks?' she said, deciding to address the 'elephant in the room'.

Fiona shrugged. 'I can't say I'm over the moon with the idea, but business is business . . . I understand that. Like I said, times are tough. I don't suppose you're in a position to turn work down either.'

Violet's business, *The Memory Box*, was almost a year old, and although things had gone remarkably well during the first twelve months of trading, she knew the situation could change in an instant. All it would take was a few fallow weeks. Fiona was absolutely right – she couldn't afford to turn work away – but that didn't prevent a feeling of guilt from burrowing its way into the pit of her stomach. *The Cuckoo's Boot* tearoom was already threatening Fiona's livelihood, and a snazzy promotional film was likely to draw even more customers away from the BBC. If Violet took on this project, she'd be faced with an agonising conflict of loyalty. Chastising herself inwardly, she realised she should never have agreed to meet the Spenbecks.

'Enquiries have been worryingly thin on the ground at *The Memory Box* over the last few weeks,' Violet said. 'But if working for the Spenbecks is going to put our friendship in jeopardy, I'll tell them to find someone else for the job.'

Fiona reached across the table and patted Violet's hand. 'Don't be silly. You must do whatever it takes to make your business thrive. Besides, if you don't make the film, someone else will. Whether I like it or not, this tearoom is here to stay, and I'd like to think at least one of us will benefit from its presence in the village.'

Violet smiled gratefully.

'And don't worry about our friendship,' Fiona added. 'I'm not going to fall out with you over this, or anything else. You and I are pals for life now, Violet. You're stuck with me, whether you like it or not.'

'That's good to know. Your friendship means the world to me.'

'I know it does, but so does your business,' Fiona said. 'Please . . . ignore my grouchiness. Honestly, Violet, I don't have a problem with you working for the Spenbecks. I'm more than familiar with the highs and lows of being self-employed, and this is a great opportunity. You should grab it with both hands.'

Violet sighed. 'I must confess, since I took Molly on as my assistant, I've felt under more pressure than ever to make a go of *The Memory Box*.'

Fiona smiled. 'That's another downside to running a business . . . having employees. They add an extra layer of responsibility. Then again, when they're as efficient as Molly, it's a price worth paying. Seriously, Violet . . . if the Spenbecks want you to make their film, you should do it.'

'What will *you* do?' Violet asked. 'How are you going to fight back against your new competitor?'

Fiona rubbed her cheeks, pondering the question. 'I haven't worked out a strategy yet. For now, I'll carry on doing what I've been doing for the last eleven years. I'll provide a friendly service in the bakery and café, and sell top-quality produce. Hopefully, that will be enough to ensure our survival.' She pushed away the plate containing what remained of her scone. 'Now . . . can we talk about something else? In fact . . . let's get out of here.'

Violet nodded and drained her teacup. As she stood up and pulled on her jacket, the main door swung open again and, this time, Hilary Spenbeck entered the tearoom. She stood with her hands behind her back, gazing at the packed tables and beaming happily. And then she spotted Fiona, and the smile dissolved. Arching her eyebrows, Hilary marched over to their table.

'Fiona?' she said, as she approached. 'What are you doing here?'

Fiona smiled politely and nodded towards the used crockery on the table. 'I would have thought that was self-evident,' she said, as she zipped up her coat. 'Violet and I have been treating ourselves to a cup of tea and a scone, although I'm not sure the word "treat" applies to *everything* we've eaten.'

Violet cringed. What on earth was Fiona playing at? So much for *let's get out of here.*

'What's that supposed to mean?' Hilary said, narrowing her eyes.

Violet braced herself, anticipating a spat.

'Nothing. It doesn't matter,' Fiona said. Having thrown down the gauntlet, she sounded immediately regretful and reluctant to be drawn into an argument. 'Come on, Violet. Let's go.'

Hilary barred their way. 'Not so fast,' she said. 'If you're unhappy with something you've eaten, I'd like to hear about it. If you've got something to say, I'd prefer you say it to my face, rather than spreading gossip around the village and damaging the tearoom's reputation.'

Fiona frowned. 'I wouldn't do that,' she said. 'I'll admit I'm not thrilled about you opening a café and poaching my customers, but I'd never disrespect you or your business.'

'Forgive me if I don't believe you,' Hilary said. 'I'm not stupid. I know exactly why you're here. You're spying, aren't you? Giving us the once-over.'

Thankfully, Fiona had the good sense to keep quiet. A denial would have been futile, as well as a downright lie.

'So, what's the plan?' Hilary asked. 'Are you going to leave a bad review on Google? Is that it?'

'Of course not,' Fiona said. 'Don't be ridiculous.'

'We came here to satisfy our curiosity, that's all,' Violet said, hoping to calm the waters. 'The tearoom is lovely, Hilary. You've done a great job.'

Blanking Violet completely, Hilary continued to glare at Fiona with a look sharp enough to cut diamonds.

'If there was a problem with what you've eaten, I want to know about it.'

Fiona released a sigh. 'If you're genuinely looking for feedback,

I'd say the scone wasn't very fresh. The jam was nice though, and the clotted cream.'

Silence had descended in the tearoom. The young waiter hovered close by. Over by the till, Clayton Spenbeck and the dark-haired woman behind the counter were exchanging nervous glances. Even the clatter of cutlery had ceased, and the faces of the people around them were all turned in their direction. Everyone was alert and listening in.

'Those scones were delivered this morning,' Hilary said, her crisp tone both defensive and argumentative.

'In that case,' said Fiona, 'I suggest you change your supplier.'

Hilary stepped closer, thrusting out her chin. 'I know your game, Fiona Nash. You want to ruin our reputation before we've even begun. I've dealt with people like you before. You're all smiles until someone steps on your toes, and then your claws come out.'

'So you admit you're stepping on my toes?' Fiona said. 'You accept that this tearoom will impact negatively on my café?'

'Poppycock,' said Hilary. 'There are more than enough customers to go round. All we're doing is providing people with more choice. We had absolutely no problem getting planning permission for the tearoom, so there's obviously demand for our services locally. Who knows, we may diversify even further in the future. Variety is the spice of life . . . isn't that what they say?'

'Perhaps I should adopt a similar approach with my business,' Fiona said, her snappy tone at odds with her easy-going nature. 'What would you say if I started selling plants?'

'I'd say, go ahead. Knock yourself out. It wouldn't bother me in the slightest. Clayton and I are used to competition. During the bedding plant season, the supermarket in Matlock always undercuts us on price – but you know what? People come here anyway, because our plants are bigger and better.'

'You're absolutely right,' Fiona said. 'Quality always sells, and my scones are top notch – far better than the ones you sell here. I don't think there's any need for me to worry, do you?'

Violet tugged Fiona's arm. 'Let's make a move, shall we?' she said. Then, under her breath, she added: 'Come on, Fiona. You're causing a scene.'

'*Scene?*' Fiona said, in her loudest voice. 'It's not me making a scene.'

It was at that point that Clayton Spenbeck bustled over, his hands clasped together.

'Hilary. Ladies. Let's not fall out. We're all local business owners . . . let's try and be a little more supportive of one another, yes? I'm sorry if you didn't enjoy your scone, Fiona. Obviously, in the circumstances, there's no need for you to pay the bill. Have this one on the house.'

Hilary twisted around and stared at her husband, her face red with fury. 'Keep out of this, Clayton. I deal with customer service issues, not you. Not that this *is* a customer service issue – it's just someone being peevish, petty and spiteful.'

Fiona threw her head back and laughed. 'If that's your idea of good customer service, Hilary, then I have absolutely nothing to worry about.'

She tried to brush past the Spenbecks, but Hilary stood her ground. Fiona began to inch around her adversary, using an elbow to gently ease her out of the way.

Violet wasn't sure how it happened, but seconds later, Hilary lurched sideways and fell to the floor, landing in an ungainly heap.

Had she lost her footing and overbalanced, or had she stumbled on purpose to cast Fiona in a bad light? Fiona had barely touched Hilary . . . She definitely hadn't pushed her over. But from the furious expression on Hilary Spenbeck's face, it was clear she didn't agree.

Chapter 2

Even though Fiona had done nothing wrong, she looked utterly contrite.

'Oh my goodness, Hilary. Are you OK?' She held out a hand. 'Here, let me help you up.'

Hilary slapped Fiona's arm away. 'You've done yourself no favours here today,' she said, as she leaned on a chair and pulled herself back onto her feet. 'Everyone in this room has witnessed the callous way you knocked me down.'

'Knocked you down?' Fiona said, remaining remarkably calm despite the unfounded claim against her. 'That's nonsense, and you know it. Violence isn't in my nature. Anyone who knows me can vouch for that.'

Clayton placed a comforting hand on his wife's arm. 'Steady on now, Hilary,' he said. 'I'm sure Fiona didn't mean you any harm.'

'Trust you to take her side,' Hilary replied, shrugging away his hand. 'That's you all over, isn't it? You see the good in everyone except me.'

Clayton looked crestfallen, but determined. 'Don't make a fuss, love. It's not good for business. You stumbled. It's not as if you've hurt yourself.'

'Clayton's right,' Fiona said. 'I barely made contact with you, let alone pushed you over. However, I'll admit I was being impatient. I should have waited for you to step aside rather than try to barge past. If I'm in any way to blame for your fall, then I apologise unreservedly. Come on, Hilary, let's call a truce and put this whole unfortunate incident behind us, shall we?'

'Easy for you to say,' Hilary replied. 'You're not the one who ended up on the floor.'

Fiona flexed her shoulders. 'Look . . . I am genuinely sorry,' she said, 'but if you're not willing to accept my apology, it's probably best if I leave. If you'll excuse me, I'll get going.'

'Make sure you pay your bill first,' Hilary said, jabbing a finger in Fiona's direction. 'And when you've done that, get out and don't bother coming back. You're not welcome here.'

Fiona opened her mouth to deliver a parting shot, but obviously thought better of it. With her lips pressed firmly together, she settled the bill at the counter and then followed Violet out of the tearoom.

'Well, that was embarrassing,' Fiona said, once they were outside in the fresh air. 'I didn't push her, Violet. Honestly, I didn't.'

'You don't need to convince me,' Violet replied. 'I know you wouldn't do that.'

'Do you think she fell over on purpose to make me look bad?'

'I'm not sure, but I'd say she was definitely playing to the crowd. If I were you, I'd keep out of Hilary's way for a while, until things have calmed down.'

'Believe me, if I never cross paths with the woman again it won't bother me. I'd heard she could be confrontational, but today's the first time I've had to put that rumour to the test. Trust me, I won't get on the wrong side of Hilary Spenbeck a second time. I'll be keeping well out of her way from now on.'

'You probably shouldn't have complained about the scone,' Violet said, thinking that Fiona was at least partly to blame for the altercation. 'What was it you said in there? *If you can't say something nice, you're better off saying nothing at all?'*

Fiona looked sheepish. 'It's not my fault the woman can't handle a bit of constructive criticism.'

'Was it constructive though?' Violet said. 'It sounded to me like you were winding her up.'

Fiona released a guilty sigh. 'Maybe I was. I suppose I felt angry and envious . . . sitting there in that pristine tearoom . . . but you're right, I shouldn't have let my temper get the better of me. I'll ring Hilary later and apologise properly. I'd buy her some flowers, but sending a bouquet to someone who runs a garden centre would be like sending coals to Newcastle.'

'Ordinarily, I'd suggest you bake her a cake by way of apology,' Violet said. 'But given the nature of your complaint, I can't imagine that would go down too well either.'

Fiona smiled. 'A phone call it is then,' she said. 'I'll wait until tomorrow . . . give her some time to cool off. Hopefully, that will be the end of the matter.'

Despite her plans to make another apology, a look of defiance still blazed in Fiona's eyes.

'Come on,' Violet said, linking arms with her friend. 'We'd better go.'

They skirted a cheerful display of yellow and purple pansies and headed towards the middle of the garden centre, where a huge selection of herbs and rockery plants were set out on low, wooden stands. Violet ran her hand across the top of a lemon balm plant, releasing its heady, citrus scent.

'Is there anything you need while we're here?' Fiona asked. 'If you fancy a browse, we shouldn't let Hilary Spenbeck's foul temper drive us away.'

'I am a sucker for herbs,' Violet said, picking up a variegated thyme and breathing in its pungent aroma. 'But please, don't let me buy any more mint. I've got four different varieties in my garden already.'

Fiona wandered off to the right, pausing to inspect a collection of stone garden ornaments, which were arranged alongside an impressive array of tinkling water features.

'This is nice,' Fiona said, as she picked up a glazed and rather comical-looking owl.

'It's very quirky,' said Violet, smiling at the owl's enormous eyes. 'Are you going to buy it?'

'Depends how much it is,' Fiona replied. 'It's well made and very heavy, but I wouldn't want to pay more than twenty quid for it.' She held the owl above her head to check the price label that was stuck to the base. 'Wow! £39.99. The Spenbecks sure know how to charge.'

'It does seem quite pricey,' Violet said.

'Too expensive for me, anyway,' Fiona said, as she returned the ornament to the display stand.

'Shall we go then, before we're tempted to buy something else?'

'Actually . . .' Fiona grinned. 'I think I'll pay a visit on my way out. I don't know if it's the sound of the water features, or whether that weak tea has gone straight through me. Either way, I need to call in at the lavvy before we head back to the village.'

Laughing, Violet waved goodbye to the stony-faced owl and followed Fiona into the garden centre's retail building, where the customer toilets were located.

Chapter 3

Violet was already awake when her alarm went off at six-thirty the following morning. A strong gale had blown into the Peak District overnight, and her sleep had been disturbed by the sound of the wind pummelling the thick stone walls of her cottage.

Having had a night to reflect on things, she had come to a firm decision: she was going to decline the Spenbecks' offer of work. Fiona may have given the project her blessing, but deep down, Violet knew it would be a mistake to take the job. Whenever she accepted a commission, she dedicated herself to delivering the best possible outcome for her client. If she agreed to produce a film for the Spenbecks, professional pride would compel her to make it a good one, something that would achieve its objective. But at what cost? An enticing promotional campaign for *The Cuckoo's Boot* tearoom would inevitably tempt even more customers away from *Books, Bakes and Cakes*, and that was something Violet didn't want on her conscience.

The truth was, she bitterly regretted having visited the tearoom at all. If she hadn't run into Clayton, he might never have followed through on his idea to make a video. The project might have been overlooked, and eventually forgotten about altogether.

Thankfully, Violet was under no contractual obligation.

The only thing she *had* committed to was a meeting with the Spenbecks. In order to maintain her reputation for reliability, she would turn up for that meeting and offer them the benefit of her professional advice. Then, and only then, would she tell them that, unfortunately, she was too busy to take on the job (even if the opposite was true).

At quarter to eight, Violet locked the back door of Greengage Cottage and got into her car. The gale was still raging, and twigs from the wind-ravaged trees were strewn across the main road through the village. Overhead, the pigeon-grey sky looked ominous, threatening rain.

Violet drove out of Merrywell, past St Luke's church, and turned right. The village roads were quiet at this time of day, and as the lane to the garden centre was well away from the main 'A' road, she didn't expect to encounter much in the way of traffic.

After a quarter of a mile, she pulled up at a crossroads and turned left into Dale Lane. Another vehicle was approaching in the distance and, as it got closer, Violet realised it was Fiona's grey Nissan. She waved cheerily, but Fiona looked straight ahead.

She must be preoccupied, Violet thought. *Otherwise she would have waved back . . . wouldn't she?*

As the car whizzed past, Violet waved more vigorously – but Fiona drove on, seemingly oblivious.

Through the rear-view mirror, Violet watched the Nissan turn right at the crossroads, towards Merrywell. Why wasn't Fiona at work? She was usually at *Books, Bakes and Cakes* by seven o'clock at the latest, baking fresh supplies of bread, pies, cakes and pastries for the day ahead. What was she doing driving through the back roads of Merrywell at this time in the morning? And, more importantly, why hadn't she waved back?

Violet told herself that Fiona must have been daydreaming, her mind on something else. She had simply failed to recognise Violet's car . . . that's all it was. She tried not to dwell on the alternative explanation – that despite all her protestations to the contrary, Fiona was feeling aggrieved, annoyed that Violet was pressing ahead with her meeting at the garden centre.

Pushing aside her misgivings, Violet drove on to her destination. Clayton had asked her to use the goods entrance, so she circumnavigated the main customer car park and made her way along the bumpy access road, climbing steadily uphill, until she was behind the main cluster of buildings. She parked her car at the rear gate and stepped out into the wind.

This part of Bluebell Hill Garden Centre was at a higher elevation than the rest of the site, and from here Violet could see the roof of the new café, as well as the four enormous polytunnels that stood alongside it. Closer to, directly behind the rear gate, was the huge retail building – a bland grey structure that was surrounded on three sides by plants, outdoor furniture, and horticultural accessories.

Behind her, further up Bluebell Hill and set slightly to one side of the garden centre complex, was Highfield House, the Spenbeck family home. According to Fiona, the property had originally belonged to Dennis Spenbeck, but it had passed to Clayton and Hilary on his death, along with the plant nursery business. The architectural style of Highfield House was typical of the Twenties or Thirties and, unusually for the area, it was built of red brick, rather than the local stone. Its tall chimneys and generous (if somewhat boxy) proportions suggested it had been designed as a spacious family home – although Clayton and Hilary were its only occupants now.

A gust of wind ruffled Violet's hair as she lifted the heavy latch of the gate – which, as promised, had been left unlocked. Once she was safely inside, she pulled her phone from her bag and rang Clayton.

'Good morning,' he said, when he answered. 'Is that Violet?'
'It is,' she said. 'I've just arrived. Where shall I meet you?'
'I'm down at the lower end of the garden centre at the moment,

where the fruit trees are,' Clayton said, sounding harassed and slightly breathless. 'The wind knocked quite a few of them over last night, so I've been setting things to rights. Let's hope the gale eases off soon, otherwise I'll have to do it all over again later.'

'Do you need any help?' Violet said. 'I'll come and find you, if you like, and lend a hand.'

'No . . . no, you're OK. I've finished here now. I'll walk back in your direction and we can meet in the middle. Hilary's around somewhere . . . She went to check on the bedding plants, I think. That part of the garden centre is a lot more sheltered so, hopefully, it won't have sustained too much damage.'

'Fingers crossed,' Violet said. 'I'll see you both in a minute then.'

She ended the call, returned her phone to her bag, and followed the path around the side of the retail unit, out of the wind. Alongside the building was a long line of exotic shrubs that had sustained a few casualties overnight. A hardy palm and a couple of yuccas were lying on their sides at the end of the row, compost spilling onto the concrete pathway. Violet stopped to restore the pots to an upright position, and then continued on her way.

She'd never really considered how the vagaries of the weather might impact on the running of a garden centre. Heavy winds and rain, or a late unexpected frost had the potential to wreak havoc and cause thousands of pounds' worth of damage. Presumably, the tender young bedding plants were housed in the polytunnels until any serious risk of frost had passed, but it wasn't always possible to pre-empt an unexpected storm or an unseasonable cold spell.

As she emerged into the main part of the garden centre and skirted a low stand of perennials, Violet rehearsed in her head what she would say to the Spenbecks. She was confident Clayton would respect her decision, and not take it personally – but if Hilary was as volatile as Fiona had suggested, *she* was likely to take umbrage. What's more, Hilary was shrewd enough to work out the real reason Violet didn't want the job. Hilary would lay the blame firmly at Fiona's door, thus scuppering any possibility of a reconciliation between the two café owners.

As she walked, Violet admired a collection of budding wisterias and clematis in tall, carefully staked pots that had, miraculously, escaped the ravages of the weather. When she got to the middle section, where the herbs and alpine plants were located, she looked around for the Spenbecks. She'd expected to run into at least one of them by now, but there was no sign of either Clayton or Hilary. Should she stay here and wait, or go looking for them?

She decided to stop and call Clayton again, to let him know where she was. But as she unzipped her bag and felt for her phone, a terrible cry sliced through the garden centre from somewhere close by. Violet froze, listening as the cry changed to a long, guttural wail.

With her breath coming in ragged gasps and her heart hammering against her ribcage, she tuned in to the sound to assess where it was coming from. Pushing aside her own fears, she hurried towards it.

As the wail subsided to a keening groan, she became aware of another background noise – the gentle flow of running water.

The tranquil, burbling cascades of the garden centre's water fountains were designed to induce a feeling of relaxation and wellbeing, but the scene set out in front of them was like a tableau from a Greek tragedy – and the antithesis of all that was calming.

Clayton Spenbeck was lying on the ground, prostrated in grief, cradling his wife in his arms.

Violet's stomach churned as she edged towards him.

Hilary's lifeless eyes were staring up at the murky sky. Her right arm was limp, and the tips of her fingers were trailing in the rippling bowl of a water feature. Clayton let out another heart-wrenching cry and looked up, his eyes red-rimmed and wild-looking.

'I . . . I can't wake her up,' he said, his face crumpling as he began to sob.

Violet's legs wobbled as she stepped closer.

Clayton was clasping his wife's body, shaking her gently in a futile attempt to revive her. 'What am I going to do?' he wept, turning his desolate face in Violet's direction. 'I think . . . I think she's dead.'

Chapter 4

Violet felt the blood drain from her face as she was hit by a sudden wave of nausea. *Come on, Violet*, she told herself. *Don't be a wuss. Pull yourself together, and whatever you do, don't pass out.*

Taking a deep breath to steady her nerves, she stepped forward and placed a comforting hand on Clayton's shoulder.

'What happened?' she said.

'I . . . I don't know,' he replied, sounding utterly bereft. 'I was on my way to meet you and I found her here . . . She was lying face down in the fountain.' He inclined his head to the right, towards the shallow bowl of a nearby water feature.

Violet crouched down and, with shaking fingers, checked Hilary's upturned wrist for a pulse. Finding no sign of a heartbeat, she placed her hand on Hilary's neck and tried again, searching desperately for even the faintest flicker of life.

'It's no good,' Clayton said, his voice aquiver. 'I've already checked. I think she's gone.'

'I don't understand.' Violet stood up and placed her hands on her head. The adrenaline thrumming through her body was making it difficult for her to remain calm. 'Why? How? Was Hilary ill? Did she have some sort of medical condition?'

Clayton let out a whimper. 'No, she's always been the picture of good health. I can't believe this is happening. Finding her like this . . . it feels unreal.' He placed a hand over his mouth and gave a slow, disbelieving shake of his head.

'I'm so, so sorry, Clayton,' Violet said, giving his shoulder a gentle rub. 'Have you let anyone know what's happened? Have you dialled 999?'

Clayton ran a forefinger along Hilary's cheekbone, gently stroking her pallid skin. 'What's the point?' he said. 'It's too late. There's nothing anyone can do for her now.'

'I think we should still call the emergency services and explain what's happened,' Violet said, giving Clayton's arm a bolstering squeeze. 'Hilary has died suddenly and unexpectedly. The paramedics will need to confirm her death, and I expect the police will want to pay a routine visit as well.'

'The police?' Clayton said, staring up at her with a dazed expression. 'Will they have to get involved? This was an accident of some sort, surely? She's obviously tripped over.' He nodded to the right, where one of Hilary's shoes lay on its side, having presumably become dislodged during a fall. 'Look . . . there's a mark on her head . . . here.'

Clayton touched the skin above Hilary's left eyebrow, and Violet leaned in to get a better look. 'You're right about there being a cut on her forehead, but she's also got an injury on the back of her head. You said you found her lying face down?'

Clayton nodded. 'She must have toppled over into the water fountain and banged her head . . . she probably knocked herself out.'

'That would account for the cut on her forehead, but not the wound on the back of her head,' Violet said. 'It's hard to fall over and hit your head on both sides simultaneously.'

Clayton raised his left hand and clenched his fingers, as if grasping for an answer to this apparent anomaly. 'I'm sorry . . . I don't . . . I can't think clearly. But you're right . . . of course you are. We should ring the police. Will you make the call? Please,

Violet. I'm not sure I'd know what to say.'

Instinctively, Violet took a step back. The last thing she wanted to do was get mixed up in another police investigation, but what choice did she have? It was obvious from the way Clayton was trembling that he was in no fit state to make the call.

Reluctantly, she pulled her phone from her pocket and dialled 999.

Chapter 5

The emergency call handler arranged for an ambulance to be dispatched, and promised that two uniformed police officers would arrive within twenty minutes.

As they waited, the wind continued to whistle through the garden centre and, from somewhere close by, Violet heard the clatter of another pot blowing over.

'Why don't we go and sit in your office?' she suggested, shivering inside her coat.

Clayton clutched his wife's body, rocking her gently back and forth. 'I'd prefer to stay here,' he said. 'I can't bear the thought of leaving Hilary on her own.'

'I can understand that,' Violet said. 'But there really is nothing more you can do for her. And when the police and the paramedics arrive, they'll want us out of the way so that they can get on and do their jobs. Come on, Clayton. You've had a terrible shock. Let's get you inside where it's warm.'

She slipped a hand around his arm and gripped the damp sleeve of his coat, urging him to his feet. He let go of Hilary and stood up grudgingly, and then allowed himself to be steered towards his office, which was located directly inside the main door of the retail building.

'Is there anyone you'd like me to call?' Violet said, as she settled him at his desk. 'A relative, or a friend?'

Clayton shook his head.

'An employee then?' she said, determined to summon help from someone who knew the grief-stricken Clayton better than she did. 'Someone who can take charge, here at the garden centre? You obviously won't be able to open up today. Is there anyone who can put up signs for the public and let staff members know not to come in?'

Clayton rubbed his eyes. 'You could contact Anne Burridge, I suppose.'

'All right. How do I get hold of her?'

He retrieved his phone and, with trembling fingers, managed to locate Anne's number in his list of contacts.

'Here,' he said, handing it over. 'She manages the tearoom, so she hasn't worked here long – but Hilary and I have been friends with Anne for years. I can trust her to do the right thing.'

Violet wondered if Anne Burridge was the dark-haired woman who'd been serving at the tearoom counter the previous day. Using Clayton's phone, she called the number and waited for an answer.

'Morning, Clay!' Anne's chirpy, sing-song voice boomed into Violet's ear, jarring with the solemn mood. 'I'm on Dale Lane at the mo . . . the signal's rubbish here, so we're likely to get cut off. I'll be there in a few minutes anyway . . . Shall we talk then? I'll make us a nice cappuccino when I arrive. What do you—'

'This isn't Clayton.' Violet cut in, bringing an end to Anne's prattle. 'I'm using his phone.'

An abrupt silence descended. Just as Violet was beginning to think the signal *had* been lost, Anne spoke again.

'Is Clayton all right?' she said. 'Has something happened to him?'

'He's fine,' Violet said, hearing Anne's gasp of relief on the other end of the line. 'But unfortunately, the same can't be said of Hilary. There's been an accident. She died this morning.'

'Died? *What?* Who is this?'

'My name's Violet Brewster. I had a meeting scheduled with Clayton and Hilary this morning, and I'm with Clayton now.'

From the other end of the line, Violet could hear the steady click of a car indicator.

'Hang on,' Anne said. 'Sorry. I . . . I'm pulling over.' Thirty seconds passed before the conversation was resumed. 'Tell me what happened. Was it a car accident?'

'No, Hilary died here at the garden centre,' Violet said, thinking it wise to hold back on the details. 'Clayton asked me to call you. Obviously, given the circumstances, the tearoom and plant nursery won't be able to open today, and he hoped you'd be able to ring round and speak to the staff . . . let them know not to come in.'

'Yes. Yes, of course,' Anne said. 'Is Clayton there? Can I speak to him?'

Clayton had obviously heard Anne's side of the conversation, because he held up his hands and waved them in front of his face, making it clear he wasn't ready to talk.

'He's very upset at the moment, and not up to chatting,' Violet said. 'I'll ask him to call you later, once he's spoken to the police.'

'The police?' Anne said. 'Why have they been called? Is there something you're not telling me?'

'No, don't worry. It's standard procedure in this kind of situation,' Violet said, doing her best to sound unruffled and matter-of-fact. 'Clayton will explain everything when he speaks to you. For now, he'd like you to ring your colleagues and let them know not to come into work. I take it you have everyone's phone number?'

'Yes,' Anne replied. 'There are only six of us in the team, and I've got the numbers saved on my phone. I'll start making the calls now.'

'Thank you,' Violet said. 'I'll let Clayton know.'

'Will you give him my love?' Anne said, sounding overcome with emotion. 'And tell him . . . just tell him I'm sorry.'

As Violet ended the call and passed on the message to Clayton, two fresh-faced police officers appeared in the doorway. The pair looked remarkably young and inexperienced – but even so, it was a relief to see them.

The taller of the two officers offered his condolences to Clayton and introduced himself as PC Turner.

'The control room told us to let ourselves in through the rear gate,' he said. 'We were expecting to find you in the garden centre, but we heard voices coming from in here.'

'We decided to retreat inside, out of the wind,' Violet explained.

'That's probably for the best,' PC Turner said. 'I understand you were the one who found your wife, Mr Spenbeck. Is that right?'

'Yes.' Clayton gave a feeble nod.

'I realise how upset you must be,' the officer said. 'And the last thing we want to do is distress you any further, but do you think you'd be able to show us where she is please?'

Clayton shuddered and looked at Violet. 'Can you show them? I'm not sure I can face going out there again.'

Violet didn't relish the prospect of seeing Hilary again either, but with Clayton in a state of near collapse, it didn't look as though she had a choice. Gritting her teeth, she stood up and escorted the officers outside.

'Has anyone touched the body?' PC Turner asked, once she'd pointed out where Hilary was.

'Yes, we both have. When Clayton found her, Hilary was face down in one of the water fountains. By the time I arrived, he'd pulled her out and was holding her in his arms. I checked her wrist and neck briefly for a pulse, but I couldn't find one.'

The other officer was bending down, examining Hilary's body for signs of life. He must have come to the same conclusion as Violet, because he shook his head at PC Turner, stood up, and began to cordon off the area with police tape.

'We noticed that Hilary has a cut above her eyebrow,' Violet said. 'She's obviously banged her forehead.'

'It probably happened when she fell.'

Violet pursed her lips and rocked her head from side to side. 'Maybe, but she also has a wound on the back of her head.'

'Does she now?' PC Turner frowned. 'Thank you for drawing that to our attention – although I'm sure we would have spotted it ourselves. Rest assured we'll assess everything very thoroughly, and if there's the slightest hint of anything out of the ordinary, we'll investigate. For now, I'd like you to go back inside and sit with Mr Spenbeck. I'll be along in a minute to take your statements.'

When Violet returned to the office, Clayton had taken off his jacket and was swivelling restlessly in his chair, looking pale and distraught. His tear-filled eyes were fixed on the clock on the wall, but his gaze was unfocused and distant.

'How are you doing?' Violet asked, as she took a seat on the opposite side of the desk.

'I feel sick,' he replied. 'I keep thinking this is some kind of nightmare and I'm going to wake up – but it's real, isn't it? Hilary's dead.'

'Yes, I'm afraid she is. I'm so sorry, Clayton. I can't begin to imagine what you must be going through.'

He ran his hands through the white streak in his hair, causing wispy tufts to sprout untidily on the top of his head.

'What will happen now?' he asked.

'PC Turner's going to come and take statements from us. Do you feel up to answering his questions?'

Clayton rested his hands on the edge of the desk and straightened his arms. 'Not really, but it has to be done. What do you think he'll want to know?'

'I expect he'll ask where Hilary was when you found her, and whether she had any known health issues. They'll need to establish when you last saw her, or spoke to her – and I imagine they'll ask about CCTV footage. I'm guessing you have security cameras here?'

'We do,' Clayton said, giving a half-hearted nod, 'but not in the area where Hilary fell. There are cameras in the car park, at the main entrance, and around the front of the retail building, but not there.'

'I suspect the police will want to see the footage anyway,' Violet said.

As she finished speaking, PC Turner reappeared and came to stand awkwardly in the centre of the room, his arms crossed over his high-vis police jacket.

'The ambulance crew has arrived, and the paramedics have confirmed what I think you already knew, Mr Spenbeck. Unfortunately, your wife has passed away.'

The officer paused respectfully to let the pronouncement sink in.

'What we need to do now, is establish what caused her death,' PC Turner added.

'Yes . . . of course,' Clayton said. 'Initially, I thought she must have tripped over and knocked herself out, but now I'm wondering if she collapsed for some other reason.'

'Those do seem to be the most likely explanations,' PC Turner said. 'But we need to be sure. A detective is on his way, as is a SOCO . . . a scenes of crime officer. They'll determine whether there are any suspicious circumstances.'

'You've called in a detective and a forensics team?' Clayton's head shot up. 'Are you saying my wife's death wasn't an accident?'

'That's what we need to find out,' PC Turner replied. 'She appears to have sustained injuries to both the front and back of her head, and we need to establish how that happened. Can you tell me whether your wife was in good health?'

Clayton nodded tearfully. 'Yes, very much so. She did mention she felt slightly nauseous this morning, but apart from that, she was absolutely fine. Hilary never complained of aches or pains, and she hardly ever went to the doctor's. She is . . . *was* . . . only forty-five. That might seem old to someone of your age, PC Turner, but as far as I'm concerned, she was in the prime of her life.'

The constable pulled an electronic notebook from the inside pocket of his jacket. 'Is it all right if I sit down while I take your statements?'

Without waiting for an answer, he pulled up a spare chair and lowered himself onto it.

'Would you like me to step outside while you talk to Clayton?' Violet asked.

'Actually, Violet, I'd like you to stay,' Clayton said, before the policeman had a chance to respond. 'If that's all right with you, Officer?'

PC Turner shrugged. 'Not a problem, providing Ms Brewster is OK with that.'

Violet's preference would have been to leave the garden centre and return to her place of work at Merrywell Shopping Village as soon as humanly possible. What she needed was a comforting hug from Matthew, and a coffee and a warm croissant from *Books, Bakes and Cakes* – but that would mean abandoning Clayton in his hour of need, and it wasn't in her nature to shy away from an obligation, especially one forced upon her by such tragic circumstances.

Nodding to express her willingness, she leaned back and listened as Clayton repeated his account of finding Hilary just before eight o'clock as he'd emerged from the other end of the garden centre.

'She was lying face down in the fountain,' he explained. 'I pulled her out of the water and tried to revive her, but it was no good. She didn't respond.'

'Prior to that, when was the last time you saw your wife?' PC Turner asked.

Clayton pulled a handkerchief from his pocket and wiped his eyes. 'It would have been around twenty past seven,' he said. 'The gale woke us in the night, and we decided to get up early and come over here to check for any storm damage. Hilary and I let ourselves into the garden centre just after seven-fifteen. I went off to sort out the shrubs and young trees at the far end of the site, and I left Hilary checking on the bedding plants. My wife and I were meeting Violet at eight o'clock, and Hilary said she'd come and find me a few minutes beforehand.'

'But she didn't do that?'

'No, obviously not,' Clayton replied, seeming upset by the question. 'It was me who found *her*. In the fountain.'

'And apart from yourself and your wife, was there anyone else in the garden centre at the time?'

'Not that I'm aware of,' Clayton said. 'I didn't see or hear anyone until Violet turned up.'

'And that was at eight o'clock?' PC Turner said, turning to direct the question at Violet.

'A couple of minutes before, actually,' she replied. 'I came in through the back gate. Clayton had left it unlocked so that I could let myself in.'

'And did you see anyone when you got inside?'

'No, I was alone right up until I found Clayton and Hilary. I heard Clayton cry out, which alerted me to their whereabouts.'

'You didn't notice anyone hanging around outside the garden centre? Or leaving the premises as you arrived?'

An image of Fiona's Nissan hurtling along Dale Lane popped unbidden into Violet's head, but she pushed it quickly aside. Her friend's proximity to Bluebell Hill Garden Centre at the time of Hilary's death was the one piece of information she wasn't willing to share with the police.

'No, I didn't see a soul,' she said. 'But that's hardly surprising. It was early. The garden centre doesn't open until nine-thirty, so I wouldn't have expected to see anyone. The customer car park was empty when I passed by, and there was no one about as I drove up to the rear gate and let myself in. However, the gate *was*

unlocked, so I suppose someone could have slipped in unseen before I arrived.'

'What time did you unlock the gate, Mr Spenbeck?' PC Turner asked.

'At seven-fifteen, when I got here. I knew I was going to be busy, so I left it unlocked to save having to walk back up later on.'

The constable frowned thoughtfully. 'So, the gate was unlocked for almost forty-five minutes,' he said, stating the obvious. 'Could someone have entered the garden centre during that time without you knowing?'

'It's possible,' Clayton replied. 'But not very likely. Violet was the only one who knew the gate would be unlocked.'

'Not necessarily,' Violet said. 'If you recall, we were in the tearoom when we arranged the meeting. There were loads of other people around at the time. Any of them could have overheard.'

'Can you tell me who those people were, please?' PC Turner said.

Clayton and Violet reeled off the names of the people they'd recognised, and PC Turner made notes. After that, he closed his electronic notebook and returned it to his inside pocket.

'Is that it?' Violet said, desperate to escape, even though it would mean leaving Clayton on his own. 'Can I go now?'

'Yes, you can leave if you wish,' PC Turner said. 'Thanks for your cooperation, Ms Brewster. We'll be in touch if we have any more questions.'

As Violet snatched up her bag and prepared to leave, a familiar figure appeared in the open doorway, blocking her escape. Her heart sank. Of all of the detectives in the Derbyshire Constabulary, it was just her luck for the case to have been assigned to Charlie Winterton.

In fairness, his presence didn't come as a complete surprise – Merrywell was part of DS Winterton's patch – and it wasn't as if she didn't like the man. Violet's contribution to solving three local murder investigations in the previous twelve months had

brought about an uneasy, if somewhat precarious truce between the two of them. DS Winterton didn't necessarily like her getting involved in his cases (and, for that matter, neither did she), but he seemed to accept she had a knack for ferreting out crucial clues. In fact, during the last murder investigation Violet had become embroiled in, she and Charlie had been on the verge of becoming friends.

Would their tentative bond survive him finding her at the scene of yet another death in Merrywell?

Chapter 7

'It was awful. Absolutely awful.'

Violet had retreated to Matthew Collis's furniture workshop – more specifically, into Matthew's arms, her head resting against the reassuring strength of his chest. He listened in shocked silence as she told him about the tragedy that had taken place at the garden centre, and her subsequent conversations with PC Turner and DS Winterton.

'You're a magnet for trouble, Violet Brewster. You do know that?'

She pulled her head back and stared into Matthew's dark brown eyes. 'I can't help it,' she said. 'I just seem to stumble into these things.'

'You can say that again.'

'I should never have agreed to meet the Spenbecks,' Violet said. 'If I'd given more consideration to my friendship with Fiona, and worried less about drumming up business for *The Memory Box*, I wouldn't have been anywhere near the garden centre this morning – ergo, I wouldn't have got myself involved in any of this.'

'You're not involved,' Matthew said, as he dragged a stool from under a workbench and lowered her onto it. 'You just happened to be there when Hilary died. It's an unfortunate coincidence, but you've done your bit and given a statement to the police. That should be the end of it. Sad as Hilary's death is, it's not your problem.'

'It will be if Charlie Winterton is lining up Fiona as his prime suspect.'

Matthew's jaw tightened. 'Don't you think you're jumping the gun? We're not even sure a crime's been committed yet.'

Violet shook her head. 'There's definitely something fishy about Hilary's death, otherwise Charlie wouldn't have been called in.'

'Let's hope for the best, rather than assume the worst, yeah?' Matthew said, as he took hold of her hands. 'I'm sure the police are just being thorough. You wait . . . the post-mortem will most likely show that Hilary died from natural causes.'

'But what if it doesn't?'

Matthew frowned. 'Even if it *does* turn out to be foul play, you can't seriously think DS Winterton will suspect Fiona? OK, she and Hilary argued – but so what? People fall out all the time. It doesn't mean they go around killing each other.'

'True, but you have to admit, it doesn't look good for Fi. She couldn't have picked a worse time to have a row.'

'If you're that worried, why don't you go and see her and give her a heads-up?'

'I've already tried to do that,' Violet said. 'The first thing I did when I got back to the shopping village was go to the bakery, but Fiona wasn't there. Sophie's running the shop this morning. Apparently, Fi's gone to Matlock to see a new supplier.'

'Well, there you are then.' Matthew grinned. 'If she's not around, there's no way she could have bumped Hilary off, is there?'

'This isn't funny, Matthew,' she said, giving him a half-hearted nudge with her elbow.

She paused, deliberating over whether to say anything about seeing Fiona on Dale Lane.

'Why the serious face?' Matthew said. 'Is there something you're not telling me?'

Violet was desperate to share what she knew, and Matthew was one of the few people she could trust with such potentially incriminating information.

'I saw Fiona earlier,' she said. 'Just before eight o'clock.'

'In Merrywell?'

Violet nodded. 'More specifically, she was driving up Dale Lane . . . you know, the road that goes past the garden centre.'

'Yes, I know where Dale Lane is.' Matthew was beginning to look uneasy. 'What was she doing there?'

Violet shrugged. 'I don't know. I'm sure there's a perfectly innocent explanation – I just wish I knew what it was.'

'Why don't you give her a call and find out?' Matthew suggested. 'Put your mind at rest.'

'I've already tried that as well. Her phone's switched off.'

Matthew frowned, causing a vertical line to appear on his forehead.

'Have you said anything to the police about seeing Fiona near the garden centre?'

'Are you kidding?' Violet pulled a face. 'I wasn't going to land her in it, was I?'

Matthew grimaced. 'I have to say, the more I hear, the worse things seem to get. Fiona had a very public falling-out with Hilary yesterday. That, on its own, doesn't mean very much – but if the police find out she was in the vicinity of the garden centre around the time Hilary died, they'll have a field day. If the death does turn out to be suspicious, there's no way your Detective Winterton will ignore such a potentially hot lead. You need to get hold of Fiona ASAP and warn her about what could be heading her way.'

Determined to follow Matthew's advice, Violet left the workshop and crossed over to the bookshop in search of Eric. His part-time assistant was at the front desk, unboxing a delivery of hardback novels with beautifully sprayed edges.

'Hi, Jill,' Violet said. 'Is Eric in?'

'No, sorry. He's over in Derby picking up some books from the auction house,' she said. 'He's due back soon though. You're welcome to stay and browse if you want to wait for him.'

'It's Fiona I'm after, actually,' Violet said. 'She's not answering her phone, and I hoped Eric might be able to get hold of her. When Fi's busy, he's about the only person she'll accept a call from.'

Jill pulled another handful of books from the box. 'Like I say, he won't be long.'

'Would you ask him to come over to *The Memory Box* when he gets back, please?' Violet said. 'There's something I need to talk to him about. Tell him it's important.'

Almost an hour passed before Eric showed up. He threw open the door and shot into Violet's office like a terrier pursuing a squirrel.

'Eric. Thank goodness,' she said, slightly taken aback by his dramatic entrance. 'Thanks for coming over. Did Jill tell you why I wanted to see you?'

'Jill?' Eric looked baffled. 'I haven't spoken to Jill. I've just got back from Derby . . . I bypassed the bookshop and came straight here. I've got a crisis on my hands, Violet, and I need your help.'

'What kind of crisis?' she said, feeling a sliver of dread inch down her spine.

'It's Fiona,' he replied. 'She's in Matlock being questioned by the police.'

Chapter 8

Eric was pacing like a caged animal, frantically crisscrossing the small area of floor space in *The Memory Box*.

'For goodness' sake, Eric. You'll wear the carpet out,' Violet said. 'Sit down and tell me what's happened.'

He let out an enormous sigh, flopped onto a chair and blurted out the story. 'Apparently Hilary Spenbeck died this morning, and for some unfathomable reason, the police are questioning Fiona about it.'

'Ah,' Violet said. 'I've been trying to get hold of Fi, to warn her that might happen.'

'Eh?' Eric said, his nose scrunched up in confusion.

'I assume she told you about the run-in she had with Hilary yesterday afternoon?'

Eric nodded. 'She talked about nothing else from the minute she got home. You don't think Hilary died as a result of the fall she had yesterday?'

He put his hands on his head. 'You hear about these things, don't you?' he said. 'People take a tumble, think they're perfectly all right, and then hours later they end up with a bleed on the brain.'

'Hilary's death was nothing to do with what happened yesterday,' Violet said. 'She definitely didn't hit her head when she fell over in the tearoom. Quite the opposite. She landed on her backside, and the only thing damaged was her pride. However, the same can't be said of what happened to her today – and I should know, because I had the misfortune of being there when Clayton discovered Hilary's body.'

She described her early morning visit to the garden centre and brought Eric up to speed on what she knew about Hilary's death.

'It sounds to me like a straightforward accident,' he said. 'But if that's the case, why are the police talking to Fiona? There's got to be more to this than meets the eye. Coppers don't line up suspects until they know for certain a crime has been committed.'

'Just because Fiona's being questioned doesn't mean she's being treated as a suspect,' she said, trying to disguise her own underlying concerns. 'The police are probably just dotting i's and crossing t's. Although I have to say, they've gone to a lot of trouble to track her down. I've been trying to get in touch with Fiona on and off for the last couple of hours, but all I've been getting is her voicemail.'

'She went to a meeting earlier and switched her phone onto silent,' Eric said. 'The police rang and left her a voicemail message, asking her to go to the station. Fiona listened to it when she came out of her meeting and, as she was already in Matlock, she decided to go straight there.'

'I assume she's being interviewed voluntarily?' Violet said. 'She's not been arrested, has she?'

'No, that's the first thing I asked her when she rang me from the station.'

'How did she sound when you spoke to her?'

Eric gave a wry smile. 'Remarkably laid-back,' he said. 'You know Fiona. She says she's done nothing wrong, and therefore has nothing to worry about.'

'Quite right too,' Violet said, sounding a lot more confident than she felt. 'Hilary may not have been Fiona's favourite person, but Fi would never have done anything to hurt her – and if that's what the police suspect, they'll soon realise their mistake. I must confess, I'm slightly annoyed that Charlie Winterton has decided to question Fiona, but I suppose he's only doing his job.'

'Fiona doesn't seem in the least bit bothered, but I am,' Eric said. 'I'm worried about her, and I don't mind admitting it.'

'She'll be fine,' Violet said, adopting her most reassuring tone. 'Fiona knows how to look after herself, and it's not as if she's got anything to hide. Except . . .'

'What?' said Eric.

Violet hesitated. She was desperate to know why Fiona had been driving along the back lanes of Merrywell at eight o'clock that morning, but if she asked Eric the question, he might think she had doubts about Fiona's innocence.

'Nothing,' she said. 'It doesn't matter. Tell me how I can help. What's the plan?'

'I was hoping you'd tell me that,' Eric said. 'You know more about these things than I do.'

Violet tapped her bottom lip. 'As far as I'm aware, there's no conclusive evidence to suggest Hilary Spenbeck's death was anything other than an accident – so hopefully, we won't need a plan.'

'But what if Charlie Winterton knows something we don't?'

'If he does, and it concerns Fiona, he needs to disclose that information.'

'That's not likely to happen, is it?' Eric said. 'He's not obliged to tell *us* anything. He must have found something though . . . something that has the potential to incriminate Fiona. Why else would the police be interrogating her?'

'Interrogating?' Violet smiled, hoping to lift Eric's spirits. 'You make it sound like the Spanish Inquisition! Fiona doesn't *have* to answer their questions. If she's there voluntarily, she can walk out whenever she wants to.'

Eric ran his hands down his cheeks. 'Do you think I should get her a lawyer?'

'Let's hope it doesn't come to that. We'll wait an hour or so and see what happens, yeah?'

'No . . . sorry, Violet.' Eric stood up and made for the door. 'I can't sit around doing nothing. I'm going to the police station. They've no right questioning an innocent woman. I'm going to demand to see Fiona and advise her to come home.'

'Wait!' Violet said, as Eric opened the door. 'You said you needed my help. If you're going to the police station, I'm coming with you.'

Chapter 9

'Fiona and I should never have gone to the tearoom in the first place,' Violet said, as Eric drove them into Matlock. 'I knew instinctively it was a bad idea. If we'd steered clear, none of this would have happened.'

'That's not strictly accurate,' Eric said. 'Hilary would still be dead.'

'True, but Fiona and I would be in the clear. We certainly wouldn't have had to answer questions from the police.'

'You've had to give a witness statement,' Eric said. 'Fiona's situation is a lot more serious. It must be, otherwise she wouldn't have been summoned to the police station.'

'Let's try and think positively, shall we?' Violet said. 'By the time we get there, Fiona will probably be on her way home.'

Eric found a parking space on Bank Road, a few yards uphill from Matlock Police Station.

'I'm hoping you can pull some strings once we get inside,' he said, as they marched towards the main entrance. 'You and DS Winterton are mates, aren't you?'

'I wouldn't describe us as "mates" exactly,' Violet said, sensing a sudden weight of pressure on her shoulders. 'Fiona's my friend though – and I'll do everything I can to help her.'

With more than a little trepidation, Violet approached the front desk with Eric and asked to speak to Fiona or DS Winterton. The duty sergeant was polite but non-committal.

'Mrs Nash is in one of the interview rooms at the moment,' he said. 'As for DS Winterton, I'll need to check whether he's available. Take a seat for now, and I'll see what I can do.'

Violet and Eric shuffled into the adjacent waiting area and sat side by side on a row of wall-mounted plastic chairs.

'If DS Winterton is interviewing Fiona, he's not likely to break off to come and see us, is he?' Eric said. 'This is crazy. We could be stuck here for hours. Sitting around, waiting.'

'According to DS Winterton, the police have specially trained officers to conduct interviews,' Violet said. 'I don't think he'll be the one asking the questions.'

'He'll be listening in though, won't he? Bound to be. Watching through one of those two-way mirrors.'

'Possibly,' Violet said, unable to suppress a smile. 'Or maybe you and I have been watching too many crime dramas on TV. This is Matlock, Eric. They might not *have* two-way mirrors.'

They lapsed into silence. Violet tapped her foot impatiently, while Eric checked his phone, which kept pinging.

'I'm guessing that's Sophie?' she said, when another message alert sounded.

'Yeah, she's all for closing up the bakery and coming down here.'

'Fiona won't thank her if she does,' Violet said. 'The best thing Sophie can do for her mum is look after the bakery and café until Fiona gets back. It won't be much longer now, surely. They can't keep her here indefinitely.'

Five minutes later, a door swished open at the end of the corridor, and Charlie Winterton strolled through it. Violet and Eric stood up as he approached.

'Charlie!' Violet said. 'What's happening? Why are you questioning Fiona?'

'Simmer down, Violet,' he replied. 'Let's talk about this somewhere quieter, shall we?'

He greeted Eric with a brief nod, and took them into a small room off the waiting area. It was surprisingly neat and cosy, furnished with modern seating and a large coffee table.

'This really isn't on, you know,' Eric said, as he dropped into one of the easy chairs. 'How much longer is Fiona going to be here for?'

'As long as it takes,' DS Winterton replied. 'There are questions we need to ask her and certain things we need to establish. We're also awaiting the results of some fingerprint comparisons.'

Eric scowled. 'Whose fingerprints?'

'Your wife's. We're checking them against prints found on an object we believe was used to assault Hilary Spenbeck.'

'Assault?' Violet said. 'So Hilary was definitely attacked?'

'Yes, traces of her blood have been found on an item at the scene,' DS Winterton replied. 'We believe she was struck on the head during some sort of altercation. We'll know more once we've received the results of the post-mortem and the fingerprint comparison.'

'And when's that likely to be?' Eric said.

'The post-mortem won't be carried out until later on today, possibly even tomorrow morning, but we should have the fingerprint results back within the hour.'

'I can tell you now, you won't find Fiona's prints at any crime scene,' Eric said. 'I'd like to speak to her, please. It's time she came home.'

'Your wife is here voluntarily, Mr Nash – which means she is, of course, free to go whenever she wants,' DS Winterton said. 'However, so far, she's expressed no desire to do so. On the contrary, she seems more than willing to answer our questions.'

'Have you cautioned her?' Violet said.

'Yes we have, but there's nothing unusual about that. We're conducting an investigation . . . It's all perfectly normal.'

'It might be perfectly normal in your world,' Eric said, 'but not in ours. Fiona is a law-abiding citizen, and I won't have you treating her like a common criminal.'

Violet shared Eric's concerns. Her ex-husband was a detective with the Met, so she was well aware that volunteering to have a 'quick chat' with the police was often the precursor to criminal proceedings.

'Unlike you, Mr Nash, your wife doesn't have a problem with being here,' DS Winterton insisted. 'She's being very helpful and cooperative, because she realises there are things we need to clear up.'

Violet and Eric exchanged a look of mutual concern.

'We've been checking with the people who were in the tearoom yesterday afternoon,' DS Winterton told them. 'The ones we've spoken to so far have confirmed that an argument took place between Fiona and Mrs Spenbeck.'

'You already knew that,' Violet said, slapping her knees impatiently. 'I told you the same thing myself.'

'You did, but there are points of view other than yours to take into consideration. *You* said the two women "had words", and that Mrs Spenbeck "slipped", but . . . as it turns out, not everyone saw it that way.'

Violet was indignant. 'I was standing right next to Fiona, which means I had the best view of what happened.'

'So, tell me about it,' DS Winterton said. 'And no whitewashing this time. I want the truth. What was the argument about?'

Violet gulped. She wanted to be honest with DS Winterton, but how could she do that without making Fiona's situation worse?

'Fiona was worried about another café opening up in Merrywell,' she said, choosing her words carefully. 'She and I went along to check the tearoom out, and Hilary accused her of spying.'

'And was she? Spying?'

'Not exactly,' Violet said. 'She wasn't wearing dark glasses and a disguise, if that's what you mean. Fiona went along as a legitimate customer to satisfy her curiosity. She knew that the tearoom would be competing directly with her own café, and she wanted to see what impact it might have. As a business owner, she likes to keep abreast of local rivals. There's plenty of opposition out there – especially in the catering trade. Bars and cafés are popping up all over the place these days.'

'Interesting choice of language,' DS Winterton said. 'Local rivals. Opposition. You make it sound very adversarial.'

Violet could have kicked herself. 'That wasn't my intention,' she said. 'Fiona is the opposite of adversarial. She's friendly. Helpful. Very community-minded.'

Eric smiled gratefully as he listened to the verbal character reference.

'And yet, she *did* argue with Mrs Spenbeck,' said DS Winterton.

'It was a minor disagreement,' Violet countered. 'About a scone.'

'A scone?'

Violet noticed that DS Winterton had rhymed the word with 'cone', whereas her own pronunciation had rhymed with 'gone'. Trust him to contradict her.

'She complained that it was stale, and Hilary took exception to that,' Violet explained. 'Hilary Spenbeck was a volatile woman. I heard her husband tell you that himself.'

The detective smirked. 'That must have been when you were listening at the door. How long were you out there for exactly?'

'Long enough to know there are other people you should be talking to,' Violet said, feeling her cheeks turn pink. 'The neighbour, Roy Geldard, for instance.'

'My officers are making enquiries as we speak. They're talking to all of the people Clayton Spenbeck mentioned, including those who were in the tearoom when Hilary Spenbeck *slipped over*, as you put it.'

'Good,' Violet said. 'I'm glad you're being thorough.'

'Not thorough enough, if you ask me,' said Eric. 'You're barking up the wrong tree if you think Fiona had anything to do with Hilary's death.'

'If that's the case, I'm sure we'll have no problem ruling her out.' DS Winterton forced his mouth into a faux smile. 'Can either of you think of anyone else who may have wanted to harm Hilary Spenbeck? Someone with a grudge, perhaps?'

'I couldn't possibly say,' Violet replied. 'As I told you earlier, I hardly know the Spenbecks.'

'What about you, Mr Nash? How well did you know the victim?'

'Not very,' Eric replied. 'And tempting as it is to put forward the names of other potential suspects, I'm not going to throw another innocent person under the bus just to get Fiona off the hook.'

DS Winterton opened his mouth to respond, but his words were quelled by a loud knock on the door.

A woman poked her head into the room. 'Can I have a word, boss?' she said, pointing towards the corridor with her chin, making it clear she wanted to speak to the detective in private.

Violet and Eric waited anxiously as Charlie Winterton left the room.

'Maybe they're letting her go,' Eric said.

'Maybe,' Violet said, feeling less optimistic. 'I hope so.'

But when DS Winterton returned, Violet could see from his expression that he wasn't about to impart good news. He looked unhappy. Embarrassed even.

'We've received the fingerprint results,' he said. 'I'm sorry, folks, but it's been confirmed. The prints on the weapon are a match for Fiona's.'

Chapter 10

Eric stood up and resumed his pacing. 'There must be some mistake,' he said, his face quivering with suppressed fury. 'There has to be. You need to check again.'

Violet had never seen the mild-mannered Eric lose his temper, but it was obvious he was close to boiling point.

'I'm sorry, but there's no mistake,' DS Winterton said, sounding genuinely regretful. 'They were partial prints, but they do belong to your wife. No question.'

Eric's shoulders sagged. 'So, what happens now?' he said, as he sank back into the chair.

DS Winterton stuffed his hands into his pockets. 'The interviewing officers are talking to your wife. It's possible there's a plausible explanation for her prints being at the scene.'

Eric rallied. 'Yes. Yes, there will be,' he said, forcing himself to sit up straight. 'You can bet your life on that.'

'Tell me about this so-called "weapon",' said Violet. 'Were there any other prints on it, apart from Fiona's?'

DS Winterton gave her a warning frown. 'I thought you said you weren't going to poke your nose into my investigation.'

'That was before you put my best friend at the top of your list of suspects,' she replied. 'So, can you please answer the question?

Were there other prints?'

'Yes, there were – although we haven't identified who they belong to yet. Right now, we're focusing on Mrs Nash. She and Hilary Spenbeck had a blazing row less than twenty-four hours before Mrs Spenbeck died, and Mrs Nash's prints are on a blood-stained object found near the body. You have to admit, it doesn't look good.'

'I don't care what it *looks* like,' Eric said. 'You haven't even had the post-mortem results back yet. Why are you so convinced this was . . . what? Manslaughter? Murder? It's ridiculous to think Fiona would get herself mixed up in anything like that. Why are you so determined to pin this on her? Are you looking to improve your clear-up rates? Is that it?'

'Calm down, Mr Nash. I'm not in the business of *pinning* anything on anyone. I'm a copper, doing my job. You're right about the post-mortem results though . . . until we know the actual cause of death, there's technically no case to answer, at least not yet. Even so, based on the forensic evidence we've discovered, things don't look great for your wife. We need to know why her prints are on the weapon. Surely you understand that?'

'What is this "weapon" you keep referring to?' Violet said. 'Is it a hammer? A brick? I don't remember seeing anything like that at the scene when I checked Hilary's pulse – although I'll admit I was somewhat freaked out by the situation, and not at my most observant.'

Charlie hesitated, as if weighing up how much information to divulge. 'As this relates to your wife, Mr Nash, I can share some information with you, but please don't disclose what I'm about to tell you to anyone else. That goes for you too, Violet.'

Violet and Eric nodded in unison.

The detective studied their faces for a moment, as if checking whether he could rely on them.

'The weapon used was a stone ornament,' he said eventually. 'Very heavy and—'

'Wait!' Violet said, hit by a sudden flash of understanding. 'Are you by any chance talking about an owl? A silly, googly-eyed, glazed owl, priced at £39.99?'

The detective gave a long, low whistle. 'Well, I'll be. I knew you were sharp . . . good at working things out . . . but how the *hell* did you know about the owl?'

'Because,' Violet said, 'yesterday afternoon, after we left the tearoom, Fiona and I wandered through the garden centre, and she picked it up. *That's* why her prints are on it – and I'm not surprised hers weren't the only ones. The owl was on public display for anyone to inspect and admire.'

DS Winterton raised an eyebrow. 'I'm not sure *admire* is quite the right word,' he said. 'As owl ornaments go, it's not the best I've ever seen.'

'And as detecting goes, this isn't the best *I've* seen either,' Violet said. 'Certainly not from you. For heaven's sake, Charlie, it's time to admit you've got this all wrong. I've given you a perfectly logical explanation as to how Fiona's prints came to be on the owl, and I'm sure she's telling the same story to whoever's interviewing her right now.'

DS Winterton released a sigh – whether of relief or frustration, Violet couldn't tell.

'I'll go and find out,' he said. 'And if you're right, we'll be able to let Fiona go home . . . at least for now.'

He turned to leave, but Violet wasn't finished with him. 'What about the CCTV in the garden centre parking area?' she said. 'Is there any sign of Fiona's car on the morning Hilary died?'

Charlie paused, his hand resting on the door handle. 'No, but she could have parked elsewhere and walked up to the rear gate. That area's not covered by CCTV.'

'Fiona wouldn't have known that, would she?' Eric said. 'How could she possibly know where the garden centre security cameras are?'

'Maybe she was just lucky,' DS Winterton replied. 'She knew

the gate would be open. Fiona was with Violet in the tearoom when Mr Spenbeck told her he'd leave it unlocked.'

'Yes, and so were dozens of other people,' Violet said. 'Anyone who was in the tearoom at the time could have heard what Clayton said. Admit it, Charlie, this is all circumstantial. You have nothing solid to implicate Fiona. In fact, apart from the owl, it sounds as if you have very little evidence that a crime has been committed at all.'

Eric got up and went to stand directly in front of DS Winterton, blocking his exit from the room.

'I'd like to take my wife home, please,' he said. 'And I don't mean in a couple of hours. I mean *now.*'

'Let me have a word with the interviewing officer,' DS Winterton said, acquiescing with a nod. 'If Fiona's account of the owl matches Violet's, she can come home with you right away.'

Chapter 11

'I appreciate your concern, love, but please don't make a fuss. The police have accepted why my prints were on the owl, and they've let me go.'

Violet was travelling back with Eric. Fiona was in her own car, one vehicle behind them – her voice booming into Eric's van courtesy of the Bluetooth hands-free kit. They were on the outskirts of Matlock, near the school, and traffic was slow – the roads clogged with cars, driven by parents and grandparents completing the afternoon school run.

'I bet they only released you because Violet backed you up,' Eric said. 'If it wasn't for that, you might still be in there.'

'Well, I'm not, am I?' Fiona said. 'I'm right behind you, on my way home, and I'm perfectly all right. No harm done.'

'Maybe not to you,' Eric said. 'But my blood pressure went through the roof while I was waiting for you to be released.'

The traffic inched forward a few yards.

'I told you not to worry,' Fiona said. 'I'll admit I was a bit flustered by some of the questions they asked, especially about my barney with Hilary – but what choice did I have, other than to tell them what they wanted to know? A woman has died. I had a moral duty to cooperate.'

'We'll have to agree to disagree on that,' Eric said, as he fiddled with the van's heating controls. 'In my opinion, the police should never have dragged you down to the station unless they had some firm evidence against you.'

'They didn't *drag* me. I went there voluntarily,' Fiona said, sounding remarkably chipper, despite her ordeal. 'Poor old Charlie Winterton is doing his best. I can totally understand why he had to eliminate me from his enquiries.'

'Never mind *poor old Charlie Winterton*,' said Eric. 'You won't catch me feeling sorry for him – not while my wife's on his list of suspects. I hope you realise they've not ruled you out completely?'

'Yes, thank you. I am aware of that,' Fiona said, her voice breaking up a little as they edged slowly forward. 'They did warn me they might need to speak to me again.'

Eric banged the van's steering wheel with the heel of his hand. 'Not if I can help it,' he said. 'And if they do call you back in, we'll make sure you have a solicitor with you next time. You should have had one today.'

'I didn't need a solicitor because I've done nothing wrong,' Fiona replied. 'Come on, love. Don't get yourself worked up. Forget it. Let's go home and have a nice glass of wine. I know it's still early, but I think I deserve a drink, don't you?'

'I think you deserve a whole bottle, never mind a glass,' Violet said, piping up from the passenger seat in an attempt to change the subject. 'I'm hoping to have a drop of the red stuff myself this evening. I'm going to Matthew's for dinner tonight. There's always a good selection in his wine rack.'

'Eric and I owe *you* a large drink next time we're in the White Hart,' Fiona said. 'I appreciate you being there today, Violet. I suspect DS Winterton was relieved to let me go in the end. The evidence may have been pointing in my direction, but I think he knows, deep down, I'm not a killer.'

They had left the environs of the school, and the traffic was flowing much more smoothly now. Violet glanced at her watch.

It was ten past three.

'Am I dropping you off at home or at the shopping village, Violet?' Eric said.

'The shopping village, please. My car's there, and I'm hoping to squeeze in a couple more hours of work before I finish for the day.'

'I'm going to drive straight home,' Fiona said, the poor signal making her sound much further away than one car behind. 'Things will have quietened down in the café and bakery by now, so I'm sure Sophie can cope without me for the rest of the afternoon. Thanks again for today, Violet. I don't know what we'd have done without you. Drop in for a cappuccino and a muffin on your way to work tomorrow . . . on the house.'

'Thanks. I'll take you up on that,' Violet said, thinking it would be the perfect opportunity to ask Fiona what she'd been doing on Dale Lane at eight o'clock that morning.

Chapter 12

Matthew lived half a mile north of the village, on Bakewell Road. His house – or, to give it it's full and proper name, Tanbeck House – was much larger than Greengage Cottage, but not quite as old. In terms of quirkiness and charm, the two properties were on a par, but Violet much preferred the light, bright, cheerful ambience of her own home. Tanbeck House was decorated in dark, masculine colours: dove and steel greys, earthy browns, and teal blue – each room spiced up with gold, turmeric and cinnamon-coloured accessories.

As she let herself into the kitchen, she was met by the delicious aroma of herbs and garlic, which were emanating from the simmering pan that Matthew was stirring on the hob.

'Whatever it is you're cooking, it smells divine,' she said, as she snuck up behind him and wrapped her arms around his waist.

He turned and smiled at her over his shoulder. 'I'm glad you approve. I'm experimenting with a new recipe. Creamy garlic chicken with herbs, served with pilau rice. Hope it's going to be OK.'

'I'm sure it'll be delicious. Was I supposed to bring a pudding?'

'It's not a problem if you haven't . . . in fact, it's probably a good thing. I've cooked far too much rice, and if we eat it all, we won't have any room left for dessert. However, if you do fancy something sweet, there's always me.'

Laughing, Violet reached for the open bottle of wine on the worktop and poured herself a glass.

'Any news on the Hilary Spenbeck situation?' Matthew said.

'I'm afraid there is,' she replied, pulling an unhappy face. Between sips of Bordeaux, she told him about her trip to the police station with Eric, reflecting on the absurdity of this latest turn of events.

'Strewth!' Matthew said, as he switched off the heat under the pan. 'Sounds like you've had an eventful day. Did you manage to find out what Fiona was doing on Dale Lane?'

'No, I didn't get the chance to ask,' Violet said. 'I'll speak to her about it tomorrow when I can get her on her own.'

'Do you think she's done enough to convince the police of her innocence?'

'I don't know,' said Violet. 'Although please don't tell Fi I said that. A lot will depend on the results of the post-mortem. The best-case scenario is that Hilary died of natural causes.'

'Is that likely, or wishful thinking on your part?'

'The latter, I suspect,' Violet said, her forehead puckering into a frown. 'If it was death by natural causes, how do we account for the blood on the owl, and the injuries on Hilary's head?'

'How *we* account?' Matthew shot her a look of mock horror. 'I hope you're not involving me in your amateur sleuthing. At the risk of sounding like a broken record, this is a matter for the police. You need to let them deal with it. You and I have better things to do.'

'Such as?'

He leaned in and kissed her. 'Let's start with dinner, shall we? If you take the wine to the table, I'll serve up.'

After they'd finished their meal (including every last grain of rice), Matthew loaded the dishwasher and they moved into the snug. The gale had long since abated, but it was chilly for the time of year, so they lit a fire and sat either side of the hearth in matching armchairs, drinking the last of the wine.

'This is nice,' Violet said. 'Very cosy.'

'My house is always warmer and brighter when you're in it.'

'Thank you,' Violet said. 'That's a lovely thing to say.'

'It's true. You light up my life, Violet Brewster.'

Giving him a beaming smile, she lifted her glass in a toast and drained the remains of her wine.

'Shall I open another bottle?' Matthew said.

'Better not.'

'Tot of whisky, then? Brandy? A cheeky Baileys?'

She sighed. 'What I'd really like is a mug of hot chocolate. Does that make me sound horribly boring?'

'Maybe a little,' Matthew said, wobbling his head from side to side. 'But who cares. Your wish is my command.'

Carrying the empty wine glasses, he retreated into the kitchen and reappeared a few minutes later with two mugs of hot chocolate.

'Thanks,' Violet said, hugging her mug to warm her hands. 'You spoil me.'

Matthew laughed. 'It's a cup of hot chocolate, Violet. It's hardly an indulgence.'

'It is to me. This and a roaring fire are all I need on a cold spring evening.'

Matthew affected a glum expression, turning down the corners of his mouth. 'Does that mean I'm surplus to requirements? Have I been cast aside in favour of a milky drink?'

Violet smirked over the rim of her mug. 'Never. You're a constant. I only want the hot chocolate and roaring fire on a cold day – whereas I need you all year round.'

'That's a relief,' he said, giving her a smile that made her stomach flip. 'It also gives me the confidence to ask about our plans for the summer.'

Violet gazed into his eyes, feeling unfathomably nervous.

'Plans? What kind of plans?' she said.

'I was thinking we could book a holiday. I know you don't like taking time off work, but it'd be nice to get away, even if it's only for a few days.'

'It doesn't seem five minutes since we came back from Paris,' Violet said, referring to the weekend break Matthew had surprised her with as a belated birthday present.

'That was a couple of months ago. By the time the warm weather arrives, we'll be crying out for another break.'

Violet nodded. 'Did you have somewhere in mind?'

'Not especially. I'm happy to go anywhere, as long as you're with me. Is there somewhere you'd like to go to?'

'I've always wanted to visit Bruges,' Violet said. 'Or we could have a staycation. Explore the Cotswolds, maybe?'

'Or both,' Matthew said. 'After all, there's no point spending all our lives at work. We owe it to ourselves to take some time out once in a while.'

'I agree,' Violet said, surprising herself, as well as Matthew. 'And it's a lot easier for me to do that, now that I've got Molly working for me. If you let me have some dates, I'll check my work diary when I'm back in the office. If I'm free, I'll block out the time as holiday. To be honest, the diary's worryingly empty at the moment, so it shouldn't be a problem finding a mutually convenient date.'

Matthew reached across and squeezed her hand. 'You're not concerned, are you? About *The Memory Box*?'

Violet shrugged. 'Yes and no. Business has been disconcertingly quiet recently, but I've got a few irons in the fire, so I'm hoping things will change for the better soon. I'm discovering that work levels have a tendency to go from one extreme to another. What I'd like to do is try and strike the right balance. As a minimum, I need enough projects on the go to occupy me and Molly and cover our wages – but I also need to avoid taking on *too* many jobs, otherwise we won't be able to cope, and I'll end up spending every waking moment in the office.'

'It's often trial and error in the early years of a business,' Matthew said. 'But you'll be OK. You're a strong, capable and very determined woman – which is why I love you so much.'

Violet's heart swelled with happiness. Matthew had never said those words out loud before. He'd hinted at them, certainly, but this was the first time he'd expressed his feelings directly.

'Thanks,' she said, moving her hand to interlock her fingers with his. 'I love you too.'

He smiled at her, and for a second Violet thought he was going to say something else – but the moment passed, and he turned to throw a fresh log on the fire. Violet sat back and watched it burn, smiling as the flames danced around it and slowly took hold.

Chapter 13

By the following morning, the weather had taken a turn for the better. It was as though the blustering gale had swept away the last remnants of winter, and spring had finally arrived in Merrywell. The village's flower-filled and slightly wind-battered gardens dazzled in the sunshine. Swathes of purple aubretia tumbled between pale yellow primroses. Post-box-red tulips opened their petals and warmed themselves in the sun.

Violet set off for work on foot. She was running late, and was in desperate need of sustenance, so she headed directly to the bakery to claim the promised muffin and coffee, and – more importantly – discover what Fiona had been doing on Dale Lane the previous morning.

Outside of the main tourist season, Tuesdays were generally fairly quiet in Merrywell Shopping Village – but today, foot traffic seemed even sparser than usual. When Violet entered the bakery, she was surprised to discover she was the only customer, and the clamour that normally emanated from the adjoining café was also strangely absent.

'Morning,' she said, greeting Fiona with a smile. 'I've come for the muffin you promised me.'

Fiona forced her lips into an unconvincing smile. 'What would you like? Triple chocolate, lemon drizzle, raspberry and white chocolate, or blueberry.'

Violet tapped her chin, deliberating over her choice. 'I'm tempted by the lemon drizzle, but I think I'll stick with my usual blueberry, please.'

'You may as well take one of each,' Fiona said, sounding noticeably downcast. 'What about Molly? Is she working today?'

'No, she's not in until tomorrow.'

Fiona shrugged. 'That's a shame. I'd have stuck a couple of extras in the bag for her, if she'd been around. The way things are going this morning, I'll have tons of stuff left over by the end of the day.'

'It's still early yet,' Violet said.

'It's twenty past nine. I've usually sold half my stuff by now. There's always a queue outside when I open up at half past eight, but today there wasn't a soul in sight. It's eerily quiet. I keep expecting to look out of the window and see tumbleweed rolling across the courtyard. It's the same in the café – by now, at least a dozen of my regulars should be tucking into a full English, but there's no sign of any of the usual gang.'

'So, where is everyone?'

'They're staying away, aren't they. It's as plain as the nose on your face what's going on.'

'Is it?' said Violet.

'News has obviously leaked out about my trip to the police station,' Fiona said. 'You know what Merrywell's like – nothing stays a secret for long. Half the people in *The Cuckoo's Boot* tearoom on Sunday were from the village and, by now, the police will have questioned each and every one of them about my row with Hilary. Combine that with my presence at the cop shop, and the good citizens of Merrywell will have put two and two together and come up with a hundred.'

'Or maybe they're just having a lie-in,' Violet said, reluctant to accept Fiona's pessimistic assessment of the situation.

'What, *all* of them?'

'You must have had some customers.'

Fiona leaned on the counter. 'I had a couple of people in the bakery earlier – they were locals, but not regular customers. They'd obviously heard the rumours and had come here hoping to hear more first hand. As for the café, there's only one person in there at the moment – a woman passing through on her way to a business meeting in Manchester – and all she's ordered is a skinny latte and a bowl of granola. I expect everyone else is rubbernecking down at the garden centre and having breakfast at the tearoom.'

'Has the garden centre reopened then?' Violet's eyes widened. 'Blimey! They don't mess about. I thought they might have stayed closed for a few more days, as a sign of respect.'

'Apparently, Clayton's team has stepped in and is running the place without him.'

Violet raised her eyebrows. 'Do you think their customers will be quizzing them about what happened to Hilary?'

'It wouldn't surprise me,' Fiona said, folding her arms. 'People can be very insensitive, even in the face of such tragedy. You know, Violet, there are times when I wish I was still living in Nottingham. The thing about being in a city is, nobody knows your business.'

'You don't mean that, Fi. You love Merrywell, and you love running the bakery. *And* you love people.' Violet winked. 'Even the gossipy ones.'

'Pffft! I can do without those kind of customers, thank you very much,' she said with a waft of her hand. 'Then again, I don't suppose I'm in a position to turn *anyone* away at the moment.'

'I'm shocked your regulars are staying away,' Violet said.

'Most of them . . . the nice ones . . . are probably too embarrassed to face me at the moment – especially those who were in the tearoom yesterday, who've been obliged to tell the police what they overheard during the fracas in *The Cuckoo's Boot*. Either that, or people are afraid to come here because they think I'm a killer. Perhaps they're worried I'll cosh them over the head with a French stick or something.'

Violet smiled. 'It's good to know you've not lost your sense of humour. Don't worry, Fiona. Things will get back to normal soon, you'll see.'

'I bloomin' well hope so,' she said. 'The police should get the post-mortem results this morning. With any luck, they'll be able to rule out foul play altogether.'

'That would be the best outcome of all,' Violet said.

'Without a doubt. It would mean my reputation could be restored, before it becomes damaged irreparably. The trouble is, nothing's ever that cut and dried. I'm sure you're familiar with the proverb *throw enough mud, and some of it will stick*. Regardless of how untrue something is, there's always someone willing to believe it – especially round here. As weird and as awful as this sounds, it might be better if Hilary's death does turn out to be suspicious. At least then the police will be forced to launch a proper inquiry. I reckon the only way my reputation can be restored completely is if they catch the real culprit.'

'If that's how you feel, then maybe *we* should make some enquiries,' Violet said. 'We could launch our own undercover investigation.'

Fiona looked dubious. 'Is that a good idea? As a suspect, I think I'm better off keeping my head down.'

'Yeah, you might be right about that – but there's nothing to stop me from asking a few questions and doing some digging,' Violet said, conscious that such a course of action would fly in the face of her promise to Charlie Winterton. She'd vowed to keep out of his investigation – but that was before Fiona had become the constabulary's prime suspect and a pariah in the village. If today's lack of customers was anything to go by, the consequences of a tarnished reputation could be far-reaching for Fiona and her business – and that was unfair. *Very* unfair.

'DS Winterton won't be happy if he thinks you're meddling,' Fiona said.

'I'm sure he won't. In fact, he'll be extremely *un*happy, but we need to do something to help clear your name.'

Fiona sighed. 'You don't think I'll be arrested, do you?' she said, sounding suddenly vulnerable. 'Charged with a crime I didn't commit?'

'I'm sure it won't come to that,' Violet said, even though she wasn't sure at all.

Fiona released another sigh. 'Even if the worst does happen, I'm not sure I'd be comfortable with you digging around for other suspects. Right now, I'm painfully aware of what it feels like to be falsely accused. I wouldn't want you putting another innocent soul in the frame just to clear me of any wrongdoing.'

'I'd never heap the blame onto an innocent person,' Violet said. 'At least not knowingly. The whole idea would be for me to find the *guilty* party.'

'It's kind of you, Violet, and I know you mean well – but let's just wait and see what develops during the course of the day.'

'OK,' Violet said. 'But you'll let me know if you change your mind?'

Fiona gave a nod as she placed the bag of muffins on the counter top. 'If you hang on a minute, I'll make you a cappuccino to go with those.'

As she turned towards the coffee machine, her phone began to ring. She pulled it out of her pocket and glanced at the screen.

'Aren't you going to answer it?' Violet said, as the jangling ring tone continued.

'It's an unknown number,' Fiona said.

'It might be the police,' said Violet.

With an exaggerated huff, Fiona swiped the screen and answered the call. As she listened, she held a finger to her lips to request silence, and then put the caller onto loudspeaker.

'To what do I owe the honour, DS Winterton?' Fiona said. 'Are you ringing to apologise?'

'No, this is a courtesy call,' Charlie said, his voice booming from the phone and echoing around the empty shop. 'I wanted you to know that we've received the results of Hilary Spenbeck's post-mortem.'

'I see,' said Fiona.

'The pathologist couldn't be absolutely certain which of the head injuries was sustained first, but the most likely scenario is that Mrs Spenbeck was struck from behind initially, and then fell and banged the front of her head. One or both of the head injuries could have caused her to lose consciousness, but neither was serious enough to kill her.'

'So how did she die?' Fiona said.

'She drowned. She must have lost consciousness and landed in the water fountain. It was fairly shallow . . . a couple of inches of water at most . . . but enough to drown in.'

'That's terrible,' Fiona said. 'Poor Hilary.'

'Poor Hilary indeed. If she hadn't passed out, or if she'd regained consciousness quickly, she'd have come through the ordeal with nothing more than a thumping headache. Instead, she lay face down and slowly breathed in water until she drowned.'

'You're saying she could have survived?' said Fiona.

'Most definitely.' DS Winterton cleared his throat. 'The post-mortem showed that Mrs Spenbeck was in good overall health – although she did have the beginnings of an inner ear infection.'

'Could that have affected her balance do you think?' Fiona said. 'Made her dizzy? Maybe that's why she fell over when I pushed past her in the tearoom.'

'Possibly,' DS Winterton said. 'But it certainly wasn't an ear infection that killed her. Someone definitely hit Hilary Spenbeck. The person responsible may have acted in the spur of the moment, in a regrettable fit of rage, but had they stayed to help . . . turned her over . . .'

'She'd still be alive,' Fiona said, finishing the sentence.

'Exactly. But if we can prove that the person who struck Mrs Spenbeck chose to walk away and leave her there to die . . . this will be a murder inquiry.'

Fiona looked worried. 'Why are you telling me this?' she said.

'I wanted to make you aware of the potential seriousness of the crime,' DS Winterton said. 'And I thought you should know that we'll need to speak to you again at some point, so you might want to find yourself a solicitor.'

'You don't honestly believe I'd leave someone to die like that?' Fiona said.

'Not if you were thinking straight, no – but people have a tendency to panic in these situations. And when they panic, they do things that are out of character.'

'I didn't hit Hilary Spenbeck,' Fiona said, sounding nervous but emphatic.

'So you say,' DS Winterton replied. 'Nevertheless, a crime *has* been committed, and I wanted to let you know, Mrs Nash, that you are a person of interest in this investigation.'

Chapter 14

Fiona ended the call and slid the phone into her back pocket.

'This is an absolute nightmare,' she said, placing her hands on her sternum to steady her breathing. 'I haven't done anything wrong. Why won't the police believe me?'

'Maybe they do,' Violet said. 'But they won't be able to rule you out officially until they've disproved the circumstantial evidence against you – or found compelling evidence that points them to the real killer.'

'Guilty until proven innocent, you mean?' Fiona exhaled through her nostrils. 'Isn't it supposed to be the other way around?'

'The police will get to the bottom of this, Fiona,' Violet said. 'In the meantime, you just need to hang in there.'

'I'm not sure that I can,' Fiona said, tears welling in her eyes. 'It wouldn't be so bad if I wasn't being touted as the village outlaw. It's not a nice feeling, Violet. Not nice at all.'

Violet made her way to the other side of the counter and gave her friend a comforting hug.

'My offer to do some investigating still stands,' she said. 'Or maybe you and I could work together? If we can come up with some alternative suspects – viable ones – Charlie Winterton will be forced to widen his investigative net.'

Fiona shook her head, looking utterly despondent. 'I'm not really cut out for sleuthing. I'd be useless.'

'Nonsense. You have oodles of local knowledge – far more than I do. Someone had it in for Hilary, and all we need to do is work out who that was.'

'Before DS Winterton takes me into custody, you mean?'

Violet huffed. 'He can't arrest you if he hasn't got any proper evidence. All you're guilty of is being in the wrong place at the wrong time. Talking of which, there's something I need to clear up . . . something that's been puzzling me.'

Fiona wiped tears from her eyes with the heels of her hands. 'If you're puzzled, I can guarantee DS Winterton will be equally baffled.'

'Actually . . .' Violet cleared her throat and steadied her nerves. 'This is something he knows nothing about.'

Fiona gave a confused frown. 'Now I am intrigued,' she said. 'Come on then. Don't keep me in suspense.'

'I saw you,' Violet said. 'Yesterday morning, on Dale Lane, as I was driving to the garden centre. It was a few minutes before eight o'clock, around about the time Hilary died. I waved to you as our cars passed, but either you didn't see me, or you chose to ignore me.' She shuffled awkwardly. 'You're usually at work at that time in the morning, so . . . I wondered . . . what were you doing there?'

Fiona gave a wry smile. 'I can see why you've been keeping that snippet of information to yourself,' she said. 'Me . . . close to the scene when the crime was committed. Were you afraid Charlie Winterton would assume the worst?'

'Something like that,' Violet said. 'I certainly wasn't going to risk telling him what I saw.'

Fiona smiled. 'You're a good and loyal friend, Violet, but you don't need to cover for me. The police already know I was on Dale Lane on Monday morning. I've made no secret about it.'

'Oh!' Violet let out the breath she'd been holding on to, relieved to know that she'd been fretting over nothing. 'So, what *were* you doing there?'

'I'd been to the petrol station.'

'The garage at Bridge Top?'

Fiona nodded. 'I had a nine o'clock appointment in Matlock. My plan was to use the BBC van for the journey – but then, on Sunday evening, Eric reminded me that *he* needed the van. He was going to the auction house in Derby, so I had to use my own car instead. When I drove to work in it the next morning, I realised I was almost out of petrol. There were things I needed to do at the bakery before I set off for my meeting, and I ended up running short on time. I used Dale Lane as a shortcut to get to the garage. As a general rule, I avoid going that way – it's really narrow at the bottom end of the lane, and the junction's on a blind bend – but it's more direct and a lot quicker than driving the long way round.'

The niggling doubts Violet had been harbouring melted instantly away – but there was still one more thing she needed to know.

'Why didn't you wave to me as you drove past?'

Fiona held up her hands. 'I genuinely didn't see you,' she replied. 'I was in a hurry, still half asleep, and I had other things on my mind. As I passed the garden centre, I got to thinking about the row I'd had with Hilary. I was mulling everything over, wondering whether to call her and apologise again, or let sleeping dogs lie.'

'You did look as if you were in a world of your own,' Violet said. 'You whizzed straight past me.'

'Trust me, if I'd seen you, I would have waved,' Fiona said. 'I was rushing back because I'd left some pies in the oven, and I needed to take them out before I set off for my meeting. I'm sorry for ignoring you, and I appreciate you keeping quiet about this, but there really is no need. The police asked about my movements on Monday morning when they interviewed me, so they know I drove past the garden centre on my way to get petrol.'

'What did they say when you told them that?'

'They asked if I'd paid for the petrol on my card.'

'Of course!' Violet smiled. 'They'll be able to check the time of the transaction with your bank.'

'Except . . .' Fiona pulled a face. 'I paid by cash, and I didn't get a receipt. However, they did say they'd check the CCTV cameras on the garage forecourt. Hopefully that will confirm I was there – although it won't automatically put me in the clear as far as they're concerned. Theoretically, I could have stopped in at the garden centre and confronted Hilary on my way back.'

'DS Winterton told me there was no sign of your car in the car park on the garden centre CCTV, so that's *something* in your favour,' Violet said. 'I don't suppose you spotted any other cars as you drove past? Or saw anyone hanging around?'

'No, the police asked the same question. Like I said, I was in a hurry and half asleep. I didn't even see you, let alone anyone else. Even if someone had been skulking around, I probably wouldn't have noticed.'

Fiona turned and set to work, making the cappuccino. As Violet watched her, she began to formulate a plan.

'Are you free this evening, Fi?' she asked.

'As things stand at the moment, I am – although I could be languishing in a police cell by this afternoon.'

'That's highly unlikely.' Violet said, shaking her head. 'Can you come to Greengage Cottage at about seven? Bring Eric. I'll cook dinner, and afterwards, you, me, Matthew and Eric will hold a council of war.'

Fiona threw back her head and laughed. 'Gee whiz, Violet! A council of war? It sounds like something out of an Enid Blyton story. What are we calling ourselves? The Famous Four?'

'Perhaps the Infamous Four might be more appropriate.' Violet smiled. 'Seriously, Fiona. Let's sit down and see whether, between us, we can come up with a way to clear your name. We'll eat at seven and then we can have our meeting after that.'

Chapter 15

By eight-fifteen they had polished off their meal, and Eric and Matthew were making light work of loading the dishwasher. When all the pots had been cleared away, Violet spread a handful of blank index cards across the kitchen table. Next, she rummaged around in her trusty leopard-effect pencil case, and extracted a Sharpie pen and a large blob of Blu Tack.

'We'll start by writing down the names of the people who were in the tearoom on Sunday afternoon,' she announced, when the dishwasher had been switched on and everyone had gathered around.

'As Eric and I weren't there, I guess we can sit this one out,' Matthew said.

'Oh no you don't,' said Violet, sounding irritatingly bossy, even to her own ears. 'Fiona and I will shout out the names. Eric can write them down – one per index card – and you can stick the cards on the wall.'

Eric scratched his chin. 'Are you sure that's a good idea, Violet? The Blu Tack will play havoc with your emulsion. If you're not careful, you could end up having to repaint the wall.'

Fiona rolled her eyes. 'Trust you to think of that,' she said. 'Ever the pragmatist.'

'Don't worry about the paintwork,' Violet said, keen to get started. 'I need to redecorate in here anyway. Come on, folks, let's crack on.'

Matthew gave a mock salute, and Eric picked up the Sharpie pen.

'All right,' he said, pen poised above one of the index cards. 'Fire away. Give me the first name.'

'The people I recognised were Judith and Andrew Talbot, Nigel and Sandra Slingsby, and my neighbour, Toby Naylor,' Violet said, watching as Eric scribbled down the names.

'And Lisa Wenham was there,' Fiona added, as Matthew stuck the first few index cards in a neat line on the sage green kitchen wall.

'So she was,' Violet said. 'I'd forgotten about her. Was there anyone else you recognised, Fi? You know far more people than I do.'

'There were a few familiar faces from further afield, but not ones I can put a name to.'

'What about the staff?' Violet said. 'The dark-haired woman behind the counter – was her name Anne Burridge?'

Fiona clicked her fingers. 'That's right. She lives in Bakewell now, but she's from Merrywell originally.'

Violet told them about the telephone conversation she'd had with Anne on the morning of Hilary's death.

'Clayton said that he and Hilary had been friends with Anne for years.'

'I'll add her to the list,' Eric said, as he wrote the name on a card and passed it to Matthew.

'Cheers, mate,' Matthew said. 'Doesn't look like you and I will be contributing much to this conversation. Shall we grab another beer?'

'You can have more beer later,' Violet said. 'Come on, guys. Focus. This is important.'

'We are focused,' Matthew said. 'And believe it or not, we're more than willing to chip in . . . if you'll give us a chance.'

Violet folded her arms. 'Feel free to butt in if there's something you want to say.'

Eric leaned against the wall and twirled the Sharpie in his fingers. 'Actually, I'm quite happy to stand back and act as scribe,' he said, looking as if he'd much rather be somewhere else.

Violet turned to Matthew. 'It's over to you then, Matty. What is it you wanted to say?'

'There's nothing I can contribute at this early stage in the proceedings,' he said, 'but I would like you to clarify something. The names on the index cards . . . are these our suspects?'

'I'd say they're more persons of interest,' Violet replied. 'All of these people were within earshot when I arranged my meeting with the Spenbecks. Any one of them could have heard Clayton say that he'd leave the gate open for me.'

'So, in theory, they'd have known how to slip into the garden centre unnoticed on the morning Hilary died?' Matthew said.

'Exactly. It's not much, I know – but we've got to start somewhere.'

'What if it's not any of these people?' Fiona said, sounding utterly defeatist. 'What if the person responsible didn't go in through the back gate? It could have been a random intruder . . . a chancer, intent on stealing whatever they could lay their hands on.'

'That's possible, but a lot less likely,' Violet said, trying to make it sound as though she knew what she was talking about. 'As far as I'm aware, there were no signs that the garden centre had been broken into. And usually, with this type of crime, there's a link between the victim and the suspect.'

Fiona gave an *it was worth considering* shrug.

'The one person who's missing from our list is Clayton Spenbeck,' said Eric.

'Good point,' Violet said, as Eric retrieved another card from the table and wrote Clayton's name on it. 'I also heard Clayton tell

DS Winterton about a troublesome neighbour called Roy Geldard. Apparently, he owns the land that backs onto the garden centre, and he was at loggerheads with Hilary for a while.'

'If it's links you're looking for, you've just found one,' Fiona said. 'Roy Geldard is Simon's grandad.'

'Simon?'

'You know . . . the young waiter in the tearoom who got a ticking-off about his shirt tails? Simon lives with Roy, has done for the last few years.'

Violet nodded. 'Let's add both their names to the list then.'

Eric scratched his head. 'If Hilary was at war with Roy Geldard, why would she employ his grandson?' he said. 'Doesn't that strike you as odd?'

'I think Hilary and Roy had agreed a ceasefire,' said Violet. 'Roy had finally decided to sell the Spenbecks some land, and they were in the process of finalising a deal. Maybe, as part of that deal, Hilary agreed to give Simon a job.'

'Perhaps they only took Simon on under sufferance,' Fiona said. 'If that *was* the case, it's possible they were looking for reasons to get rid of him. Remember how snappy Clayton was about Simon's shirt?'

'You're right, Clayton's reaction was a bit over the top,' Violet said. 'It's something to bear in mind, but let's not get bogged down in speculation. What we really need is a strong lead. We need to find clues, or – even better – hard evidence, otherwise we could end up going down all sorts of blind alleys.'

Matthew added Roy and Simon's names to the list and then stood back and gazed at the wall. 'Is that the lot then?' he said. 'Is there anyone you've missed?'

'No, I think that's everyone,' Violet said.

'Good,' said Eric, 'because that's ten names already, and we're running out of index cards.'

'Ten persons of interest does seem rather a lot,' Fiona said. 'Is there any way we can whittle that number down?'

'That will happen automatically when we move on to our next topic,' Violet said. 'Motive.'

Matthew and Eric exchanged a smirk.

'Before we start on that,' Eric said, 'is there any chance we can replenish the beers?'

With fresh drinks in their hands, the quartet considered each of the names in turn. Within a few minutes, Nigel and Sandra Slingsby and Toby Naylor had been removed from the wall, on the grounds that they had no obvious motive, means or opportunity.

'That's not to say we're eliminating them completely,' Violet said. 'But for now, we'll concentrate our efforts on the other people on the list.'

'We ought to take the Talbots off the wall as well,' Eric said. 'I can't imagine any possible scenario in which Judith or Andrew would want to do away with Hilary.'

'We can remove Andrew's name,' Violet said. 'But I'd like to keep Judith on the list for the time being.'

Matthew screwed up his eyes. 'OK, bossy boots,' he said. 'Would you like to explain why?'

Violet scratched her nose. 'During Hilary's diatribe on Sunday afternoon, she mentioned how easy it had been to get planning permission for the tearoom. I'm assuming approval for that would have gone through the parish council?'

Matthew was well placed to answer the question. He'd been a parish councillor for almost eight years, and was therefore fully conversant with local planning procedures. Violet was also aware that Judith Talbot had been the leader of the parish council for at least a decade.

'The Spenbecks would have applied directly to Derbyshire Dales District Council for planning permission,' Matthew said. 'The parish council did have a say on the matter, but only as representatives of the community. As part of the general decision-making process, we comment on any proposals or applications that might have an impact on Merrywell.'

'How strong an influence is Judith Talbot during those kinds of discussions?' Violet said. 'Could Hilary have been lobbying Judith, or one of the other councillors to push the application through? Or worse, exerting undue influence?'

Matthew downed another mouthful of beer before replying. 'I can assure you, Hilary didn't try anything like that with me.' He smiled. 'Even if she had, it wouldn't have worked . . . not with me, or any of the other parish councillors. We're an honest bunch, and pretty robust too – especially Judith. She's not the sort of person who's easily swayed, if that's what you're implying.'

'I'm not implying anything,' Violet said. 'Just thinking aloud.'

She could see from the set of his mouth that Matthew didn't believe her.

'I realise you're in full "amateur sleuth mode" right now, Violet, but you're also in danger of letting your imagination run away with you,' he said. 'I know Judith can be officious and a stickler, but actually, those are great qualities for a council leader – particularly if someone is trying to put pressure on you. Not that Hilary *was* guilty of doing that. I can assure you, the application for *The Cuckoo's Boot* was treated with due diligence. It was discussed at several parish council meetings, and we also consulted with the community. In the end, there was very little opposition to the idea, so it went through pretty quickly.'

'You said very *little* opposition. Does that mean there was some?' Violet said. 'Who are we talking about?'

'There was one objection,' Matthew said, lowering his gaze.

Into the uncomfortable silence that followed, Fiona released a heavy sigh.

'He's talking about me,' she said. 'I objected the minute I heard about the planning application – although I may as well not have bothered for all the good it did. I expect my objection is on record somewhere though, which will be another strike against me as far as DS Winterton is concerned.'

Violet slipped an arm around Fiona's shoulder and gave her a sideways hug.

'I'm sure I'd have done the same in your position, Fi. Thinking about it, I'd be more surprised if you hadn't objected – it just didn't occur to me that you'd done it officially.'

'It was a complete waste of time,' Fiona said. 'Didn't make a blind bit of difference. Even so, Matthew's right to defend Judith. She is a cantankerous so-and-so at times – but when it comes to her position on the council, she does everything by the book.'

'I agree,' said Eric. 'Plus, it's patently obvious that Judith's not taking backhanders. She'd be living a far more lavish lifestyle, if she was.'

'It's not like Judith has any hidden skeletons either,' Matthew said. 'She's not connected to any scandals that would make her susceptible to blackmail, or bribery. And if there was even a whiff of anyone else on the council taking a bribe or being subjected to undue pressure, Judith would get to know about it – and she'd call it out.'

'OK,' Violet said, accepting that she was outnumbered. 'Between you, you've done a great job of defending Judith. She might not be my favourite person, but it sounds like she's a decent, scrupulous woman, and I agree we should rule her out.'

Matthew plucked Andrew and Judith's names from the wall and threw the cards onto the table. Five names remained: Clayton Spenbeck, Anne Burridge, Roy and Simon Geldard, and Lisa Wenham.

'Can we justify leaving Lisa's name on the list?' Violet asked. 'She and I have never been properly introduced, but I've encountered her a few times when she's been out walking her dogs, and she always nods or says "hello". She seems like a friendly sort, albeit rather gruff. I've got her down as a fairly straightforward kind of person.'

From the look on Fiona's face, it was clear she didn't agree. 'I wouldn't necessarily describe her as straightforward,' she said.

'Really?' Violet narrowed her eyes. 'I imagine her as being rather passive . . . the quiet type, someone who's at one with nature. Definitely not the sort of person who'd attack another Merrywellian in broad daylight.'

'At one time I would have agreed with you,' Fiona said. 'But Lisa and Hilary had a proper humdinger of an argument a while back.'

It was obvious from the way Matthew raised his eyebrows that this was news to him. 'When was this?' he asked.

'Towards the end of last summer,' said Fiona. 'It happened in the café, so I witnessed it with my own eyes. They were too far away for me to hear what was being said – but it was obvious from their body language that they were really going at it.'

'We've already established that Hilary was volatile,' Violet said. 'Maybe Lisa just happened to be the person Hilary picked a fight with on that particular day.'

'That wasn't the impression I got.' Fiona shook her head. 'From what I could tell, it was Lisa who instigated the argument. Mind you, Hilary gave as good as she got . . . no surprise there. There were raised voices, and it started to get extremely heated. I was on the verge of going over and asking them to leave, but then Lisa marched away and I was saved the bother.'

'I'd love to know what they argued about,' Violet said, making a mental note to speak to Lisa Wenham at the earliest opportunity. 'I'd like to talk to Roy Geldard as well. Clayton said Roy's long-running dispute with Hilary had been resolved, but what if that wasn't the case? Maybe they were struggling to agree a price on the land deal.'

'You need to be careful about wading in with those sorts of questions, Violet,' Matthew said. 'From what I know of Roy, he's the kind of guy who'll send you away with a flea in your ear.'

Eric cleared his throat. 'If you want my ten penn'orth, I'd say we're overlooking the most obvious suspect of all.'

They stared at him expectantly.

'I'm talking about Clayton,' Eric said. 'I read online somewhere that sixty per cent of women killed by men in the UK are killed by a current or ex-partner. I bet the police will have Clayton on their radar, even if we haven't.'

'He was in a dreadful state when he found Hilary's body,' Violet said. 'If that was an act, it's worthy of an Oscar. However, you could be right about him being on the police's radar. I do know he's had his fingerprints taken for elimination purposes. I'm assuming the police will have checked him out and run a comparison to see whether his prints were on the owl.'

'I think we'd have heard about it by now if they were,' said Fiona.

'Even so, let's keep his name on the list for the time being,' Eric insisted. 'I've always assumed the Spenbecks were happily married, but sometimes, when you scratch beneath an apparently smooth surface, you get a surprise.'

'I imagine Charlie Winterton will be doing plenty of scratching, round about now,' Violet said. 'He's like a terrier. More of a digger than a scratcher, actually. Maybe I should have a word with him, see what I can find out.'

'He's not likely to tell you much,' Fiona said. 'Not when your best friend is his prime suspect.'

'I'll give him a call tomorrow anyway, see what I can wheedle out of him,' Violet said. 'For now, I suggest we reconvene this council of war.'

'Suits me.' Matthew smiled. 'Do you want me to make coffee and bring it into the living room?'

Violet was more than happy to go with the consensus. She knew the four of them would spend what remained of the evening laughing and joking, and talking about things other than the Hilary Spenbeck case and – right now – that kind of easy conversation seemed very appealing.

Tomorrow would be a different story, though. That's when she would begin to make a few tentative enquiries of her own.

Chapter 16

'I'm really sorry, Violet. Would you prefer it if I took him home and worked a different day?'

Violet's part-time assistant, Molly Gee, was sitting at her desk looking flustered and utterly contrite. The cause of her consternation was her Jack Russell, Alfie, who was currently writhing happily on his back in the middle of *The Memory Box*.

The nine-year-old dog belonged to Molly, but lived at her parents' pub. When Molly had moved into her own place three years earlier, she had decided it would be easier to let Alfie stay at the White Hart, rather than uprooting him from the home he'd known since puppyhood. But today a team of decorators had descended on the pub, called in to repaint the customer toilets – hence Alfie's guest appearance at *The Memory Box*.

'He's as good as gold with the customers – aren't you, Alfie, darling?' Molly gazed lovingly at the dog and made a kissing sound by sucking air through her lips. 'Unfortunately, when something out of the ordinary happens – like the loos being painted – he kicks off big time. Mum and Dad tried keeping him upstairs, but Alfie knew the workmen were around, so he just kept barking and howling and wouldn't shut up. After an hour of that, Mum was at the end of her tether, which is when she rang me. She told me to go and get Alfie after I'd dropped Jamie off at nursery – gave me a right earful, she did. *He's your dog, our Molly. You'll have to have him for the day.* I told her I was at work, but she wouldn't take "no" for an answer.'

'Don't worry about it,' Violet said, leaning down to tickle the bristly white fur on Alfie's chest. 'Let's call today *Bring-Your-Dog-To-Work-Day*. I quite like having an animal in the office, and hopefully Alfie won't feel so territorial here.'

Hearing his name, the dog stood up and shook, his head and body swinging rapidly from side to side. After a quick sneeze, he trotted over to the door, stood up on his hind legs, and gazed out into the courtyard through the glass panel.

'I want to get the accounts done today,' Molly said. 'There are a couple of invoices to send out and some bills that need paying, but once I've done that, I thought I'd make a few calls . . . try to drum up some new business.'

Violet smiled gratefully. 'Thanks, Molly. That's very proactive of you. I spent an hour yesterday doing the same thing. There's a community group over in Belper that I heard about. They've been awarded some lottery funding for a local history project, and I've offered to put a proposal together for them. I'm going to make a start on it today, but maybe you could follow up with that charity in Buxton? The last time I spoke to them, they were keen to do a film to help with fund-raising. Why don't you give them a nudge, and see if they've made up their minds?'

'No problem, I'll give them a ring in a bit,' Molly said. 'If you can keep an eye on Alfie for a minute, I'll go and make us a cuppa. Then, while I'm doing the accounts, you can tell me about Hilary Spenbeck. A little bird told me you were at the garden centre when the poor woman popped her clogs.'

Over strongly brewed cups of Ringtons tea, Violet and Molly sat at their desks and tackled their respective tasks. As they worked, Violet explained what had happened at the garden centre, and why Fiona had been questioned.

'So it's true what they're saying?' Molly said. 'Hilary died in suspicious circumstances?'

Violet assumed that by *they*, Molly meant the village gossip machine.

'It looks that way,' she replied. 'I might give DS Winterton a call later . . . see if he's willing to give me an update.'

'I hope they find whoever did it, and quick,' Molly said. 'Because you and I both know it wasn't Fiona.'

Violet nodded. 'Let's hope the police reach the same conclusion.'

As they focused on their work, they lapsed into companionable silence. Over the next hour, Violet wrote the first rough draft of a proposal for the community group in Belper. It was a contract she was desperate to win – not just because it would provide some much-needed income, but also because it promised to be an interesting project to work on.

At eleven o'clock, Alfie interrupted the quiet calm in the office with a long, low growl. He'd settled by the door and had been observing the comings and goings in the shopping village. The growl suggested something had caught his attention.

'Be quiet, Alfie,' Molly said, as the rumbling growl changed to a loud, repetitive bark. 'What's the matter with you?'

Violet went over to the door and looked out across the courtyard. Tied up outside the shopping village's deli were three dogs. One was a Border terrier with a shaggy coat, and the other two were Patterdales – one black with a white flash on its chest, and the other chocolate brown. Violet recognised them as Lisa Wenham's cherished pack.

'I'm just going to pop out for a minute, Molly,' she said, determined to make the most of this fortuitous opportunity. 'Is it OK if I borrow Alfie?'

'Course it is,' Molly replied. Then, switching to the high-pitched voice she used to address the dog, she said: 'You're due a walkies,

91

aren't you? Are you going to be a good boy?'

At the mention of the 'w' word, Alfie's ears pricked up and he began to prance around in a circle.

'Aunty Violet's going to take you for a little stroll, Alfie,' Violet said, whispering into the dog's ear as she attached the lead to his harness. 'Let's see if you and I can sniff out some information.'

As soon as they stepped into the courtyard, Alfie yanked Violet towards Lisa Wenham's terriers. He was obviously acquainted with them, because his tail was wagging furiously, and he was met with plenty of enthusiastic sniffing and posturing. As Alfie greeted his canine friends, Lisa Wenham emerged from the deli carrying a packet of Derbyshire oatcakes.

'Oh, hello,' she said, staring quizzically at Alfie and then at Violet. 'Are you looking after Alfie today, then?'

Violet nodded. 'Molly brought him to work with her,' she explained, pointing towards *The Memory Box*. 'I'm on a quick break, so I volunteered to take him for a walk. I'm assuming from the wagging tails that he already knows your dogs?'

'My three are acquainted with almost every mutt in Merrywell,' Lisa said, as she unhooked the trio of leads. 'They're a lot more sociable than I am, that's for sure.'

Violet laughed. 'I've seen you around, but I don't think we've been properly introduced. I'm Violet Brewster. I run *The Memory Box* and I live at Greengage Cottage.'

'I know who you are,' Lisa said, her tone warmer than her choice of words. 'Everybody knows everybody in this village.'

'That's true,' Violet said. 'We all cross paths sooner or later, don't we? As a matter of fact, I saw you at the new tearoom on Sunday. I take it you've heard about what happened to Hilary?'

Lisa nodded, her face expressionless.

'Shocking, isn't it?' Violet said, determined to keep the conversation going.

'Aye, I suppose it is,' Lisa replied, as she steered the dogs across the courtyard towards the exit. When Alfie dashed after them, Violet could have hugged him.

'Looks like Alfie wants to tag along,' she said. 'I hope you don't mind.'

Lisa shrugged apathetically. 'We'll be going over the fields in a minute,' she said. 'There's a lot of mud. You're welcome to come with us, but you'll ruin your shoes.'

She pointed to Violet's immaculate brogues, and then to her own muddy boots.

'We'll come as far as the stile then,' Violet said. 'Is that OK?'

Lisa's only response was a listless twitch of her shoulders. With the dogs close at heel, she walked on, out of the shopping village and onto the main road. At the speed Lisa was moving, Violet realised she'd have to be quick if she wanted to ask any questions. Once they had reached the footpath that led onto the fields, this serendipitous meeting would be over.

'Did you know Hilary well?' she said, running to catch up, and all the while thinking about how to keep Lisa talking.

'Can't say that I did,' Lisa replied. 'Didn't really want to, if I'm honest.'

'Didn't you like her?'

'Why are you asking me that?' Lisa said, pausing briefly to upbraid the Border terrier for tangling the dog leads.

'I'm interested, that's all,' Violet said, slightly unnerved by the thunderous expression on Lisa's face. 'I didn't know Hilary well, but from what people have told me, I gather she could be difficult.'

Lisa lifted her chin and looked straight ahead. 'I'm not one for gossip,' she said. 'Never have been. Never will be.'

Having unravelled the dog leads, she set off again.

'I understand you and Hilary fell out,' Violet said, increasing her pace to keep up. 'Back in the summer, wasn't it?'

Lisa turned and glared. 'What's that got to do with you?'

'I . . . I'm curious,' Violet said, disappointed that the conversation wasn't going the way she'd hoped.

'Curious? Is that a euphemism for meddlesome?'

'Sorry. I meant no offence,' Violet said. 'I just wondered why you and Hilary didn't get on.'

'It's none of your business,' Lisa said, pressing her thin lips together and closing down the conversation.

Violet watched her stalk away along the lane. Even if Alfie hadn't chosen that moment to cock his leg, there was no way she would have dared to follow.

Chapter 17

Violet trailed after Alfie as he sniffed his way around the village. It was clear that he was taking *her* for a walk, rather than the other way around. His chosen route took them on a veritable tour of Merrywell – one that Violet was more than happy to go along with. It was good to have a break from the office and breathe in some fresh air.

When he spotted the decorator's van parked in front of the White Hart, Alfie's ears pricked up. He tugged Violet towards it and proceeded to snuffle his nose against one of the tyres. She was surprised by the little dog's strength and determination, and was temporarily outwitted by his reluctance to return to the shopping village.

'I think he was planning to drag me into the pub,' Violet said, when she and Alfie finally got back to the office.

'He probably wanted to bark at the workmen again,' Molly said. 'Little scamp.'

Violet smiled. 'He's quite stubborn, isn't he? I only managed to get him back here by promising a treat. I hope you've brought some with you.'

Molly searched in her bag and pulled out a brown, twisted dog snack, which Alfie accepted gently between his teeth. He lay down, holding it carefully between his front paws, and began to chew it, smacking his chops happily.

'Thanks for taking him out,' Molly said, as she smiled lovingly at the dog.

'It was my pleasure,' Violet replied. 'Although, I must confess, I did have an ulterior motive. I saw Lisa Wenham and her dogs in the courtyard, and I wanted an excuse to engage her in conversation. I thought Alfie would give me an "in", but unfortunately, Lisa wasn't very talkative. Quite the opposite, in fact. She gave me the brush-off.'

Molly laughed. 'Don't take it personally. She's like that with everyone. Lisa's not really a people person.'

'No, she obviously prefers animals of the four-legged variety.'

'What was it you wanted to talk to her about anyway?' Molly said.

'Hilary Spenbeck. Fiona told me that Lisa and Hilary fell out in the café a while back. I wanted to know what their argument was about, but Lisa as good as told me to get lost when I broached the subject. She shot off over the fields and left me and Alfie standing.'

Molly grinned. 'I bet your face was a picture. You're not used to people telling you to buzz off, are you, Violet?'

Violet grinned. 'It's not the first time it's happened, and I doubt it'll be the last.'

'You know, I could have saved you the bother,' Molly said. 'It just so happens that *I* was in the café when Lisa and Hilary had their set-to. I didn't witness the whole thing, but I heard enough to know the argument was something to do with one of Lisa's dogs. You've seen for yourself how fanatical she is about her pets . . . She's extremely protective of them, and from what I could tell, Hilary had done something to Buster, Lisa's Border terrier.'

'Done what?' said Violet.

Molly lifted her shoulders. 'No idea. Sorry. Whatever it was, I can't imagine Hilary would have done it on purpose. She could be insensitive at times, but she wasn't the sort of person who'd be cruel to an innocent animal. At least, I don't think she was.'

'I suppose I could ask Clayton about it,' Violet said. 'But I don't want to pry. The shock of Hilary's death has hit him hard, and I wouldn't want to upset him any more than he already is.'

'I'm sure he'd appreciate you giving him a call anyway,' Molly said. 'Just to see how he is, I mean. Say what you like about Hilary, but Clayton will be lost without her.'

As it turned out, Violet was far too busy to make extraneous phone calls to either Clayton Spenbeck or Charlie Winterton. She spent the next few hours polishing the draft proposal for the community group, and then – after Molly and Alfie had gone home and the afternoon was drawing to a close – she received a telephone enquiry from the director of a local arts project. He was following up on a pitch made to him by Molly the previous week. The organisation was launching a creative event for young adults and, thanks to Molly, they'd decided to appoint *The Memory Box* as its official videographer. Violet was thrilled that business was picking up again, and she made a mental note to celebrate by treating Molly to lunch later in the week.

She arrived home that evening feeling tired, but happy – safe in the knowledge that *The Memory Box* had secured enough work to keep her and Molly occupied for at least the next few weeks.

Matthew had messaged her to say he was having dinner with his parents, so Violet decided to knuckle down to some housework before preparing her own evening meal. As she dusted the living room, a message from Fiona popped onto her phone.

Any news? Have you heard from Charlie Winterton today? xxx

Violet typed out a reply.

No, sorry. I haven't spoken to him. But no news is good news, yeah? How are things with you? Has business picked up at the bakery? xx

Fiona's reply landed as Violet ran a feather duster along the top of the curtain rail.

It's been slightly better today. Judith called in to show her solidarity, which was kind of her – and we already had a group booked in for afternoon tea, so at least the café has been busy. xxx

After scooting around the living room with the Hoover, Violet went into the kitchen and made herself a tuna salad. As she settled down to eat it on a tray in front of the television, her phone pinged again. She glanced at the screen, assuming it would be from Matthew or Fiona, but it was a text from Clayton Spenbeck.

Hi Violet. Just to let you know, I'd still like to go ahead with the film for the garden centre. Perhaps you could come over to chat about how we can take the project forward? It would be good for me to have something else to focus on, other than my grief. Best wishes. Clayton.

Violet balanced her phone on the arm of the settee, wondering how best to break the news to Clayton that she wouldn't be taking the job. Frankly, she was surprised he wanted to go ahead at all. Didn't he have enough to worry about? The funeral arrangements, for example? Not to mention the police investigation into who had killed his wife.

When she'd finished her salad, she started to compose a text.

Hi Clayton, I took on a major project today, so I'm not

She paused for a moment, and then deleted what she'd written. The cursor blinked judgementally as she deliberated over what to say. *Why am I fiddle-faddling around?* she wondered. Surely, the best and only way to deal with this situation was to be honest. Instead of making excuses, she should simply tell Clayton the truth: that she didn't want to take on his project because of her loyalty to Fiona and *Books, Bakes and Cakes*.

Of course she sympathised with Clayton's desire to keep himself occupied, and could understand why he might look for something to take his mind off Hilary's tragic death – but her mind was made up. She didn't want to make his film. All she had to do now was relay that decision to Clayton. However, given his current circumstances, it seemed insensitive to do that via text. The least she could do was visit him and break the news in person. She would go and see him, ask how he was doing, offer her condolences once again, and then explain – as gently as possible – why she had chosen not to take on his project.

She began the text again.

Can I come and see you at the garden centre tomorrow? There's something I need to tell you. I do hope you're OK, Clayton. I know this is a difficult time for you, and if there's anything I can do to help, please let me know.

She sent the message, conscious that the words were trite and inadequate, but unable to think of anything else to say. She felt even more guilty when she received his reply, which was gushing with gratitude.

Thanks so much, Violet. I really appreciate it. As you've probably heard, the garden centre has reopened, but it's my team that is running things. I'm not sure when I'll go back to work. For the time being, I'm staying at home, but you're welcome to visit me here at the house. I'm free all day tomorrow. Would you be able to get here for 11am?

She texted back immediately to confirm the arrangements, uncomfortably aware that Clayton would be feeling a lot less appreciative once she'd told him she wasn't going to make his film.

Chapter 18

Violet was surprised to discover that Clayton's hallway was in need of a fresh lick of paint. She had arrived at Highfield House fully expecting the interior of the Spenbeck residence to be pristine, finished to Hilary's exacting standards – but as soon as she stepped over the threshold, she realised that wasn't the case.

'You'll have to excuse the state of the place,' Clayton said, as if reading her mind. 'Over the last few years, we've spent all of our spare time improving the garden centre, and we've totally neglected the house. Hilary planned to make a start in the summer. She was going to refurbish the whole of the ground floor.'

'I imagine a big house like this takes a lot of maintenance,' Violet said, as they entered a spacious sitting room. 'If you're not careful, it could easily turn into one long, continuous cycle of home improvements.'

She looked around at the sitting room's high ceilings and outdated furniture. An enormous but well-worn rug lay in front of a vaguely art deco fireplace, which was juxtaposed by the daisy-patterned wallpaper on the chimney breast. The latter's orange, gold and brown design suggested it had been hanging there since the 1970s. In the middle of the room, facing the fireplace and arranged in a U-shape around the rug, were three large settees, which were upholstered in mushroom-coloured Dralon.

'This was the room Hilary was going to tackle first,' Clayton said, wafting a hand at the tired décor. 'I inherited Highfield House from my parents, you see, and Dad did very little to it in the last decades of his life. He didn't like changing things . . . preferred to keep everything the way it was when Mum was alive.'

'It's very . . .' Violet hesitated, wondering if she was speaking out of turn. 'Retro. Very retro, and therefore bang on trend.'

Clayton laughed. 'Retro wasn't quite what Hilary had in mind. This house was built in the late Twenties, so she was keen to go with an art deco theme. She'd even picked out the wallpaper.'

'Will you go ahead with her plans?'

'Maybe . . . eventually, but I'm in no rush.' Clayton sat down on one of the settees and invited Violet to do the same. 'Quite honestly, I couldn't face the upheaval at the moment. Besides, strange as it may sound, I like this room the way it is. My parents used to sit in here in the evenings, watching TV together – so it reminds me of my childhood. For me, this room is homely . . . familiar and comfortable. That's what I need right now.'

'I can understand that,' Violet said. 'This is a sad time for you. How are you bearing up?'

He shrugged. 'As well as can be expected. I still don't think it's sunk in properly.'

'Have you heard any more from the police? Are they any nearer to finding Hilary's attacker?'

Clayton shook his head. 'Detective Winterton has rung a couple of times to update me, although there hasn't been much progress for him to report. Hilary's death is being treated as suspicious, but the police have very little evidence to work with, so I'm beginning to wonder whether the case will ever be solved. The problem is, until I know what happened, I don't feel I can mourn properly. Does that make any sense?'

Violet nodded sympathetically. 'I'm sure I'd feel the same if I were in your position.'

'At least the post-mortem is out of the way,' Clayton said. 'That's something, I suppose. It means I've been able to arrange the funeral.'

He mentioned a date in May, explaining that there would be a church service at St Luke's, followed by a private cremation.

'I haven't decided where to hold the funeral reception yet,' he added. 'I don't want to have it here. Hilary would come back and haunt me if I let anyone get even a glimpse of this awful décor.'

'The White Hart has a function room,' Violet said. 'Maybe you could hire that.'

Clayton pulled a face. 'I don't think so . . . Hilary wasn't a fan of pubs. I did try to book the Merrywell Manor Hotel, but they're hosting a mid-week wedding on the same day as the funeral, so all their function rooms are in use.'

'What about the tearoom?' Violet said. 'Hilary worked jolly hard to set it up. It might be a fitting tribute to hold the wake there.'

A slow smile crept across Clayton's face. 'That's an excellent idea, Violet. Why didn't I think of that? Thank you. I'll have a word with Anne . . . see what she thinks. The garden centre will be closed on the day of the funeral anyway, as a mark of respect – so the tearoom will be available, and it's plenty big enough. I want the wake to be a celebration of Hilary's life and all that she achieved – which makes *The Cuckoo's Boot* the perfect venue.'

'Hopefully, the funeral will bring you some closure, and a chance to say a proper goodbye,' Violet said.

'I'd like to think so,' Clayton replied. 'Although DS Winterton has warned that the case is attracting some press attention. I've been told to expect a media presence at the church, both before and after the funeral service.'

'I suppose the press will take an interest while ever the case remains unsolved,' Violet said, 'but I hope they don't make a nuisance of themselves. The sooner the police apprehend the person responsible, the better.'

'I don't have high hopes for an early resolution,' Clayton said.

'So far, the only suspect DS Winterton has come up with is Fiona Nash.'

'I can assure you that Fiona wasn't responsible for Hilary's death,' Violet said. 'I *know* her . . . and she wouldn't hurt a fly.'

'I tend to agree with you,' Clayton said. 'But if it wasn't Fiona, then who was it?'

'I've no idea – and if the police don't know, what chance do we have of working out who the perpetrator is?'

Clayton steepled his fingers and tapped them against his chin. 'I must confess, I've been racking my brains, wondering who might be capable of doing such a terrible thing.'

Violet took the opportunity to ask a question. 'This may not be relevant,' she said, shuffling to the edge of the settee, 'but I gather Hilary had an argument with Lisa Wenham a while back. Do you know what they quarrelled about?'

Clayton released a huff of air. 'Hilary was always falling out with someone,' he said. 'I know we're not supposed to speak ill of the dead, and I don't like to be disloyal, but the truth is, my wife could be thoroughly disagreeable at times. She was always picking an argument with someone, although I didn't know that she and Lisa Wenham had crossed swords. You'll have to ask Lisa if you want to know what they argued about.'

Violet smiled. 'I already have. She told me in no uncertain terms to mind my own business.'

'Based on what I know of Lisa, that doesn't surprise me at all. Having said that, I can't believe she had anything to do with Hilary's death, if that's what you're suggesting.'

'I'm sure you're right,' Violet said. 'I suppose I'm grasping at straws, trying to make sense of what happened to Hilary.'

'You and me both,' said Clayton. 'For my own peace of mind, I need to know who was responsible for her death.'

'Sometimes, in order to find an answer, it's necessary to gather and cross-check several pieces of seemingly unrelated information,' Violet said. 'The main problem for the police will be working out what information is relevant, and which isn't. For instance . . . your neighbour, Roy Geldard – you told DS Winterton that he and Hilary had patched up their differences.'

Clayton nodded.

'Are you absolutely certain about that?' Violet said.

'Yes . . . yes, of course.'

'And what about the land he's agreed to sell to you? Is that transaction signed and sealed?'

'The paperwork was in the process of being drawn up,' Clayton replied. 'Hilary and I were due to visit the solicitor's office next week to sign the contract and complete the purchase, but I've cancelled that appointment for now. I need time to decide whether to go ahead. Acquiring the land was Hilary's idea . . . It was to be her next big project, and I'm not sure I have the energy or enthusiasm to implement her master plan on my own.'

'If you don't mind me asking, what was her master plan?'

Clayton leaned back and draped his right arm along the top of the settee.

'She wanted to create an event space. There's an old barn on the plot we're buying from Roy. Hilary was going to renovate it and use it as a venue for barn dances, Halloween parties, and such like. She also planned to transform the barn into a Grotto at Christmastime – with Santa, reindeer, tweely-dressed elves . . . the whole shebang.' He pulled a face, as if he found the concept distasteful.

Violet laughed. 'I take it you're not a big fan of Christmas?'

'No, I'm not, and neither was Hilary – but she was smart enough to know when something made good business sense. Her strategy was all about getting customers through the doors. She assured me that the people who came to an event at the barn would also spend time and money in the garden centre and tearoom. She even talked about using some of the land we were buying to grow Christmas trees and pumpkins. Apparently, pumpkin picking is big business these days.'

'Did she tell Roy Geldard what she was planning to do with the field?'

'Yes, he knew all about it.'

'And he had no objections?'

'Why would he have? The land in question is on the very edge of Roy's property. It's right next to the garden centre, well out of sight of Roy's house, and far enough away for noise not to be an issue. Believe me, he can't wait to seal the deal.'

'Has he contacted you since Hilary died, to check whether the sale is going ahead?'

'Not yet, but it's only been a few days. He probably doesn't want to intrude.'

'He'll be disappointed if you decide not to proceed,' Violet said. 'But you're under no obligation – not if you haven't signed a contract.'

'True, but Hilary did give her word, and although a verbal agreement isn't legally binding, I'll probably end up doing the honourable thing, even if it means buying the land and doing nothing with it.'

'I wonder if Roy Geldard is a person of interest in the investigation?' Violet said.

'I very much doubt it.'

'DS Winterton suspects Fiona – why not Roy?'

Clayton frowned. 'I know you mean well, Violet, but I think we should leave the investigation to the police, don't you?'

'Sorry,' she said. 'I have a habit of letting my curiosity get the better of me.'

'It's all right – there's no need to apologise. I appreciate you're only trying to help, and I must confess Roy's name has crossed my mind as a possible suspect, but that's pure conjecture on my part. There's absolutely no evidence to suggest he was involved.'

'You don't think Hilary could have invited him over on Monday morning to discuss the land deal?'

'If she did, she didn't mention it to me,' Clayton replied. 'Then again, she often did things without consulting me.'

'If Roy did go to the garden centre that morning – and I realise that's a big *if* – perhaps he and Hilary fell out and came to blows.'

'No . . . no.' Clayton flicked his fingers, dismissing the notion. 'That theory's a non-starter. Thinking about it, Hilary wouldn't have had time to meet Roy, or anyone else for that matter. We were busy that morning. We went into work early to sort out the damage caused by the gale. We wanted to get everything tidied up before we met you at eight o'clock.'

'Roy could have turned up uninvited,' Violet said, trying a different tack. 'His land backs onto yours. Can he access the garden centre directly from his property?'

'Certainly not. The perimeter is securely fenced off. It has to be, for insurance purposes.'

Violet sighed, as her latest, desperate theory crashed and burned.

'I know you're eager to deflect suspicion away from Fiona,' Clayton said. 'She's your friend, so that's understandable – but I honestly can't believe Roy Geldard had anything to do with Hilary's death. His grandson, Simon, on the other hand . . . well, let's just say he'd be a far more likely candidate.'

'He works at the tearoom, doesn't he?'

'Yes.' Clayton rolled his eyes. 'Hilary only employed him to appease Roy. I was against the idea.'

'Oh?' Violet said, alert to any possibility of a motive. 'Why was that?'

Clayton shrugged. 'Simon's a troubled young man. He's had some problems recently.'

'What kind of problems?'

'He lost his mother to cancer a few years ago,' Clayton replied. 'His father's never been around, so Simon had no choice but to move in with Roy – which is when he began to act up. Roy arranged grief counselling for the boy, and the school offered support – but none of it seemed to do any good. Simon became very argumentative with his teachers and disruptive in class, and eventually he started skipping lessons altogether. I understand the final straw came when he was caught defacing school signage. He was suspended and ended up leaving with no qualifications. It was a shame, because he's actually a very bright lad.'

'Hilary obviously spotted his potential,' Violet said. 'It was kind of her to employ him and give him a chance.'

Clayton smiled. 'Trust me, she didn't do it as an act of philanthropy. Hilary knew Roy was coming round to the idea of selling some land, and she hoped she could tip the balance in our favour by offering Simon a job. Roy worships his grandson, and he's desperate for Simon to get his life back on track.'

'Getting a job is a step in the right direction,' Violet said.

Clayton scoffed. 'I'm not sure Simon would agree with you. Since he left school, he's shown zero interest in doing any work. It was obvious to Hilary that Roy was at his wits' end – so, in order to smooth the negotiations, she promised to employ Simon on a trial basis when the tearoom opened. Roy was over the moon with the arrangement. Simon, less so.'

Violet smiled wryly. 'How is it working out?' she asked. 'Is he a good worker?'

'I wouldn't go that far. Simon's extremely capable, but belligerent. He works hard enough to keep himself from being sacked, but he's not likely to win "employee of the month" anytime soon. I suspect he only took the job to please Roy and keep him onside . . . but in fairness, he's not all bad. Deep down, Simon has the makings of a good kid, and he does think the world of his grandad.'

'Perhaps he'll settle down eventually,' Violet said. 'Some people need time to mature before they become their best selves.'

'I hope he does go on to fulfil his potential,' Clayton said, 'but right now, he's not a happy chappie. He doesn't like working in the tearoom, and he's dead set against his grandad selling any land to us.'

'Why's that?'

'Simon's mum spent a lot of time at the barn. She kept horses in that field, and went there every day to take care of them. Simon helped her sometimes, so I suppose the place holds a lot of memories for him.'

'Poor lad,' Violet said. 'He's young. He might not know it yet, but he'll always have his memories, even if he can't keep the field.'

Clayton sighed. 'The Geldards haven't always been the best of neighbours, but they've had a lot to deal with recently, and I hope things work out for them,' he said. 'On reflection, I can't believe either of them had anything to do with Hilary's death, and I know the police have spoken to them – so presumably, they've come to the same conclusion. The sad truth is, DS Winterton and his team are a long way off catching Hilary's attacker.'

'It's early days,' Violet said. 'Police investigations take time.'

'I appreciate that, but it doesn't make it any less frustrating – which is why I need something to take my mind off things – something other than the investigation and the funeral arrangements. I was hoping you and I could make a start on the promotional film next week. Are you available to do some work on it?'

Violet felt a sharp stab of guilt. 'Actually, I need to talk to you about that . . .'

As diplomatically as possible, she let him know her decision, explaining the reasons why she didn't want to work on the film.

'I'm sorry to let you down, Clayton,' she concluded, 'but Fiona has been a good and loyal friend to me since I moved to Merrywell, and I wouldn't feel comfortable helping to promote a business that competes directly with *Books, Bakes and Cakes*.'

He gave a brief nod of acceptance.

'I won't pretend I'm not disappointed,' he said, smiling resiliently. 'But I understand your reasoning, and I appreciate you being candid with me. Maybe we could work together on something else instead? I'll have a think . . . perhaps a project that promotes the garden centre, rather than the tearoom? After all, flowers and plants *are* our core business. I think Hilary lost sight of that sometimes.'

Clayton's reaction was gracious and polite, his words a face-saving manoeuvre that discharged both of them from their tentative agreement. Violet was happy to consider an alternative project, but gut instinct told her it was unlikely to happen.

Chapter 19

There wasn't much left for them to talk about after that. Clayton suggested making a pot of tea, but Violet declined the offer, using the excuse that she had to get back to work.

As she left the house and walked to her car, she noted the lay of the land around the Spenbecks' home. Uphill on the left was a thicket of trees behind a dry-stone wall. Further down Bluebell Hill the vast expanse of the garden centre was clearly visible, as was the high fence around its perimeter. In stark contrast, the landscaped garden around Highfield House was open plan and far less secure. The vast, sweeping lawns were exposed, and easily accessible from the surrounding area.

Violet drove down the tarmacked driveway and exited onto the lower section of the bumpy access road she'd used on Monday. Today, instead of turning left and heading up towards the rear gate behind the retail building, she turned right, continuing down Bluebell Hill to join the lane that ran directly in front of the garden centre. As she drew alongside the customer car park, she felt an inexplicable urge to pull in and stop.

What am *I doing*? she wondered, as she reversed into a parking space. The only sensible answer she could come up with was that she needed to revisit the garden centre to lay to rest the ghost of the events that had taken place there on Monday.

She was trembling as she walked through the main entrance. The plant aisles were busy, packed with green-fingered shoppers, but as Violet weaved her way through the crowds, all she could think about was Clayton cradling a lifeless Hilary in his arms.

By the time she reached the display of water features, she was visibly shaking, so it was something of a relief to find that everything had returned to normal. The fountains were switched on, and the air was filled with the gently soothing sound of running water.

Violet closed her eyes, breathed deeply and forced herself to recall Monday's tragic scene. Was it possible she'd missed something? Some tiny detail that might offer a clue to the identity of Hilary's assailant?

'Hello, Violet.'

She opened her eyes, recognising Charlie Winterton's gruff-but-friendly voice.

'What are you doing here?' he said. 'Returning to the scene of the crime?'

She turned and smiled at him. 'I'm not entirely sure why I'm here,' she replied. 'In theory, I'm facing up to a difficult memory, but now that I'm back, it feels as though I imagined the whole thing.'

'Yes, the place looks innocuous enough today, doesn't it?' DS Winterton said, as he glanced to the right, towards the eclectic display of garden ornaments. 'It feels wrong somehow . . . the customers back in their droves, pottering around as if nothing's happened.'

'It does seem to be business as usual,' Violet said, not sure if she fully approved. 'It's astonishing isn't it – how quickly things go back to normal? It'll be a while before I do. I felt quite shaken when I first walked in here.'

'What happened on Monday isn't the sort of thing you forget in a hurry,' DS Winterton said. 'I'm a seasoned copper . . . twenty-five years on the force . . . but even I don't take things like that in my stride.'

'Are you any nearer to finding out who was responsible?' Violet asked.

'Let's just say we're pursuing a number of enquiries.' He gave a wry smirk, as if embarrassed by the triteness of his own words.

Violet smiled. 'I have every confidence in you.'

'That's reassuring to know . . . and, actually, I do have some good news I can share with you.' He tilted his head towards *The Cuckoo's Boot*. 'Do you have a minute to chat? We can grab a cup of tea, if you want?'

'It's kind of you to offer, Charlie, but if it's a cuppa you're after, I suggest you buy it from *Books, Bakes and Cakes*. They have a shortage of customers, thanks to you. Since you made Fiona your prime suspect, people have been boycotting the café.'

'I'm sorry to hear that,' Charlie said, looking genuinely shame-faced. 'I'll try and make amends by calling in there on my way back to the station.'

He nodded to an area beyond the garden ornaments, where a selection of outdoor furniture was on display. 'If you don't want to go into the tearoom, perhaps we could chat over there for a minute.'

Violet sat at one end of a rattan sofa, and Charlie chose the lounge chair directly opposite her.

'You'll be pleased to hear that your mate Fiona is in the clear,' he said, as he adjusted the brightly printed cushion that was pressing into his back.

'Really? That's a relief,' Violet said, letting go of some of the tension she'd been holding on to. 'Not that you're telling me anything I hadn't already worked out for myself. I assume you've told Fiona the good news?'

'Yes,' Charlie replied. 'I rang and spoke to her myself a short while ago.'

'So, what's changed? Why has she suddenly been vindicated?

Are you allowed to say?'

'I don't see why not. I'm sure Fiona will tell you anyway.' He smiled. 'We found something on the garden centre CCTV footage . . . or, should I say *someone*. It's the person we believe to be the perpetrator.'

Violet's pulse quickened. 'Have you identified who it was?' she said.

'No. The person was wearing dark clothing and a hooded jacket, so their face was hidden – plus, the quality of the image isn't great. They only put in a brief appearance . . . a quick dash across the front of the retail building. Mysteriously, there's no sign of them on the cameras at the main entrance or the car park.'

'Was it a man or a woman?'

'One of those.' DS Winterton grinned. 'Impossible to tell. They were of average height and build, with a slightly hunched posture – but moving fast . . . as if they were in a hurry. Running away from the scene of their crime, most likely. Other than that, there's nothing to help us with an ID.'

'But you think it's the person who assaulted Hilary Spenbeck?'

'Yes, we're pretty confident about that. The timing fits.'

'So, if you haven't managed to identify this person, how do you know it wasn't Fiona?' Violet said.

'There's a time stamp on the CCTV. The image was recorded at 7.44. Fiona told us she was at the Bridge Top garage around 7.45. The security cameras from the garage confirm she was buying petrol there between 7.43 and 7.47. It stands to reason she couldn't have been in two places at once.'

'I did tell you she was innocent,' Violet said. 'But I know you're duty-bound to investigate every possibility.'

Charlie held up his hands. 'For what it's worth, I'm glad we've been able to clear Fiona's name. She's a nice lady, and a talented baker.' He smiled. 'I'm glad you understand why we had to question her.'

Violet returned his smile to show there were no hard feelings.

'So, have you lined up any other suspects, now that Fiona's been eliminated?'

'We're working on it,' Charlie said, 'but this isn't a straightforward case. Other than the owl and the CCTV footage, there's a distinct lack of evidence . . . nothing that points us in any particular direction. All we can do is continue to ask questions and keep investigating.'

'Have you checked the other fingerprints on the owl?'

'We have, but unfortunately, we've not been able to match them to anyone on our database. They most likely belong to other shoppers who picked up the owl, took one look at it, and put it straight down again – and who can blame them? It's an ugly thing.'

Violet smiled.

'Obviously we'll continue to check the prints against those of any future suspects. However, depending on the degree of premeditation, the attacker may have been wearing gloves. Like I say, we'll just have to keep looking for new leads. We'll find something eventually.'

'Well, I'm glad Fiona's in the clear anyway,' Violet said. 'And, if you're interested, I do have the names of a couple of other people you might want to talk to.'

Charlie folded his arms, but listened attentively when Violet told him about the argument between Hilary and Lisa Wenham. She also took the opportunity to remind him about the long-running dispute between Hilary and Roy Geldard.

When she'd finished speaking, Charlie looked deflated.

'We've already spoken to Lisa Wenham,' he said. 'In fact, we've talked to everyone who was in the tearoom on Sunday afternoon. It's not relevant now, but Ms Wenham claims she didn't see the argument between Fiona and Hilary. She admits to hearing raised voices, but she had her back turned, so she didn't actually see anything.'

'That's not true,' Violet said. 'Lisa saw what happened. I know she did. She was completely agog, just like everyone else. Why would she say she had her back turned when she didn't?'

Charlie stuck out his bottom lip. 'I don't know,' he said. 'Perhaps she didn't want to point the finger of blame at Fiona. If, as you say, she's been on the receiving end of a backlash from Hilary Spenbeck herself, maybe she sympathised with Mrs Nash.'

'Did Lisa tell you that she and Hilary had fallen out?'

'No, this is the first I've heard of it. Then again, it's not something we'd have asked about, and she obviously decided not to volunteer the information. You're right though – if there's a history of ill-feeling between Lisa and Hilary, it's something we should ask her about. I'll send an officer over to have another word with her.'

'And what about Roy Geldard? And/or, his grandson, Simon?'

'Would it surprise you to learn that someone's already spoken to the Geldards?' Charlie said, giving her an indignant half-smile. 'What is it you think we've been doing over the last few days, Violet? Sitting around on our backsides, contemplating our navels?'

She blushed, aware that she had pushed things as far as she dared for the time being.

'We're fully aware that Mr Geldard was in the middle of selling a plot of land to the Spenbecks,' Charlie added. 'And yes . . . with those kind of deals, there's always the potential for problems, but he's assured us the legalities were proceeding smoothly – and that's been confirmed by Mr Spenbeck and the solicitors working on behalf of both parties. The contract is due to be signed next week.'

'Actually, when I spoke to Clayton this morning, he told me he's put the sale on hold for the time being.'

Charlie shrugged. 'I can't say that I'm surprised. However, it was definitely going ahead when Mrs Spenbeck was alive, and there's no indication of any recent animosity between her and Roy Geldard. Mr Geldard isn't a well man, so he's eager to get his hands on the money from the sale. He says he wants to use it to help his grandson out.'

'Right . . . so it would have been in his interest to keep Hilary onside to complete the sale,' said Violet. 'Is that what you're saying?'

'That's about the size of it. She was no good to him dead . . . and now that she is, I expect he'll be worried about delays, or the sale being cancelled altogether.'

'What about Simon Geldard, then?' Violet said. 'Apparently, he isn't too happy about his grandad selling the land.'

'Says who?'

'Clayton Spenbeck.'

DS Winterton looked unconvinced. 'If Roy Geldard intends to give Simon the money from the land sale, I'd have thought the lad would be all for it. There's no mention of him being disgruntled about it in his statement – but again, I don't suppose it's something we would have asked about. At the time, we were more interested in what Simon had witnessed during Hilary's argument with Fiona.'

'Is it worth having another word with him, perhaps?' Violet said. 'The Geldards and the Spenbecks live alongside each other. Roy or Simon could have climbed over into the garden at Highfield House – and made their way from there to the rear gate of the garden centre. Simon was standing at the next table when I arranged my meeting with Clayton, so he'd have known the gate was going to be unlocked. And, as a garden centre employee, he'll know where the CCTV cameras are positioned. More importantly, he'd know how to avoid them.'

DS Winterton seemed dubious. 'The lad's only worked at the garden centre for a few days. He's hardly an old hand, is he?'

'No, but the person on the CCTV didn't manage to avoid the cameras altogether. And Simon does fit the description you gave earlier. He's of average height and build, and he's young . . . so he'd be more than capable of moving quickly to avoid being recognised on camera.'

DS Winterton nodded. 'OK, I take your point. I'll talk to him again, but it won't be today.'

'Why not?' Violet said, ignoring the frown of irritation on Charlie's face. 'He works in the tearoom. You could go and see him now, while you're here.'

'You're not my boss, Violet, and this isn't the only case I'm working on. I need to get back to the station.'

As Charlie spoke, Violet leaned to the right and peered over his left shoulder. Spiralling upwards from behind the retail unit was a thin plume of white smoke.

'Charlie! Look.'

The urgency in her voice halted the detective mid-sentence. He turned and stared at the growing column of smoke.

'Do you think it's someone burning rubbish?' Violet said.

'I'll go and check,' said Charlie. 'And to be on the safe side, you'd better alert whoever's in charge of the garden centre.'

Chapter 20

As Charlie raced towards the source of the fire, Violet hurried towards the tearoom, hoping that Anne Burridge would be there, and able to take responsibility for the situation.

Thankfully, someone must have already seen the smoke and raised the alarm, because when Violet reached the door, she almost collided with a panic-stricken Simon Geldard, who burst out of the tearoom like a greyhound breaking free of its trap.

'There's a fire,' Violet said, as he shot past. 'Up near the retail unit. I'll go in and tell Anne.'

'She already knows about it,' Simon replied. 'Don't worry. I'm on it.'

'Shall I ring the fire service?' Violet said, as he hurtled away.

'No need,' he said, shouting over his shoulder. 'I'll sort it.'

Violet watched him sprint towards the smoke. Not knowing what else to do, she decided to follow him. As he ran, Simon snatched up a pair of hose reels, and it soon became apparent that he intended to tackle the fire himself. Violet thought it an imprudent thing to do. Things didn't look particularly serious now, but if the fire took hold it could easily spread to the retail unit. If that happened, the entire building would be ablaze within minutes.

Clayton Spenbeck has enough on his plate as it is, Violet thought. *The last thing he needs is for the garden centre to burn down.*

She pulled out her phone, wondering whether to call the emergency services anyway – but then, as she studied the drifting plume of smoke, she realised it was white. She'd read somewhere that white smoke meant a small fire. When things became serious, the smoke changed to billows of grey or black. She was also reassured by DS Winterton's presence at the scene. If Simon's attempts to get the fire under control were unsuccessful, Charlie wouldn't hesitate to call in the emergency services.

Violet tucked her phone back into her bag and caught up with Simon by the metal security fence. Charlie was already helping him attach the hoses to a couple of stand pipes connected to the mains water. When Simon switched the first one on, he was able to direct a pressurised stream of water onto the source of the fire – which she now realised was on the other side of the fence.

Charlie followed suit with the second hose, and as Violet edged closer, she spotted the ridge of a roof peaking up over the top of the spiked fence. The building looked to be in reasonable repair, but there were several missing tiles, and the smoke was drifting out from between the gaps. It was into these spaces that Simon and Charlie were directing the hoses.

'What is that building?' Violet asked.

'It's my grandad's barn,' Simon said, his blue eyes wide and agitated.

'Has someone called 999?' said Charlie. 'These hoses are OK for keeping the fire under control, but we need to get the professionals on the job.'

'No!' Simon shouted. 'We don't need firefighters. There's no point wasting their time . . . We've got this.'

Based on the diminishing spiral of smoke, Simon's confidence seemed well founded. The dampening down was working, and it looked as if the makeshift hoses would be enough to tackle the emergency.

'You need to step back, Violet,' Charlie said, as he turned and caught sight of her. 'As fires go, this might not look like much, but it's not wise to get too close.'

She did as she was told, backing away and moving along the fence. From her new position she had a better view of Simon Geldard's face. His cheeks were blotchy, and was it her imagination, or did he look tearful?

Charlie was peppering him with questions. 'What's in the barn, Simon? Does your grandad keep any fuel in there? Or anything that could explode?'

'Nah.' Simon shook his head. 'We used to stable the horses in there, but it's empty now. There are a few strands of hay maybe, but nothing much else.'

On her left, through the slats in the fencing, Violet noticed a sudden flash of movement on the other side. She caught a glimpse of what seemed to be a blue overall, and then she heard a string of expletives uttered by an angry male voice. Whoever was on the other side of the fence was not a happy man.

'Grandad?' Simon said. 'Is that you?'

'Yeah, of course it's me. Who else is it going to be?'

'Don't . . . don't worry.' Simon said, his words coming out in a stutter. 'We've got everything under control.'

'You could have fooled me!' Roy Geldard said. He was leaning against the fence now, and shouting through one of the narrow gaps. 'What the hell is going on? What have you done this time?'

'What do you mean? Why are you saying that?' Simon said, as he continued to direct the arc of water onto the roof of the barn. 'Why do you always assume it's my fault when something goes wrong?'

'Because, me laddo, it usually is,' Roy replied. 'Have you been smoking in there again?'

'No. I haven't. Shut up, Grandad, and tell me what's happening over there. Is the fire out?'

'It seems to be, but I won't know for certain until I've had a look inside.'

'Whoa!' DS Winterton called out a warning. 'Whatever you do, mate, don't open the barn door. There could be embers still burning. If you open the door and let in a fresh supply of oxygen, the whole thing could flare up again.'

'I couldn't open the door, even if I wanted to,' Roy said. 'It's padlocked, and I don't have the key. The only thing I can do is go and have a gleg through the window on the other side.'

'No, Grandad.' Simon sounded desperate now, verging on tears. 'Leave it. It's not safe.'

Violet had been joined at her vantage point by several other onlookers, including Judith Talbot and Sandra Slingsby.

'What's going on here then?' said Sandra.

'I would have thought that was obvious, dear,' Judith said, before Violet had a chance to respond. 'There's a fire. There's no smoke without one. Has anyone called the Fire Brigade?'

'Not yet,' Violet said. 'And, hopefully, we won't need to. It looks as if it's under control.'

The smoke had dissipated, and was now little more than a curling wisp high above the roof of the barn.

'All credit to Simon for having the good sense to act quickly,' Judith said.

They stood and watched for a few more minutes – but as the prospect of a dramatic inferno faded and the last tendrils of smoke drifted away, so did Judith and Sandra. On the other side of the fence, there was another flicker of blue as Roy Geldard returned from assessing the damage through the barn window.

'How's it looking over there?' DS Winterton said. 'Is the fire completely out?'

'Yes. Crisis over,' Roy said, sounding subdued but extremely angry. 'No need to call the emergency services.'

'Were you able to tell what started it?' DS Winterton said.

'No, but it'll be what I said . . . a cigarette butt, carelessly discarded by my irresponsible grandson. Isn't that right, Simon?'

'Ye . . . yes,' Simon said, capitulating reluctantly. 'I'm sorry, Grandad.'

Roy Geldard pushed his face against the fence, pressing his right eye against the gap.

'You're *sorry*?' he said, as he glared at Simon. 'You'll be more than sorry if you carry on as you are. You'd better get yourself round here, lad, and fast. This is a mess of your making, and you need to get it sorted, once and for all. The sooner this barn is cleared away and sold, the better. I'm trying my best to do right by you, Simon, but you're not making things easy.'

'Give the kid a break,' DS Winterton said. 'If it wasn't for his quick thinking, the fire would have really taken hold by now, and there'd be no barn left for you to sell.'

'Aye, and if it wasn't for 'im, there'd have been no fire in the first place – so you'll have to excuse me if I'm not gushing with praise for his heroic actions.' Roy stuck an index finger through the gap in the fence and used it to beckon Simon towards him.

'You get yourself home, lad. *Now.* You understand?'

'But I'm working, Grandad . . . I don't finish till four.'

'Never mind that. Tell them there are extenuating circumstances. You need to come home and start taking responsibility for your actions. You've caused a problem here, and it needs fixing. I'm not going to do it for you. Not this time.'

DS Winterton regarded Simon sternly. 'If the fire was your fault, Simon, then you should count your blessings. You've got off lightly here today. Things could have been a lot more serious. If you're daft enough to smoke, you should at least dispose of your nub ends responsibly.'

'Yeah,' Simon said, head bowed. 'Sorry.'

'You and I need to have a chat,' DS Winterton added.

'About the barn?' said Simon.

'No, I'd like to know where you were on Monday morning,' DS Winterton had lowered his voice, and Violet strained to hear what he was saying. 'But let's not have this conversation here,' he added. 'We'll catch up later and talk then. OK?'

'I can tell you now where I was,' Simon said. 'I was at home. The tearoom was closed because of what happened to Mrs Spenbeck, so I had the day off.'

'What about early on? Say between half seven and eight o'clock?'

Simon pushed his hands into his pockets. 'Like I said, I was at home.'

Roy's voice boomed from the other side of the fence. 'I can vouch for the lad,' he said. 'Simon was with me, at the house – and, if you can spare 'im, that's precisely where I'd like him to be now.'

DS Winterton stared at Simon for a few more seconds, and then tilted his head towards the exit.

'Off you go then,' he said. 'You'd better do as your grandad says, but you and I will be talking again, young man. You can count on it.'

As he turned to go, Simon cast an almost imperceptible glance in Violet's direction, his eyes appealing for something. Help, maybe? The poor kid reminded her of a cornered animal. Beneath all of the bravado, she was sure he felt scared and vulnerable.

What is it that's troubling you, Simon? she wondered. *What are you afraid of?*

Chapter 21

With the evening sun warming her face, Violet followed the path around the side of Greengage Cottage and entered her back garden. Next door, her neighbour, Toby, was pottering about in his flower bed.

'Evening, Toby,' she shouted, as she dug around in her bag for her door key. 'Are you OK?'

He stopped what he was doing and came over to lean on the wall. 'Not so bad, thank you, Violet. Thought it was time to get the bedders in,' he said, pulling off a pair of compost-covered gardening gloves. 'I've gone for petunias, nicotiana and mesem-bryanthemums this year. Plus the usual geraniums, of course. Should look nice and colourful in a few months.'

Toby was an avid gardener and a font of knowledge when it came to plants and flowers.

'There's been some excitement down at the garden centre this afternoon,' he added. 'I missed it by about half an hour, but appar-ently it was all hands to the pump . . . quite literally.'

'You're talking about the fire?'

'Aye, Roy Geldard's barn. You know about it, do you? As I understand it, the whole thing was over almost before it began, and young Simon was the hero of the hour.'

Violet smiled, thinking it wise to keep quiet about Simon being the person who had started the fire in the first place.

'I was there when it happened,' she said instead. 'And, yes, Simon acted very quickly and sensibly.'

'Well, he would do,' Toby said. 'His mam used that barn to stable her horses. I reckon the place means a lot to the lad.'

'It's a good job there were no animals in the barn today,' Violet said. 'Otherwise, things could have been a lot worse.'

'Yeah, lucky really. Roy only let the horses go a month or so ago. I know he was reluctant to part with them, on account of them having belonged to his daughter – but he's got Parkinson's, so he's scaling everything down to minimise the work.'

'What happened to the horses?' Violet said.

'I'm not sure, but Roy will have found a good home for them – that I do know. It's a shame, but taking care of horses . . . any kind of animal . . . can be hard work, and Roy knows he can't carry on as he has been doing, not indefinitely.'

'It sounds like he's done the sensible thing in the circumstances,' Violet said. 'Best to get these things sorted before they become too much of a struggle.'

'Things might have been different if that grandson of his had been willing to pitch in and help,' Toby said. 'If Simon had shown more interest, they could have hung on to the horses – but Roy can't rely on the lad. He told me so himself, the last time we met up for a pint. Simon was expelled from school, you know . . .'

'I heard he was suspended, not expelled,' said Violet.

'Same thing, isn't it?'

'Not really,' Violet replied.

Toby shrugged. 'All I know is, Simon was chucked out for vandalising school property. The lad's a troublemaker and a maverick – likes to do things *his* way, at his own pace, which sometimes means not doing them at all. All the young 'uns are the same nowadays.'

'He works full-time at the tearoom now,' Violet said, feeling an instinctive need to defend Simon's reputation, as well as that of young people generally.

'I know he does,' Toby said. 'I saw him there on Sunday. He served me my tea.'

'Maybe Simon just wasn't cut out for taking over Roy's small-holding,' Violet said. 'Working the land isn't everyone's idea of the perfect job.'

'To be frank, I don't think Simon's cut out for very much,' Toby said. 'He's what you might call *work-shy*. As for Roy's place, it's a stretch to call it a smallholding these days. It's become very run down over the last couple of years, and I heard on the grapevine he's hoping to sell a chunk of land to the Spenbecks . . . although, I guess it'll be Clayton he sells it to, now that Hilary's gone. A real shocker that, wasn't it? I heard the police are treating her death as suspicious.'

'Yes, I believe they are,' Violet said, unwilling to elaborate and suddenly eager to get inside.

'I don't know what Merrywell's coming to,' Toby added. 'There's always summat kicking off these days.'

'Tell me about it,' Violet said, as she slipped her key into the lock. 'And there was I, thinking I'd moved to a quiet, sleepy village.'

Toby laughed. 'Appearances can be deceptive,' he said. 'In my experience, you can't afford to take anything at face value.'

The first thing Violet did when she got inside was feed her cat, Rusty, and put the kettle on. As she stroked the cat and waited for her mug of tea to brew, her phone rang.

It was her mother.

Knowing there was no such thing as a short conversation with Rachel Middleton, a.k.a. her mum, Violet added a splash of milk to her tea and sat down at the kitchen table before answering the call.

'Hi, Mum. Are you OK?'

'Yes, thank you, darling. I've been out for lunch with the girls today.'

The 'girls' to which her mother was referring were all septua-genarians, and members of the same bridge club.

'That sounds nice,' Violet said.

'Actually, it wasn't. The restaurant we went to was absolutely ghastly. The food was dreadful and the service was even worse. We won't be going there again.'

'Oh, well. Even if the food was lousy, I'm sure you enjoyed spending time with your friends.'

Her mother released a heavy sigh. 'For the most part,' she said, 'although Jacqueline Rheinhart spent most of the after-noon swanking about the Caribbean cruise she'll be going on at Christmas. That woman is insufferable at times.'

Jacqueline Rheinhart was her mother's one-time bridge partner, but a few months ago there had been a 'cooling' of their friendship. Violet assumed there'd been some sort of quarrel, but as her mother hadn't volunteered any information, she had decided not to pry.

'Of course, she wanted to know what I was doing at Christmas,' her mother continued. 'Not that she was in the slightest bit inter-ested. Her only reason for asking was to show me up. She knew I couldn't possibly compete with a Caribbean cruise.'

Violet laughed. 'I shouldn't imagine many people can,' she said.

'In the end, I was forced to tell her that I didn't *have* any plans.'

'That's hardly surprising,' Violet said, acutely aware of where this conversation was heading. 'Christmas is eight months away, Mum. It's far too early to be making plans.'

'Nonsense,' her mother said. 'When you get to my age, it's nice to have something to look forward to. Of course, if you don't *want* me to come and stay with you, I can always make alterna-tive arrangements.'

And there it is, Violet thought. *Her mother's reason for ringing . . . to secure an early invitation for Christmas.*

'I've never said I don't want you to come,' Violet said. 'In fact, this is the first time we've even discussed Christmas.'

'Trust me, darling, these things are best sorted early, rather than leaving everything until the last minute.'

'If you say so. Personally, I'm not big on long-term planning these days,' Violet said. 'I prefer to live in the moment.'

Her mother tutted. 'I appreciate you like to take things in your stride, now that you're living in the countryside, but there is such a thing as being too laid-back, you know.'

Violet gritted her teeth. 'Look, Mum, if you'd like to come here for Christmas, you'd be very welcome – but let's work out the details nearer the time, shall we?'

'Thank you, darling, that's very kind of you,' her mother said. 'What about Amelia? Will she be staying as well?'

Violet sighed impatiently. 'Like I said, let's worry about the details nearer the time. I've no idea what Amelia will be doing for Christmas. Knowing her, she'll decide a few days beforehand. However, you've asked first, so don't worry . . . you've bagged the spare room. If Amelia does turn up, she'll have to sleep on the sofa.'

'I'm sure she won't object to her old gran being given priority. How is my lovely granddaughter, anyway? I've not spoken to her for ages. Is she enjoying her new job?'

'Yes, it's certainly keeping her busy. You should ring her and have a chat.'

'Good idea. I'll give her a bell now.'

Violet was astonished. Was her mother bringing the call to an end already? If she was, it would be their briefest telephone conversation in a long, long time.

'So, that's settled then?' her mother added. 'I'll be coming to you for Christmas?'

'Yes . . . yes, I look forward to it. Although I hope I'll see you before then.'

'Of course you will. I'll come and stay for a long weekend. Maybe in a few months, when the weather's warmed up.'

'Great,' said Violet. 'Give me some notice though, because Matthew and I are hoping to have a weekend away some time in the summer.'

'Are you now?' Her mother's words were delivered with an underlying chuckle. 'It sounds as though things are getting serious between the two of you.'

'Yes, I guess they are,' Violet replied. 'Matthew's lovely.'

'I'm glad, because you're also a lovely person, Violet, and you deserve some happiness.'

Compliments from her mother were as rare as hen's teeth, so Violet paused to savour the moment.

'Thanks, Mum,' she said. 'Matthew and I *are* happy, but we're taking things slowly.'

'That's very sensible, but don't take too long. After all, neither of you are getting any younger.'

Violet laughed. *There we are*, she thought. *A rare compliment, followed by a snide remark. That's the mother I know and love.*

Chapter 22

The next day, Violet walked the long way to work, to get in a few extra steps. As she looped behind the back of the village hall and past the school, she spotted Lisa Wenham coming towards her with her three dogs.

Violet's first instinct was to dash across the road to avoid another frosty exchange, but she forced herself to keep going and not be silly.

Brave it out, Violet. You live in the same village as this woman. It's not as if you can avoid her forever.

As Lisa drew near, Violet fixed a smile to her face. 'Morning,' she said, in her cheeriest voice. For good measure, she bent down to greet the dogs, who seemed thrilled to see her, even if their owner wasn't.

'Good morning, Violet,' Lisa replied. 'I'm glad I've bumped into you.'

One of the Patterdale terrier's ears had blown inside out, and Violet took a moment to flip it back to its correct forward position before standing up.

'I was sharp with you the other day,' Lisa said, the words tumbling out in a rush. 'I'm sorry. It was uncalled for.'

Violet smiled. 'Don't be sorry. I'm the one who should be

130

apologising. I have a habit of poking my nose in where it's not wanted – I'm afraid it's one of my many faults. In my defence, I was trying to help a friend, but that doesn't excuse my rudeness.'

'I assumed that's what you were doing,' Lisa said. 'And although your loyalty is commendable, you were pointing the finger of blame in the wrong direction if you were suggesting *I* attacked Hilary.'

'I apologise,' Violet said, giving a slow nod. 'And for the record, I'm relieved to say that Fiona has now been cleared. She was the friend I was trying to help.'

'I know that.' Lisa managed a cynical smile. 'The whole village knows that Fiona has been questioned by the police – and most of us were convinced of her innocence long before the police got around to clearing her name.'

Violet was puzzled. 'If that's true, then why have the locals stopped going to the bakery and café?' she said. 'Why would they do that, if they know she's innocent?'

'Because people don't want to get dragged into the speculation that's being bandied about,' Lisa said. 'The only sure way to avoid it is to keep a low profile and stay away from the BBC.'

'And yet now is precisely the time when Fiona's friends and customers should show their support,' Violet said. 'If what you say is true, and people are convinced of her innocence, the best way for them to express their loyalty is to shop at the bakery and eat at the café.'

'Don't worry, she'll be inundated with customers, now that her name's been cleared and the gossip has fizzled out,' Lisa said. 'Speaking personally, I don't frequent the café very often. I prefer to sit quietly in my living room, with a pot of home-brewed coffee. The truth is, I'm not big on socialising. The longest conversations I have these days are with my dogs.'

Violet grinned. 'I'm sure they're very good listeners,' she said. 'And at least they won't give you any backchat.'

Lisa flashed a smile that transformed her whole demeanour.

'Don't you believe it,' she said. 'They have their own special ways of making their opinions known, and they usually have the last word as well.'

Lisa's love for her dogs was evident in the way her face brightened whenever she spoke about them. Violet leaned down and gave each of the dogs one last stroke before moving on.

'Rumour has it you're quite the amateur detective,' Lisa shouted, as Violet walked away. 'If that's true, don't you want to hear why I fell out with Hilary Spenbeck?'

Violet stopped and turned. 'Not if you don't want to tell me.'

'Having had some time to reflect, I think it's best that I do,' Lisa replied. 'I don't want you to have any lingering doubts about my innocence.'

Violet smiled. 'You've said you had nothing to do with what happened to Hilary, and I'm happy to take you at your word,' she said. 'Although I must admit, I would like to understand why Hilary was so unpopular with the locals. It sounds like she fell out with a lot of people, and I'm interested to know why that was.'

'Does there have to be a "why"?' said Lisa. 'Can't you just accept that Hilary's mean streak was part of her personality? The sad truth is, she was a self-centred, unpleasant woman. The only thing she really cared about was making money.'

'In my experience, there's always a "why",' Violet said. 'People behave as they do for a reason. Our personalities are shaped by our upbringing and background. Hilary's desire for money, for instance, may have stemmed from a childhood tainted by financial insecurity.'

'Forgive me, but that sounds like psychobabble to me,' Lisa said. 'As regards Hilary's life before she came to Merrywell, I'm afraid I know nothing about that. She was friends with Anne Burridge at university, though. She might be able to tell you about Hilary's early life.'

'Is that how Hilary met Clayton? Through Anne?'

'Yes, it was quite the topic of conversation in the village at the time. You see, there'd always been an unspoken expectation that Clayton and *Anne* would eventually get together. They were great friends when they were teenagers – but then Anne went off to university and, on one of her visits home, she brought Hilary with her. Clayton was instantly smitten. Anne didn't get a look-in after that.'

Lisa joined Violet and they walked on together, the dogs leading the way.

'Tell me about your argument with Hilary, then,' Violet said. 'What did you fall out about?'

'I had a go at her about a plant she sold me,' Lisa said. 'My garden's only small, and most of it is given over to lawn for the dogs, but last summer I decided to add a splash of colour to the patio. I took myself off to the garden centre and bought half a dozen geraniums in terracotta pots – and as I was leaving, I ran into Hilary. She said I should buy something else to give my garden a Mediterranean feel. She tootled off and came back with a small, pretty-looking shrub with dark green leaves and little clusters of purply-peach flowers. It was nice. The colour of the flowers reminded me of those Fruit Salad chews I used to buy as a kid. I'm no expert, but it was an attractive plant – so I took Hilary's advice and bought it.

'As it turns out, it was a lantana. It's a beautiful shrub, but what I didn't realise was, it's toxic to dogs. The next day, Buster . . .' She pointed towards her dogs. 'He's the one in the middle there, the Border terrier . . . I caught him chewing some of the leaves. I told him off . . . shouted at him for ruining my new plant, but I had no idea it would do him any harm. Thankfully, the other two never went near it. The only greenery they'll eat is grass, and even that has to be a certain kind. Buster's a lot less fussy. He's into everything. Much more mischievous.'

'What happened, after he'd eaten the lantana?' Violet said.

'The first thing I noticed was that he'd stopped eating. Buster loves his food, so I knew straight away there was something wrong. Then he started vomiting, and he had the trots. Really, really poorly, he was. I rushed him to the vet and right away she asked whether Buster had eaten anything he shouldn't. I told her about the lantana, and that's when she explained how toxic it is to animals. Buster ended up having to go on a drip and stay at the vet's overnight. The poor little mite was badly dehydrated, and it was touch and go at one point. As you can imagine, I was beside myself with worry.'

'And that's why you had a go at Hilary?'

'Yes. I'm pleased to say, Buster made a full recovery, but after I'd brought him home, it hit me just how close I'd come to losing him – and all because of an ill-advised recommendation from Hilary Spenbeck. My dogs are my family, and Hilary knew that. She should have warned me about the plant, or better still, not sold it to me in the first place.'

'Maybe she didn't know it was toxic,' said Violet.

'It was her *business* to know,' Lisa said, her eyes flashing with renewed anger. 'Her father-in-law would have known. When Dennis ran the garden centre, it wasn't the mammonish retail outlet it is now. He understood horticulture, and he cared about people. He really took the time to get to know his customers. He knew how precious my dogs were to me, and he would never have put them at risk like that. Hilary, on the other hand, didn't give a damn. All she cared about was making a sale.'

'So, you decided to give her a piece of your mind?'

Lisa gave a crooked smile. 'I didn't set out with that intention,' she said. 'I saw her in the café and thought I'd go over and tell her what had happened with Buster, so that she could avoid anything similar happening to other pet owners.'

'Did she apologise?' Violet asked.

'Did she heck as like. She told me she wasn't responsible for the welfare of my dogs . . . said *I* was their owner, and it was my job to make sure they were properly looked after. *What about your responsibility as a plant seller?* I said, but she just sneered at me.

Even when I described how close I'd come to losing Buster, she just shrugged her shoulders and said it wasn't her fault. *Sue me if you think it'll do any good*, she said, knowing full well I couldn't afford to do any such thing.'

'I can understand why that would make you angry,' said Violet.

'I was furious,' Lisa said. 'It's not often I lose my temper, but I had an overwhelming urge to swing for Hilary Spenbeck that day.'

'But you didn't?'

'No, of course not. I backed down and walked away. Things might have been different if Buster had died. If that had happened, I probably would have clonked her one – I might even have wanted to kill the woman – but, of course, wanting to do something, and actually doing it are two very different things.'

'You're right,' Violet said. 'Even the angriest of people are loath to cross that particular line.'

'I'm not an aggressive person, but I confess I wanted to throttle Hilary,' Lisa said. 'The truth is, it was the thought of my dogs that held me back and stopped me from doing the unthinkable. If I had assaulted her – or worse – I'd have been convicted and possibly sent to jail, and who would have looked after my dogs then? My animals mean the world to me, and I intend to be there for them while ever they need me.'

They had rejoined the main road through Merrywell and were heading towards the shopping village.

'I admit I was fuming that day, but I would never have caused Hilary any physical harm,' Lisa said, her expression intense and serious. 'Loving and nurturing my dogs will always be my priority. Their welfare takes precedence over any negative feelings I might have towards other people, or life in general.'

There was no doubting Lisa's sincerity, or the strength of the emotional bond she had with her pets. Even so, Violet couldn't shake the feeling there was something she wasn't saying.

Was this sudden desire to volunteer information Lisa's way of getting everything off her chest, or simply an attempt to get Violet off her case? Had Lisa revealed the whole story, or just the part she was willing to share?

'This is the longest conversation I've had for a long time,' Lisa said, as they came to a halt outside the shopping village. 'I'm glad we've had an opportunity to get to know each other a little better, Violet. As anyone in the village will tell you, I'm not big on joining in, but I'm always around, walking the dogs – so next time you see me, be sure to say hello.'

'I will,' Violet said. 'Goodbye, Lisa, and thanks for explaining what happened with Hilary.'

As she strolled through the courtyard towards *The Memory Box*, Violet mulled over what Lisa had said, wondering whether to take her off the list of suspects.

I don't think she did it, Violet told herself. *But she's definitely holding something back. There's a wariness about her. Lisa Wenham may not be a murderer, but she's guilty of something. I'm sure of it.*

For the time being at least, she decided to keep Lisa's name on the list.

Chapter 23

'How come we're going to *The Cuckoo's Boot* tearoom?' Molly said.

It was midday. Violet had been home to collect her car, and she and Molly were now heading along Dale Lane towards the garden centre.

'I didn't think you wanted to go there again, ever,' Molly added.

'What I said was, I wished Fiona and I hadn't gone there on Sunday,' Violet said, as she pulled into a passing place and gave way to an approaching car. 'I didn't say I never wanted to go back.'

'But what about being loyal to the BBC? Shouldn't we be giving our custom to the café, rather than spending money at the tearoom?'

Violet smiled. 'First of all, *you* won't be spending any money today. Lunch is my treat, as a thank you for securing the contract with the arts project.'

'Aww, Violet. That's kind of you, but you don't have to do that. I was only doing my job.'

'No, you weren't. You went above and beyond – and it's thanks to your proactiveness that we got the gig. Lunch is on me, and I won't hear another word about it.'

'All right, then. Thank you, but you still haven't told me why we're going to the tearoom.'

'We always go to the café, and I wanted to take you somewhere different. I'll admit *The Cuckoo's Boot* wouldn't necessarily have been my first choice, but I have an ulterior motive.'

Molly giggled. 'And what might that be? Are you, by any chance, in "investigation" mode?'

Violet grinned. 'I'm always in investigation mode,' she said. 'You should know that by now.'

'And what is it you're planning to investigate at the tearoom? Or should that be *who*?'

'I'm hoping to talk to Anne Burridge. She's the manager.'

'Yeah, I know she is,' said Molly. 'My mum knows Anne. They were at school together.'

'In that case, depending on what I find out today, I may need to have a word with your mum. It'll give me an excuse to visit the pub.'

Molly leaned against the headrest and laughed. 'Since when did you need an excuse?'

To their surprise, *The Cuckoo's Boot* was almost deserted.

'And there was me, thinking we might not get a table,' Molly said, leaning in to whisper into Violet's ear. 'Where is everyone?'

'Search me,' Violet said. 'Do you think they've all gone back to the BBC?'

'Let's hope so, for Fiona's sake,' Molly said. 'I'll grab a table. Do you have any preference as to where you'd like to sit?'

Aside from two occupied tables by the door, they had the whole tearoom to choose from.

'You decide,' Violet said. 'I'll go and get a couple of menus. It'll give me an excuse to talk to Anne.'

As Violet approached the front counter, Simon Geldard emerged from the kitchen carrying two platefuls of artfully presented food. In what may have been an act of protest against his uniform, he'd rolled his shirt sleeves up – and as he whisked the plates to one of the two pairs of waiting customers, Violet noticed several large purple bruises on his forearms. She winced, recalling how furious Roy Geldard had been about Simon starting the fire. Was it possible he'd inflicted those bruises as some kind of punishment? Violet sincerely hoped not. Roy had come across as grouchy and ill-tempered, but she was struggling to believe him capable of such cruelty, especially to a member of his own family.

Anne Burridge was watching her from behind the counter.

'Could I have some menus, please?' Violet said.

'Yes, of course.' Anne gave a half-hearted smile as she handed them over. 'The specials are on the board. If you take a seat, someone will come over and take your order.'

'OK, thanks,' said Violet. 'You're Anne, aren't you?'

'Yes?' she replied, narrowing her eyes and regarding Violet suspiciously. 'That's me.'

'I'm Violet Brewster. We spoke on the phone the other morning . . . on the day Hilary died.'

Anne's watery smile froze in a terrified rictus. Violet couldn't decide whether it was an expression of nervousness, or overwhelming sadness.

'My condolences,' Violet said. 'I was told you and Hilary were old friends.'

'Yes, we were at university together.'

'Her death must have come as a terrible shock.'

Anne nodded. 'It has, but I'm trying to hold myself together so that I can keep the tearoom ticking over. Everyone here at the garden centre is extremely fond of Clayton, and we're doing our best to keep the business running smoothly while he takes some bereavement leave.'

'I'm sure he appreciates that. It must be a difficult time for him, having to organise the funeral and deal with his grief.'

'I'm helping with the funeral,' Anne said, sounding distinctly proprietorial. 'Clayton's decided to hold the wake here, in the tearoom, so I'll be arranging the catering.'

'You'll still be able to attend the funeral service though?' Violet asked.

Anne nodded. 'Oh yes, I'll be there. Clayton will want me by his side. He doesn't have any family, you see. He'll be relying on my support.'

Suddenly, Anne jerked her head, craning her neck to look over Violet's left shoulder, her eyes fixed on a spot in the corner of the tearoom. Violet turned and looked in the same direction, but as far as she could tell, there was nothing there.

Anne gave a tight smile. 'I'm sorry, you'll have to excuse me. There are things I need to do. Please, sit down, and I'll get someone to come over and take your order.'

'Did you find anything out?' Molly said, when Violet joined her at a centrally located table for two.

'Absolutely nothing,' she said. 'We exchanged a few niceties, but she didn't tell me anything I didn't already know. She seemed distracted, as if something was bothering her. Perhaps she was afraid I was going to ask some awkward questions.'

'Or maybe she's just feeling emotional about everything that's happened?' Molly said. 'I mean, she's bound to be upset, isn't she?'

Violet smiled. 'That's one of the things I like most about you, Molly. You always see the good in people. You put me to shame. Here, have a menu. Let's decide what we're going to eat.'

'Is there anything you recommend?'

Violet grinned. 'No, but if I were you, I'd steer clear of the scones.'

They both made the same selection: hot steak baguettes, served with blue cheese, Dijon mustard and a mixed-leaf salad. They also ordered a side of triple-cooked chips to share. The food, when it came, was served by Simon, whose eyes darted from side to side as he carried over the plates, his focus eventually settling on the vacant area by the window.

'Ey up, Simon,' Molly said. 'What's up? You look worried.'

'You've not spotted more smoke, have you?' said Violet.

Simon placed their food on the table and then stood with his hands behind his back. 'Nah, there's no danger of that now. At least not on my grandad's land.'

'It's very quiet in here, Si,' Molly said. 'Where is everyone today? I was expecting the place to be heaving.'

Simon gave a brief shrug and then glanced surreptitiously to where Anne Burridge was standing. When he was sure she wasn't listening, he leaned in and, in a stage whisper, said: 'I'm surprised to see you two here, to be honest. You've obviously not heard.'

'Heard what?' Molly said.

'Simon!' Anne Burridge's shrill voice pierced the room. 'I need you over here please. Now.'

'Sorry, ladies.' Simon gave an apologetic smirk. 'Duty calls. Enjoy your food.'

He sauntered back to the front counter, where Anne hissed something inaudible into his ear.

'What do you suppose that was about?' Violet said.

'No idea,' said Molly, who seemed far more interested in sprinkling salt and vinegar onto the chips than speculating about what might be amiss in the tearoom.

'Is it me, or does Anne Burridge look stressed?'

'No more than usual,' Molly said, glancing over at Anne, who was biting a thumbnail. 'That's her default expression. According to my mum, she's a proper fusspot. Always has been, apparently.'

'Even so, she looks a complete bundle of nerves.'

'I reckon we should stop worrying about Anne Burridge and start thinking about how we're going to get our chops around these baguettes.' Molly said, using her knife to point to the food on her plate. 'They're enormous.'

'They are,' Violet said. 'But they do look delicious. Come on, let's tuck in.'

Chapter 24

'I'm going to call in at the bakery,' Violet said, when they returned to the shopping village after lunch. 'I need to buy some rolls.'

'You mean cobs?' said Molly. 'You're a Derbyshire girl now, Violet. We call bread rolls cobs round 'ere.'

Violet laughed. 'Sorry, I forgot. *Cobs.* I need to buy some cobs. I'll catch up with you in a minute.'

The first thing Violet noticed when she entered the BBC was the hubbub coming from the café. The place was packed, and there were several customers lined up at the bakery counter.

'It's good to see things back to normal,' Violet said, when she reached the head of the queue. 'I take it the news is out? About you being in the clear?'

Fiona was smiling from ear to ear. 'Yes, but that's not the only reason for the sudden influx of customers.'

'Oh?' said Violet. 'Has something else happened?'

Fiona chuckled. 'You've not heard then? About the tearoom?'

'No . . . what about it?'

Fiona was trying not to laugh, her mouth twitching with the effort. 'It would appear they have an infestation of vermin,' she said.

'What!?' Violet said. 'You've got to be kidding. Molly and I have just come from there.'

That unexpected piece of news was enough to wipe the smile off Fiona's face. 'Have you?' she said, frowning.

Violet held up her hands. 'I took Molly there for lunch,' she explained. 'But only because I needed an excuse to talk to Anne Burridge.'

'What did you want to talk to her about?' Fiona said. 'You're not still investigating, are you?'

'Kind of,' Violet said. 'Although I didn't get very far with Anne. She wasn't giving much away.'

Fiona leaned forward and lowered her voice. 'Listen, duck, I'm in the clear. My reputation and my customer base have been restored. You need to let it go.'

Violet shrugged guiltily. 'I'm finding that tricky,' she said. 'You know what I'm like when I'm curious about something. But never mind all that . . . tell me more about this infestation at *The Cuckoo's Boot*. An infestation of what?'

'Rodents,' Fiona said, unable to suppress a smirk. 'More specifically, mice. Apparently, one of the customers saw one running under her chair.'

Violet pulled a disbelieving face. 'How can that be?' she said. 'It's a brand-new building.'

'I know, but there are bound to be loads of mice in the garden centre,' Fiona said. 'Maybe they were disturbed when the tearoom was built and now they're reclaiming their territory. Who knows? I'm just glad to have my customers back.'

'It does explain a few things,' Violet said. 'Anne Burridge was acting very oddly when Molly and I had lunch. Now I understand why.'

'Were there many people there? In the tearoom?'

'No, the place was almost empty. News of the mice infestation has obviously swept through the village like a dose of salts.' Violet rolled her eyes.

'They'll need to get the problem sorted, and fast,' Fiona said.

'Otherwise they'll be closed down by the environmental health team. I'll admit to being quietly amused by the situation, and I'm a great believer in karma, but I do feel sorry for whoever has to deal with the issue.'

'You can't blame people for staying away if the place is overrun with mice,' Violet said. 'But I'm afraid this sudden stampede away from the tearoom is yet another example of the capricious nature of the great British public.'

'I doubt very much whether they've been *overrun*,' Fiona said. 'But you're right about the great British public. Having been on the receiving end of consumer fickleness myself recently, I can't help but sympathise with Clayton. He's got enough on his plate at the moment.'

'Actually, it's Anne Burridge you should feel sorry for,' Violet said. 'She's the one who's running things on Clayton's behalf. No wonder she kept looking over my shoulder when I was in the tearoom. She was probably on the lookout for Mickey and his friends.'

Fiona laughed. 'What was the food like?' she asked.

'Very good,' Violet said. 'Excellent, in fact. Although I wouldn't have enjoyed it half as much if I'd known about the mice.'

That evening, Violet sat on the sofa with the cat and a copy of the latest Richard Osman novel, which had been languishing on her reading pile for far too long. There was a casserole in the oven and a pan of peeled potatoes on the hob, waiting to be cooked. Matthew would be joining her for dinner, but it would be at least half an hour before he arrived. While she waited, Violet intended to read at least one chapter, if not two.

Sighing contentedly, she turned to the first page of the book – but as she absorbed the opening paragraph, she was interrupted by the irritating rattle of the door-knocker, followed by the sound of a banging fist. Rusty jumped off her knee and fled into the kitchen with her tail in the air, and in the time it took for Violet to go into the hallway and open the front door, Lisa Wenham had raised her right knuckle, ready to knock again.

'Hello, Lisa,' she said, stepping back instinctively in case the knuckle landed on her, instead of the door. From the furious expression on Lisa's face, that seemed a distinct possibility.

'I want a word with you,' Lisa snapped. 'Just what do you think you're playing at?'

Violet cocked her head. 'Sorry, but I have no idea what you're talking about.'

'Don't play the innocent with me,' Lisa said. 'You know jolly well why I'm here. I had a visit this afternoon from the police. You told them about my argument with Hilary, didn't you?'

Violet stepped aside and opened the door wide. 'Please, Lisa. Come in and let me explain.'

Lisa bristled as she stepped into the hallway.

'Let's go into the living room, and sit down,' Violet said, leading the way. 'Would you like a cup of tea? Coffee?'

'I've not come to socialise. I'm here to say my piece. Who do you think you are, going around telling people my business?'

'I haven't told anyone your business,' Violet said. 'Please, Lisa. Take a seat and hear me out.'

'I prefer to stand, if you don't mind.'

'Fair enough, if that's what you want, but I have to say, glaring at me with your arms folded is extremely confrontational. I'm sure we'd both feel a lot more comfortable if we sat down.'

Reluctantly, Lisa unfolded her arms and perched her bottom on the edge of the armchair.

'You've been blabbing to that DS Winterton,' Lisa said. 'Don't try and deny it, because I know it was you. It stands to reason. The pair of you are thick as thieves, and everybody in the village knows how much you like to poke your nose into police business.'

Violet bristled but said nothing. She was, after all, guilty as charged.

'I'm disappointed in you,' Lisa said, her voice trembling with emotion. 'After the conversation we had earlier, I thought we'd reached an understanding. I'm hurt that you thought it necessary to send the police round to talk to me.'

'I told DS Winterton about your argument with Hilary *before* you and I talked properly,' Violet said. 'I suggested he might want to speak to you, but I didn't insist on it. Even if I had, he wouldn't have listened. Charlie Winterton is his own man. He does things *his* way, if and when it suits him.'

'Well, thanks to you, it did suit him. He sent a couple of bobbies to my house and I got a right grilling about my row with Hilary, even though it happened months ago. I had no choice but to tell them about it – which means I'm now a suspect in Hilary's murder.'

'Did the police say you were a suspect?'

'Not in so many words, but now that Fiona Nash has been cleared, they'll be desperate to lay the blame on someone – and it looks as if I'm their prime candidate.'

'They'd let you know if you were being treated as a suspect,' Violet said. 'I'm sure questioning you was just a routine part of the investigation. Let's face it, if you'd wanted retribution for what happened to Buster, you'd have done something about it at the time. You wouldn't have waited months before exacting your revenge . . .'

Lisa was staring at the carpet, trying (and failing) to hide the red flush that was creeping across her cheeks.

Violet raised an eyebrow. 'Unless, of course, there's something you're not telling me?'

'I racked up quite a vet's bill when Buster was ill,' Lisa said, ignoring Violet's question. 'Nearly eight hundred quid it cost me. Not that I begrudged him. I'd do anything for my animals – sell the clothes off my back if I had to – but I don't have a huge income, and I could have done without the expense.'

'I'm sure you could, but why are you telling me this now?'

Lisa put her head in her hands. 'I don't know. I suppose I'm trying to explain why I was so angry with her.'

'You don't have to justify yourself to me,' Violet said. 'Hilary acted unprofessionally when she sold you that plant. Her lack of care cost you and Buster dearly, and I don't suppose she offered to pay your vet's bill?'

'You suppose right.'

'I can see why you'd resent that.'

Lisa nodded. 'I was seething about the whole thing, and I've kept out of Hilary's way ever since.'

'So why were you in the tearoom on Sunday?' said Violet, who was mentally reviewing a few possible reasons. 'It didn't register with me at the time, because I had no idea how you felt about Hilary – but knowing what I know now, I'm surprised you'd want to patronise her new venture. Why give your custom to a woman you couldn't stand?'

Lisa shifted her feet, clearly unnerved by the question.

'I was there for the same reason as you and Fiona,' she muttered. 'I was satisfying my curiosity.'

The unimaginative response didn't ring true. Lisa was hiding something. Violet felt sure of it.

'You sat in the corner, as I recall,' she said. 'Again, it didn't hit me at the time, but I remember you seemed rather laden down. Your coat was draped across the back of your chair, and you had a large shopping bag with you, which was tucked under the table.'

'So?'

Violet's mind was racing. 'If you were there purely to take tea and satisfy your curiosity, why were you carrying a huge bag?'

'I was going to have a look around the garden centre afterwards. I brought the bag in case I decided to buy something.'

'*Buy* something? From Hilary Spenbeck, a woman you despised?' Bit by bit, Violet was slotting the pieces together. 'If you'd wanted plants, you'd have gone to another garden centre – *any* other garden centre – rather than giving your custom to the Spenbecks. Besides, if memory serves me correctly, the bag under the table was already full. There was something inside it. Something bulky, like a box.'

Lisa lowered her eyelids.

Violet nodded slowly. 'I'm pretty sure I know what was in that box,' she said, finally understanding the real reason for Lisa's visit to *The Cuckoo's Boot* tearoom.

Lisa got to her feet. 'You think you know it all, don't you, Violet Brewster? The contents of that bag are none of your business.'

'Mice,' Violet said, pronouncing the word confidently and crisply. 'That's what you were carrying, isn't it?'

'Mice?' Lisa said, looking a lot like a mouse herself – one who was well and truly caught. 'What are you on about?'

'I'm talking about getting your own back on Hilary Spenbeck. You had to bide your time and wait for an opportunity – and the tearoom opening was your big chance. You went there and released a mouse.'

Lisa said nothing, but her hangdog expression was proof enough of her guilt.

'I was at the BBC earlier,' Violet continued. 'Apparently Fiona has been inundated with customers this morning, mainly because of a rodent problem in the tearoom.'

Lisa flopped back onto the armchair, all bravado gone.

'It would appear they have a mouse infestation,' Violet continued. 'Although I guess you're the only one who knows the true extent of the problem. Was it just one mouse you released on Sunday? Or two? Three? More? How many did you manage to fit into that box you were carrying in your bag?'

Lisa capitulated with a heavy sigh. 'How did you know?'

'I didn't know for sure, until now,' Violet said. 'When we last spoke, I sensed there was something you weren't telling me, but I didn't know what it was. Later, when I heard about the problem at the tearoom, I began to have my suspicions.'

'Have you told anyone?'

'No, I've only just arrived at the correct conclusion, so I haven't had a chance – and I don't intend to tell anyone either, on one condition.'

Lisa folded her arms. 'And what might that be?'

'As you were the one who caused the problem in the tearoom, it seems only fair that you should be the one to sort it out. I think you should go over there. You don't have to admit to anything . . . just tell them you've heard about their problem and want to help.'

Lisa jerked her head back. 'Who do you think I am? The Pied Piper of Hamelin? Why would they accept an offer of help from me?'

'You're good with animals,' Violet said. 'I'm assuming you caught the mice in the first place? How hard would it be to recapture them and release them back into the wild?'

'There are only two,' Lisa said. 'They're field mice from my garden. I kept finding droppings in my greenhouse and shed, so I set a humane trap for them, and that's when I got the idea.

'You're right, I wanted to teach Hilary a lesson, but I didn't mean to cause any serious harm. I just hoped to spoil things a little . . . inconvenience her. I put the mice in a cardboard box and set them loose in the tearoom, when no one was looking. As a matter of fact, I did it while Hilary was having her slanging match with Fiona. It was the perfect diversion. Everyone was staring at Hilary, which meant no one was looking at me. It was silly of me, a stupid act of revenge. It felt good at the time – but it was childish. I realise that now.'

'Well, if you'd like to make amends, I suggest you get in touch with Anne Burridge and offer to catch the mice humanely,' Violet said.

'I'd be drawing attention to myself if I did. She'd be suspicious. She'd want to know why I was offering to help, and I'd probably end up giving myself away.'

'Everyone in the village knows how much you love animals,' Violet said. 'You can tell Anne you're doing it to help the mice, not her. You'll need to act quickly though, before she puts down spring traps, or calls in the exterminators. In fact, she may already have done that.'

'Actually, the mice have probably made their escape by now,' Anne said. 'They're field mice, not house mice. They eat seeds and plants and caterpillars. They won't want to live on a diet of scones and lemon drizzle cake.' She gave a shy smile. 'Do you promise not to tell anyone what I did?'

'I do,' Violet replied. 'Providing you go and see Anne and offer to help.'

'All right, I'll talk to her first thing in the morning,' Lisa said. 'But I want to make it clear that releasing the mice is the only thing I'm guilty of. I was nowhere near the garden centre when Hilary died. You do believe that, don't you?'

'Yes, Lisa, I do, and I appreciate you being honest with me. I won't tell DS Winterton what you did . . . not if you don't want me to. Besides, he won't be interested in an apparent infestation of mice – not when he has a murder to solve.'

After Lisa had gone, Violet went into the kitchen and lit the burner under the potatoes. When she'd done that, she went over to the wall and stared long and hard at the index cards. That's where Matthew found her a few minutes later.

'Are you OK?' he said. 'You looked like you were in a trance when I came in. Were you staring into space, or considering the names on the wall?'

'The latter,' Violet said. 'I've just had a visit from Lisa Wenham. I'm going to take her name off the list.'

Matthew located the card with Lisa's name on it, plucked it from the wall, and placed it on the table.

'Shall I take the rest down as well?' he asked. 'Now that Fiona's been exonerated, there's no reason for us to be sticking our oar in, is there? There's been a steady stream of customers at the bakery and café today, so I think we can safely say things are back to normal.'

Violet gave a brief nod of agreement, and then watched as Matthew removed the remaining cards from the wall.

'Looks like Eric was right about the Blu Tack,' he said, as he stacked the index cards on the table. 'You might want to bring forward your plans for redecorating. I'll help you, if you like.'

'Thanks, but there's no rush. I haven't decided what colour to go for yet. I might stick with green, or maybe I'll choose a nice pale blue next time, or even plain white.'

'What have you got planned for the weekend?' Matthew asked.

'Nothing much, but I don't want to go to the DIY superstore if that's what you're hinting at. I'm not in the mood for home improvements.'

'Actually, I was going to suggest a walk,' Matthew said. 'The forecast is good for both Saturday and Sunday. We could take a picnic and head into the Peaks . . . get some fresh air and exercise.'

Violet smiled. 'That sounds wonderful,' she said. 'Let's go tomorrow. I'll make the picnic, if you plan the walk.'

Chapter 25

The morning sky above Merrywell was bright and blue and optimistic. A swathe of flat-bottomed cumulus clouds hovered in the distance, but they were puffy and cotton white and beautiful.

They had stashed their walking boots on the back seat of Matthew's car, along with a backpack containing the picnic, and they were currently heading north. Their destination was Castleton, in the High Peak district of Derbyshire, at the western end of the Hope Valley. The village was the starting point of a circular walk that would take them up into the Dark Peak.

'Rhys FaceTimed me late last night,' Matthew said, as they drove through Bakewell and headed towards Ashford in the Water. 'He's coming back at the end of next week.'

Matthew's son, Rhys, had spent the last two and a half months travelling around Australia and New Zealand.

'That's great news,' Violet said. 'You'll be glad to have him home.'

'Actually, he's not coming home. He's got a job with a big design agency in Bristol.' Matthew sounded proud, but also a little wistful. 'Apparently, he applied online, submitted his digital portfolio, and they interviewed him via Zoom.'

Violet was impressed. 'Job hunting international style, eh?' She smiled. 'Well done, Rhys. I bet he's thrilled.'

'Yeah, he's loved travelling, but I think he's ready to come back and focus on his career. It's going to seem weird though, him being in Bristol. It's not exactly round the corner, is it?'

'No, but it is an amazing city, one that you'll be able to take full advantage of when you visit him.'

Matthew nodded. 'I don't suppose I can expect him to live at home forever.'

'I take it he's coming back to Derbyshire first, before he heads for the big city?'

'No, actually, he's heading straight from the airport to Bristol. He needs to find somewhere to live. Once he's done that, he'll come home for a few days, and then we'll load all of his worldly possessions into my works van, and I'll drive him back to Bristol.'

'Will all of his stuff fit into your van?'

'Easily,' Matthew said, laughing. 'He hasn't accumulated much in his twenty-four years, and I can guarantee he'll be picky about what he takes with him to his new place. If there's any junk, he'll leave it behind at my house.'

When they got to Castleton, Matthew drove to the Visitor Centre. After he'd parked the car, he unfolded an Ordnance Survey map to show Violet the walk they'd be taking.

'We're going along the Great Ridge from Lose Hill to Mam Tor,' he said, trailing a finger along the proposed route. 'It's one of the most popular walks in the Peak District. You're going to love it.'

'Actually, I think I did this walk when I was a student,' Violet said, remembering the hiking group she'd joined when she was at university in Sheffield. 'It wasn't too challenging, as I recall – although admittedly I was a lot younger in those days.'

Matthew smiled. 'We'll take it steady,' he said. 'It's only about seven miles, and we can rest at the halfway point and eat our picnic.'

They pulled on their hiking boots, and once Matthew had hoisted the backpack onto his shoulders, they set off. The sun was surprisingly warm, but there was also a refreshing breeze blowing in from the south.

After walking along the main road through Castleton, past Ye Olde Cheshire Cheese Inn, they joined the footpath that led up to the summit of Lose Hill. From there they followed the flagstone path along the Great Ridge. It was an easy track to follow, and they walked in companionable silence, breathing in the fresh air and taking in the stunning views of the surrounding hills and villages.

They passed other walkers on the route, as well as a flock of bleating sheep, but when they reached Back Tor, they had the place to themselves. Standing side by side, they admired the spectacular scenery in awed silence.

'It's breathtaking,' Violet said, eventually. 'And the perfect spot to eat our picnic.'

They sat down to share a flask of coffee and eat ham and tomato sandwiches from a lunchbox, all the while appraising the smooth, green bulk of Great Ridge. The footpath ran along its top like a spine, giving it the semblance of a huge, sleeping, prehistoric animal.

Matthew pointed towards Mam Tor, explaining that the name meant 'mother hill'.

'It's beautiful,' Violet said. 'And very serene. We should come here more often.'

Matthew nodded, and then turned away, staring into the distance with a faraway look in his eyes.

'What are you thinking about?' Violet asked.

It was a few seconds before he replied. 'The past,' he said, his eyes fixed on the horizon. 'Katy and I used to bring Rhys up here when he was little.'

Violet waited, wondering if he'd say more – but he lapsed back into silence. Tilting back his head, he looked up at the sky.

'You've never really spoken to me about Katy,' she said, prompting him to continue.

Matthew straightened his back and rested his forearms on his knees. 'Rhys and I talk about her a lot,' he said. 'I've never said much to you, because I wasn't sure you'd be interested.'

'Of course I'm interested,' Violet said. 'She was your wife.'

'Yeah, but you didn't know her, and the last thing I want to do is bore you with stories of the old days.'

'Whatever stories you have, I'm sure they're not boring. I'd like to know more about your past. It would help me understand you better.'

Matthew laughed. 'Am I really that unfathomable?'

'No . . . of course not, but if you and I are going to make *new* memories, we need to be able to talk freely about the past.'

He gave a slight frown. 'For me, that's not as easy as it sounds. I want to keep Katy's memory alive, and I love remembering all the good stuff we did – but when I talk about her, the happy memories end up reminding me of the pain of losing her.'

Violet squeezed his hand. 'I don't suppose the grief will ever go away completely.'

'No,' Matthew said. 'Although it does hurt a little less as each year rolls by. Trouble is, as the grief recedes . . . that's when the guilt moves in.'

'Guilt? What have you got to feel guilty about?'

'It's stupid, I know, but I can't help it.' He smiled sadly. 'Katy's gone, and I'm still here, getting on with my life. It seems unfair that I get to do that, and she doesn't.'

'She'd have wanted you to be happy, wouldn't she?' Violet said.

'Yes . . . yes of course she would . . . which is why I've been thinking . . . thinking about asking you something.' He rubbed his hands together as if psyching himself up for an important announcement.

Violet regarded him quizzically, her fingers resting against her mouth as she ate her sandwich.

'When Rhys moves out, I'll be rattling around the house on my own,' Matthew said, casting a nervous glance in her direction.

'I wondered how you'd feel about us moving in together at some point?'

He bit his lip and waited.

Violet stared out towards Mam Tor, chewing the last of her sandwich and taking several much-needed seconds to consider her reply. She prided herself on her observational skills, but she hadn't seen this coming.

'Your silence speaks volumes,' Matthew said, looking increasingly deflated as the seconds ticked by.

She gave his hand another squeeze, eager to drive away the sadness in his eyes.

'I just need a minute to think,' she said. 'You've surprised me.'

'Have I?' he said, his eyes searching her face for a reaction. 'Are you saying the idea's never crossed your mind?'

'Fleetingly perhaps, as something that *might* happen. Eventually.'

'OK,' he said, running a hand through his hair. 'But if you feel about me the way I feel about you, what's the point in waiting? I'd say we're both old enough and wise enough to recognise happiness when it comes along.'

Violet smiled, remembering her mother's comment about how she and Matthew weren't getting any younger.

'You *do* make me happy, Matthew, but moving in together is a huge commitment. Don't get me wrong . . . I like the idea . . . I'm not saying "no" . . .'

'But it's not an instant "yes"?'

She leaned against him and slipped her hand into the crook of his arm. 'Only because it's a big decision . . . something I want to be completely sure about before I commit myself. I was under the impression we were taking things slowly, so you've caught me unawares.'

He put his arm around her shoulders and kissed the top of her head. 'Sorry, I shouldn't have sprung it on you. You're right – there's no rush. Take as long as you need.'

He was trying to sound unruffled, but the flatness in his voice betrayed his disappointment.

'Don't be upset,' she said. 'I'm as committed to our relationship as you are – you're just a few steps ahead of me, that's all. Moving to Merrywell was a massive change for me, and I'm still getting used to my new lifestyle . . . plus, I must admit, I do like having my own house and space.'

Until she'd moved into Greengage Cottage, Violet had never lived on her own. For most of her adult life, she'd been in a relationship with her ex, Paul. They'd got together at university and moved in together after they graduated. Soon after that, they'd married, and then Violet had fallen unexpectedly pregnant . . . and before she knew it, twenty-three years had flown by. In the aftermath of her divorce, she'd realised how much she enjoyed the sense of freedom that came with being newly single. For the first time in years, she'd been in a position to make radical, life-changing decisions based purely on what *she* wanted and needed – her move to Merrywell being a prime example. Was she willing to give up that independence and move in with Matthew? Was she ready to take that leap of faith?

'When I came to Merrywell, I was determined to make the most of my new-found freedom,' she said, resting her head against him. 'And then I met you.'

'You make that sound like a bad thing,' he said. 'I'm not trying to take your freedom away from you, Violet. I don't want to trap you, or change you, or force you in a different direction. I just want to share my life with you. Is that so very wrong?'

'Of course it isn't,' she said. 'And I'm sure we will move in together eventually, just not necessarily right now.'

He acknowledged her decision with a nod.

'I need a little more time to think about it,' she clarified.

'OK, I get it, and don't worry . . . I'm not going to put pressure on you. We won't discuss it again until you're ready.'

'I don't mind talking about it,' Violet said, 'just so long as I don't have to make up my mind right away. And actually, if it is going to happen at some point, we probably *should* talk – about the practicalities.'

'What practicalities?'

'Well, for instance, would I move in with you, or would you move into Greengage Cottage? Unlike Rhys, you and I have accumulated a lot of stuff over the years, and I'm not sure how we'd fit all of that into one house. There's a lot to consider, things we'd need to work out. That, my darling, is why I need time – time to think things through and get used to the idea of sharing a house with someone again.'

'Righty-ho,' Matthew said, sounding slightly more optimistic. 'I'll let you set the pace. Take as long as you need. And if, in the end, you prefer to keep things the way they are, then I guess I'll have to learn to live with that. I'll always love you, Violet, no matter what you decide.'

When they had eaten all the sandwiches and packed away the empty flask, they made the steep descent from Back Tor. At Hollins Cross they kept on the main path, walking uphill to Mam Tor summit, which was marked with a structure that looked a lot like a stone-built chimney, but which Violet knew to be a triangulation pillar. It was one of the many trig points that had been used by the Ordnance Survey to determine the lay of the land and the shape of the country.

Violet leaned against the pillar and gazed at the undulating landscape around her. *If only life's ups and downs were as easy to map out*, she thought. Falling in love with Matthew had been a personal high point, but it was impossible to predict what lay ahead. The future was a journey – and Violet hoped that she and Matthew would continue to navigate its mysteries together.

Chapter 26

There was a shower of light rain overnight, but by Sunday morning the skies had cleared again and the sun was out, warming Merrywell in its cheerful golden light. Violet had been invited over to Matthew's parents' house for lunch, and she was looking forward to it immensely. It was always fun spending time with Joyce and Brian Collis, especially when gathered around their dining table for a full roast with all the trimmings.

'Come on in, love,' Joyce said, when Violet arrived at Well View Cottage, the quaint, stone-built property the Collis family had owned for more than fifty years. 'Matthew's already here. He's in the garden with his dad.'

Joyce's kitchen smelt of roasting beef and parsnips. A home-made, lattice-topped apple pie was waiting on the worktop, ready to put in the oven, and there were pans of expertly prepared vegetables on the hob.

'Need any help with lunch?' Violet said, making the offer even though everything looked to be in hand.

'Only with eating it,' Joyce replied. 'It's all done and ready to go, and now that you're here, I'll put the veggies on. Then we'll pour a glass of wine and join the boys in the garden.'

'Thanks for inviting me today,' Violet said, as Joyce lit the gas under the saucepans. 'It's a nice way to end an otherwise difficult week.'

'Yes, I was sorry to hear about what happened with Hilary,' Joyce said, as she wiped her hands on her apron. 'It's a real shame. Poor woman.'

Using a tea towel to protect her fingers, she opened the oven door and pulled out a piping-hot Yorkshire pudding tray, which she placed on the kitchen worktop. From a Pyrex jug, she poured a small quantity of Yorkshire pudding batter onto the oil that had been heating at the bottom of each compartment.

'Do you know if a date's been fixed for the funeral?' Joyce said, as she slid the tray back onto the top shelf and closed the oven door.

'It's three weeks tomorrow,' Violet said. 'Will you go?'

'Probably not,' Joyce replied. 'Hilary and I didn't run in the same circles. What about you? Will you be attending?'

Violet frowned. 'Ordinarily, I wouldn't have bothered, but because I was at the garden centre when she died, I feel I should go along and pay my respects. I'll attend the church service, but it's a private cremation. There's a gathering afterwards at the tearoom, but I don't think I'll go to that.'

'I'm surprised they're holding the wake at the tearoom,' Joyce said, as she untied her apron.

'It was me who suggested it, actually. Clayton was struggling to find a venue locally, so it seemed the obvious choice. Anne Burridge is organising the catering – in fact, she's stepped up and completely taken over the running of *The Cuckoo's Boot*.'

Joyce gave a half-smile. 'That doesn't surprise me. Anne's been hovering in the wings for years.'

'Really?'

'Oh, yes,' Joyce said, with a knowing look. 'Primed and ready to step into Hilary's shoes. It's common knowledge that Anne carries a torch for Clayton.'

Given what Violet had already learned about Anne Burridge, this particular revelation came as no real surprise, but it did provoke a few new questions. Was it possible that Anne had grown tired of her role as understudy? Had she fantasised about getting rid of Hilary so that she could claim centre stage?

'Anne and Clayton were really close when they were kids,' Joyce explained. 'They were never girlfriend and boyfriend . . . at least, not officially . . . but as a teenager, Anne was like a love-sick puppy whenever Clayton was around. It was pretty obvious she was in love with him, but I don't think the feeling was ever reciprocated. Even if it was, everything changed the day Clayton met Hilary. From that moment on, he only had eyes for her. Anne was devastated at the time . . . but there's been a lot of healing water under the bridge since then.'

'Anne's maintained a friendship with the Spenbecks over the years, so she must have got over her disappointment.'

'I suspect the friendship has been her way of keeping in contact with Clayton,' Joyce said. 'I don't think there's ever been much love lost between Anne and Hilary – especially in recent years – but I don't know them all that well, so who am I to judge?'

'Do you think the police suspect Anne?' Violet said. 'Given her attachment to Clayton?'

'Oh no, I shouldn't think so,' Joyce said, looking immediately regretful. 'Goodness me, I didn't mean to imply anything like that. Ignore me, Violet. I'm prattling, as usual. I really don't think Anne's the sort of person who'd attack someone – least of all, Hilary. The two of them might not have been the best of friends, but they were always respectful of one another.'

'They must have been,' Violet said. 'Otherwise, I don't suppose Anne would have taken a job at the tearoom.'

Joyce chortled. 'I bet that's a decision she's come to regret. The place has only just opened, and I hear they've already got a food hygiene problem.'

'I believe it's mice, actually,' Violet said, choosing not to

161

elaborate. 'But I'm sure Anne's more than capable of sorting the problem.'

'I hope so . . . She certainly can't rely on Clayton to do anything about it.'

'I don't think she'll be expecting him to,' Violet said. 'Clayton's taken a step back from the business for the time being, understandably so.'

'I'm afraid he'd be useless, even if he hadn't stepped back temporarily,' Joyce said, as she wiped a damp cloth across the worktop. 'I don't wish to sound mean, especially in light of what's happened, but Clayton Spenbeck has been taking a back seat for a long while now. He's always relied far too heavily on his wife.'

'Hilary was a forceful character,' Violet said. 'Maybe she didn't leave him much choice.'

Joyce shrugged. 'You're right. She was forceful . . . and ambitious, but she was also intelligent and energetic and competent. Hilary's never been popular with the locals, but despite what people might say about her, it's important to remember that she wasn't all bad. The police need to make haste and catch whoever was responsible for her death.'

'I agree,' said Violet, 'but unfortunately, there's not a lot of evidence for them to work with.'

'It's a crying shame that Hilary was never well liked,' Joyce said. 'The problem was, she was strong and opinionated, and also very successful – and those are dangerous qualities if you're not willing to endear yourself to the locals. Hilary lived in Merrywell for the best part of twenty-five years, but unfortunately, she made very little effort to fit in – and that's created a lot of resentment and jealousy. The locals have always viewed her as an intruder, an unwanted incomer.'

'Oh, dear,' Violet said, pulling a face. 'That doesn't augur well for me.'

'Nonsense,' Joyce said. 'You're a different kettle of fish altogether, love. You've only been here for a year, and you're already part of the community. You're friendly, you throw yourself into local activities, and you have a positive attitude – attributes that Hilary was sadly lacking.'

'I wonder why that was,' Violet said. 'Do you think she'd had a difficult childhood?'

'I don't know, love. I'm sorry. All I can tell you is that Hilary turned up in the village, hooked up with Clayton, and married him within six months. She joined the family business from the off, but there was always an air of superiority about her, as if she thought she was too good for Merrywell. I believe she was a city girl, so perhaps she struggled to adjust to life in a quiet village. Maybe she'd have been better off living somewhere a bit livelier.'

'Did she get on all right with her father-in-law?' Violet asked.

'Yes, surprisingly, they got on like a house on fire,' Joyce replied. 'I knew Dennis Spenbeck quite well, and he was a good judge of character. I think he could see that Hilary had her faults, but he also recognised and valued her strengths. She was a natural-born businesswoman – far more commercially minded than Clayton – and I think Dennis came to regard her as his natural successor.'

'I shouldn't imagine Clayton was too happy about that,' said Violet.

'He was fine about it, actually. In fact, I think he was relieved to step aside and let Hilary take the reins. As a young man, Clayton hankered after a different career path altogether. As a teenager, he was a member of the local am-dram group, and I think he'd set his heart on a job in theatre or television . . . acting, maybe . . . or writing.'

'So, why didn't he pursue that dream?'

'I don't know, maybe he wasn't talented enough. Plus, there'd always been an expectation that he'd work in the family business. Clayton was an only child, so the onus was on him to keep the garden centre going. Maybe that's what he found so attractive about Hilary. Perhaps Clayton spotted her potential as a business partner, as well as a wife.'

'He'll miss having her around, then.'

Joyce smiled. 'I'm sure he will, but knowing Clayton, he'll be content to sit back and let Anne step into Hilary's shoes. Anne'll jump at the chance, of course, although she's nowhere near as talented as Hilary was.'

'She seems more than capable of running the tearoom.'

'Aye, and she'll settle for that to begin with – but Anne's not daft, she won't let Clayton slip through her fingers a second time. She'll do what Hilary did all those years ago . . . attach herself to Clayton and the business and make herself indispensable. You mark my words. In a few months, Clayton Spenbeck won't be able to function without Anne by his side.'

Joyce's no-holds-barred assertion that Clayton was reliant on a strong female partner was prompting Violet to have a rethink. Theoretically, Anne had a lot to gain from Hilary's death. The big question was, after two decades of playing second fiddle, had Anne finally taken measures to reclaim what she perceived to be her rightful position? And if so, why now, after all this time?

And what about Clayton? Was Joyce's assessment of his character a fair one? Had he become fundamentally lazy over the years, happy to sit back and relax? Or had he grown resentful of Hilary's supremacy at Bluebell Hill Garden Centre?

Joyce opened the fridge door and retrieved a bottle of Chenin Blanc. 'Is white OK?' she said. 'There's red, if you prefer it?'

'White's fine,' Violet said, accepting a generously filled glass. 'Thank you.'

'Sunday lunch, a glass or two of wine, and good company,' Joyce said. 'You can't beat it.'

'And a Sunday roast,' Violet said. 'That's a rare treat for me. Thanks again for the invitation.'

Joyce smiled. 'Violet, love, you're welcome any time. The truth is, I'm grateful to you. Matthew's had a real spring in his step since you moved to the village. Long may it continue.'

'I'll drink to that,' Violet said, raising her glass.

The back door opened and Brian Collis ambled into the kitchen, with Matthew a few steps behind.

'Hello, hello, what are you two cheersing?' Brian said.

Joyce and Violet smiled conspiratorially.

'Nothing you need to know about,' Joyce said. 'As a matter of fact, we were about to come and join you in the garden.'

Brian rubbed his stomach. 'And I've come in to carve the beef,' he said. 'Matt and I are starving. Is it ready, love? Shall I get it out of the oven?'

'Don't you dare, Brian Collis,' Joyce warned. 'The Yorkshires are only half risen – you'll ruin them if you open the oven door now. Give it another ten minutes and we'll serve up then. In the meantime, you'll have to make do with a glass of wine.'

'All right then,' Brian said, planting a kiss on Joyce's cheek. 'I know better than to argue with the cook.'

As they carried their drinks out onto the sunny patio, Violet processed all the things that Joyce had told her. Anne Burridge's name had been on the now defunct 'suspect board' since the impromptu council of war. Until today, Violet hadn't given any serious consideration to her being the perpetrator, but if Joyce was right, and Anne *had* been harbouring feelings for Clayton, a rethink was in order. In fact, it was fair to say that Anne Burridge had shot straight to the top of the suspect list.

Chapter 27

When she got out of bed on Monday morning, Violet's calf muscles were sore – the aftereffects of her hike up to Mam Tor. Although invigorating, the weekend's exertions had highlighted precisely how unfit she'd become. As she made the short walk to work, she chastised herself for not exercising more regularly. Perhaps she could take up running, or some other form of workout – anything, providing it didn't involve going to a gym.

Molly arrived at *The Memory Box* at ten o'clock, humming quietly to herself as she walked through the door.

'You sound very chirpy this morning,' Violet said.

'I feel chirpy,' Molly said, as she switched on her computer. 'I'm going away for two nights next month. Robert made the booking at the weekend. He's taking me and Jamie to Center Parcs in Sherwood Forest.'

Robert Doleman ran an antique shop in the shopping village, and he and Molly had been seeing each other since earlier in the year.

'Sounds great,' said Violet.

'I know.' Molly grinned. 'I'm so lucky . . . I still don't know what Robert sees in me.'

'Are you kidding?' Violet said. 'You're funny and interesting, and a very kind person. Robert's the lucky one, Molly, and I'm sure he knows it.'

'But he's loads cleverer than I am . . . He knows about so many things. He must think I'm dead boring.'

'I doubt that very much,' Violet said, thinking that the socially awkward Robert was undoubtedly thrilled to be dating someone as bubbly and outgoing as Molly. 'Besides, Robert's not the only one who's intelligent. You might not know a lot about antiques, but you're just as smart as he is.'

Molly smiled modestly. 'I don't know about that, but it's kind of you to say so. I hope you're right because I really, *really* like Robert. I just hope things don't fizzle out after a few months like all my other relationships have done.'

'From what I've seen of the two of you, I'd say you're in it for the long haul,' Violet said.

Smiling contentedly, Molly shrugged off her jacket and hung it on the back of her chair.

'You've not forgotten I'm at the dentist this afternoon, have you?' she said.

'No, it's in my diary. You're finishing at one o'clock, right?'

'Yeah. It makes it a short day, but I'll make up the hours later in the week.'

'There's no need to do that, Molly. You're allowed time off to visit the dentist.'

'Are you sure?' Molly said.

'Absolutely.'

Violet made a pot of coffee and, as they worked, she and Molly chatted about the Merrywell Village Fete, which was due to take place at the end of May.

'Bluebell Hill Garden Centre was meant to be the main sponsor this year,' Molly said. 'Hilary Spenbeck was going to cut the ribbon, or whatever it is they do to officially open the event. I'm not sure who'll do it now.'

'Perhaps Clayton will say a few words instead,' Violet said. 'Or, more likely, he'll ask Anne Burridge to stand in for him. She's taken on most of Hilary's other tasks, so I'm sure she'll be more than happy to add PR to her list of duties.'

Molly laughed. 'Do I detect a hint of sarcasm in that remark?'

Violet grimaced. 'Sorry. I was thinking aloud, mulling over something Joyce Collis told me. I didn't mean to mock.'

'Don't worry about it,' Molly said. 'In fact, you could be right about Anne. Rumour has it she's been enjoying being in charge a little bit too much. I take it you've heard what happened at the tearoom yesterday?'

'No, what?'

'Anne tore a strip off Simon Geldard for talking back at her, and it ended with her giving him a verbal warning for taking time off after the fire the other day. Made a right show of him in front of everyone, she did . . . although, in fairness, there weren't many customers in the tearoom at the time, given the ongoing situation with the mice.'

'Blimey,' Violet said. 'Poor Simon. He seems to be getting it in the neck from everyone.'

'I wouldn't feel too sorry for him, if I were you,' Molly said. 'He brings most of it on himself. He's a cheeky git . . . always sassing people.'

'Who told you about this latest run-in?' Violet said. 'How come you're always up to date with the gossip?'

Molly winked. 'When your parents run a pub, it's amazing what you get to hear. One of the White Hart regulars was in the tearoom when Anne threw her wobbly, so everyone in the pub had got to hear about it by the end of the day. Apparently, she was giving Simon a hard time for "abandoning his post" in order to sort out what Anne described as *a personal issue* . . . i.e. the aftermath of the fire.'

'That was a bit harsh,' Violet said. 'Simon was only doing what his grandad had asked him to do.'

'That's what he said, but Anne wasn't having any of it. In the end, Simon told her to stick her job, and then he stormed out.'

'Oh dear,' Violet said. 'That's not good news. By walking off, he's played right into her hands. I suspect Anne and the Spenbecks have been looking for an excuse to get rid of Simon since the day he started work. Clayton didn't want him there in the first place.'

'To be honest, I can't say I blame him,' Molly said. 'Simon's . . . how can I put this politely? He's a handful. As my gran would say, "trouble with a capital T".'

Violet sighed. 'Which makes it even more of a shame that he's lost his job. If Simon's got time on his hands, he's likely to get himself into trouble again.'

'There is a part of me that feels sorry for him,' Molly said. 'But in many ways, Simon's his own worst enemy. He's a bright lad, but he hangs out with the wrong kind of people – the sort who make it their business to find trouble. The word on the street is that Simon was the one who started the fire.'

Violet nodded. 'I'm sure it wasn't intentional, but he did admit to smoking in the barn. He must have dropped a cigarette end that was still alight.'

'What an idiot.' Molly shook her head and rolled her eyes. 'That's so irresponsible, as well as downright careless – and knowing Simon, I bet it wasn't tobacco he was smoking either.'

'Seriously?' Violet's ears pricked up.

'Yeah,' Molly said, giving the word a rising inflection. 'Everybody knows he likes the occasional spliff.'

'Everybody? Even his grandad?'

'Probably. There's not much gets past Roy Geldard.'

Violet cast her mind back to the day of the fire. Roy had been annoyed from the moment he showed up. It had been easy to understand why he was so upset – his barn was on fire – but later, when Simon had admitted to smoking, Violet had been surprised at how much Roy's anger had intensified. Rather than being relieved that the fire was out, he'd been absolutely furious. Was that because he'd guessed it was cannabis Simon had been smoking?

'Roy's the one I sympathise with the most,' Molly said. 'He took Simon in and looked after him – no questions asked. He'd do anything for the lad, anything at all, but there's no getting away from the fact that Simon's caused him a lot of grief.'

'It's a pity Simon can't get himself a proper job,' Violet said. 'Something more exciting that would appeal to him and keep him interested.'

'Where Simon Geldard is concerned, I'm not sure the words *job*, *appeal* and *interest* can be used in the same sentence,' Molly replied. 'The kid really does need to get his act together . . . and fast. Let's hope the near disaster with the fire is a wake-up call for him.'

Five minutes after Molly had set off for her dental appointment, Violet received a call from Clayton Spenbeck.

After their last conversation at Highfield House, she was surprised to hear from him again so soon. Even more surprising was that he was ringing to discuss the 'alternative project' he'd hinted at – the one that Violet had assumed would come to nothing.

'I meant what I said about needing something to occupy myself,' Clayton said.

Violet thought his time might be better spent going back to work and taking responsibility for his business. Then, chiding herself for being uncharitable, she tuned in properly to what he was saying.

'I've had an idea that I'd like to run past you,' he said. 'It's a project that would be an outlet for my creativity, and it would also allow me to focus on the core business that my father established all those years ago.'

'OK,' Violet said. 'Go ahead. I'm listening.'

'I'd like to film a series of short gardening videos,' Clayton said. 'You know the kind of thing . . . growing tips, advice on what to plant, seasonal jobs in the garden et cetera. I appreciate I'm no

Monty Don, but I'm more than capable of doing some research and putting a few interesting segments together. I thought we could make a video for every month of the year. That way, there'll always be something new to put on the garden centre's website and social media channels. I could post the videos alongside some buying recommendations. What do you think?'

'I think it's an excellent suggestion,' said Violet, who was genuinely impressed with the idea. 'You could even get the customers involved . . . do an online poll to let them choose what subject they'd like you to cover in the next video, for instance.'

'Why not?' Clayton said. 'That'd be a great way to encourage people to engage with the posts. What about you, Violet? Can you think of any suitable topics? I'd be very grateful for your input.'

Violet thought about her own gardening dilemmas. 'Maybe some advice on plant choices, based on soil type,' she said. 'There's a lot of clay in my back garden, which makes growing certain types of plant very challenging.'

'That's a good one,' Clayton said. 'I'll make a note of it.'

'And what about a video for pet owners,' she said, throwing the idea into the mix to gauge Clayton's reaction. 'You could mention the plants that pets like – such as catnip – but also warn against those that are potentially toxic to animals.'

She waited, but the reaction she'd hoped to elicit from Clayton failed to materialise. There was nothing to indicate that he had connected the suggested topic to what had happened to Lisa Wenham. On the contrary, Clayton's enthusiastic response suggested he knew absolutely nothing about the problematic lantana plant.

'Good stuff!' he said. 'I've written it down, and I'll dig out some information on the subject.'

Violet was pretty sure Dennis Spenbeck wouldn't have needed to research the topic, but obviously Clayton was nowhere near as well informed as his father had been.

'This is wonderful,' Clayton said, excitement lifting his voice a couple of octaves. 'I can't wait to begin. When can we make a start on the filming?'

'Let's meet first to draw up a proper plan and filming schedule,' Violet said. 'It's probably best if we shoot one video a month. That way, the weather and the plants will be appropriate for the season you'll be talking about.'

'That makes sense,' Clayton said. 'When are you free to come over?'

Violet opened her diary.

'How about Wednesday?' she said. 'Ten o'clock?'

'Perfect,' Clayton said. 'We'll meet at Highfield House again, if that's all right. I know I'll have to go back to the garden centre at some point, but I'm not ready to face it yet.'

'OK,' said Violet. 'Wednesday. Ten o'clock. Highfield House. I'll see you then.'

Chapter 28

By the following day, Violet was feeling distinctly upbeat about the steady stream of enquiries that had started to filter through to *The Memory Box*. All of a sudden, the future of her small business looked much, much rosier.

Molly didn't work on Tuesdays, and without her effervescent presence, the office seemed empty. The flip side to that was that the enforced silence was proving a useful aid to concentration. Violet had spent the last hour selecting some new sample reels to add to *The Memory Box* website.

As she waited for her chosen files to upload, the door opened and Charlie Winterton strolled in, carrying two takeaway coffees on a cardboard tray.

'Hello,' Violet said, greeting him with a smile. 'What are you doing here?'

'You made me feel guilty the other day, and seeing as I was in the area, I've been over yonder for lunch.' He tipped his chin towards the window in the direction of *Books, Bakes and Cakes*. 'I went in there expecting to find the place empty, but it was full to the rafters. I thought you said they hadn't got any customers.'

Violet grinned. 'That was before . . . when you were treating

Fiona as a suspect. Now that she's in the clear, the café's busier than ever.'

She made no mention of the 'mouse' situation at the tearoom. The last thing she wanted to do was draw Charlie's attention back to Lisa Wenham.

'I bought a couple of extra coffees on my way out,' Charlie said, as he placed the cardboard tray on Violet's desk.

'And is one of them for me?'

'It is. I thought we could have a chat while we drink them.'

'OK. In that case, you'd better take a seat,' she said, gesturing towards Molly's empty chair.

'I wanted to give you an update,' Charlie said, as he tipped the contents of several sachets of sugar into one of the coffees. 'And, if I'm honest, I'd also appreciate getting your views on a couple of things.'

Violet smiled. 'No problem,' she said. 'I'm more than happy to give you the benefit of my opinion. I'll start by pointing out that too much sugar's not good for you. You really should start using sweeteners, you know.'

'You sound like my missus,' Charlie said, as he stuck a wooden stirrer into his cup. 'Now, do you want this update or not?'

'You know I do, providing you've got something worth reporting.'

'I certainly have,' Charlie said, smiling uncertainly. 'As a matter of fact, there's been a major development.'

'That is good news.' Violet picked up her own coffee and removed the lid. 'Does it mean you're about to solve the case?'

Charlie shrugged. 'Looks like I won't have to. Someone walked into the station last night and confessed.'

Chapter 29

Violet almost choked on her coffee.

'You're joking,' she said, coughing to clear her throat. 'Who?'

Charlie continued to stir his drink, eking out the suspense.

'Would you like to guess?' he said.

'*No*,' Violet said. 'I wouldn't. Just tell me, will you?'

Charlie blew on his coffee, took a sip, and leaned back.

'Roy Geldard,' he said. 'He's admitted to assaulting Hilary Spenbeck, but he says he had no intention of causing her any serious harm.'

Violet placed her hands on the desk and did a double take. 'Roy?' she said. 'Roy Geldard has confessed?'

'That's what I said.'

'And you believe him?'

DS Winterton pulled a face. 'I like to keep an open mind about these things, but I've no obvious reason to doubt him. Why would he confess to a crime he didn't commit?'

'I don't know,' Violet said, breathing rapidly as she absorbed the news. 'I'm surprised, that's all. He doesn't seem the type.'

Charlie wrinkled his nose. 'With a crime like this . . . something committed in the spur of the moment . . . there isn't necessarily a "type". And if Mr Geldard is telling the truth about what took place, we're looking at manslaughter, rather than murder.'

'What has he told you?'

Charlie pressed his lips together and shook his head.

'Oh, come on, Charlie,' Violet said, tapping her fingers on the desk. 'You can't waltz in here and say that Roy's confessed and then leave it at that.'

The detective made a slurping noise as he drank his coffee.

'There must be something you can tell me?' she said.

He looked at her, frowning as he considered his response.

'My DCI would give me a right rollicking if she knew I was here, talking to you like this.'

Violet tapped the side of her nose. 'I won't tell her about it, if you don't. Now, be honest, Charlie. Aside from bringing me a cup of coffee, why *are* you here?'

He drummed his fingers on the top of the desk. 'I'm interested in hearing your opinion,' he said. 'You seem to have good instincts – our previous encounters have taught me that.'

Violet experienced a warm glow of pride. Knowing that Charlie valued her opinion meant a lot.

'Correct me if I'm wrong, but you seemed sceptical when I told you about Roy Geldard's confession,' he said. 'Why was that?'

Violet shrugged. 'Gut instinct, I suppose. Roy's gruff and curmudgeonly, there's no denying that – but he's had a lot to deal with lately. I can understand him feeling disillusioned and cranky, but I'm really not convinced he's a killer. Having said that, I'm not in possession of the facts – so it's hard for me to judge whether his confession is genuine.'

'You want the facts?' Charlie cleared his throat nervously. 'All right – but what I'm about to tell you, I'm telling you in confidence. Are we clear on that?'

'Crystal clear.' Violet nodded.

'Mr Geldard claims he entered the grounds of Highfield House at around seven-thirty,' Charlie said. 'From there, he made his way to the goods road and entered the garden centre through the rear gate.'

'OK,' Violet said. 'But how did he know the gate would be open?'

'Hilary Spenbeck told him. He says he'd spoken to her the previous day and they'd agreed to meet to finalise the details of the land sale. He arranged to see her at the garden centre at seven-forty-five. She told him the back gate would be open and that he should let himself in.'

'So why didn't Clayton know about this meeting?'

DS Winterton shrugged. 'Maybe Hilary didn't want him involved. It sounds to me like she was firmly in the driving seat when it came to running the family business.'

'Even so, you'd think she'd have mentioned it to him.'

Charlie raised a bushy eyebrow. 'It sounds like you're deliberately trying to poke holes in Roy's confession.'

'I'm testing its strength,' Violet said. 'Seeing whether it holds together.'

'And how do you think it's faring so far?'

'Not very well,' Violet said. 'There are things that don't make sense. For instance, didn't you say the CCTV footage showed a person who was, and I quote, *moving fast*? Roy Geldard has Parkinson's.'

'True, but he only received his diagnosis a few months ago,' DS Winterton replied. 'As far as I can tell, the Parkinson's hasn't yet affected his mobility.'

'Even so, he's not a young man. I'd hardly describe him as lithe and fast-moving.'

'You're right, and it's one of the details we'll be clarifying with him.'

'What about his fingerprints? Do they match any of those found on the owl?'

'We're running a comparison, but Mr Geldard says he wore gloves.'

Violet frowned. 'It was a chilly morning, so that's not beyond the realms of possibility,' she said. 'On the other hand, he could just be saying that because he knows full well his prints aren't on the owl.'

'Because he never handled it in the first place, you mean?'

Violet gave a slow nod and sipped her coffee. 'Do you intend to charge him?'

Charlie shrugged. 'For now, he's being interviewed under caution,' he said. 'We'll need to verify a few things before we press charges.'

'So, you're not convinced he's telling the truth either?'

Charlie stared at her, his face inscrutable. 'Let's just say we're proceeding cautiously . . . keeping an open mind until we've checked the veracity of his statement. But thank you, Violet – this chat has been useful. It's helped me clarify a few things, and I'm grateful to you.'

'Always happy to help, if I can,' she said.

'I appreciate that – but don't worry, I won't be troubling you again. This investigation is my responsibility, and not something you need concern yourself with. I'll take it from here. Understood?'

Feeling increasingly doubtful about Roy Geldard's confession, Violet opened her mouth to object, but the determined expression on Charlie's face left her no option but to stay silent and nod obediently.

On her way home from work, she called at Merrywell Stores to stock up on a few provisions.

'Did you find everything you needed?' asked Will, the shop-keeper, as she plonked her selection of groceries onto the counter. In recent weeks, she'd noticed that he'd been upping his game in terms of customer service, presumably in a bid to increase turnover.

'Yes, thank you,' Violet replied. 'I'm also extremely tempted by a family-sized bar of Dairy Milk, but my waistband's telling me that wouldn't be a good idea. I will take a *Peak Times* though.'

'There you go,' Will said, as he handed over a copy of the local newspaper. 'At least there are no calories in that . . . and, if my wife's to be believed, nothing worth reading either. According to her, people follow the news online these days. She reckons newspapers will be a forgotten memory before too long.'

'That does seem to be the way things are going,' Violet said. 'But call me old-fashioned, I prefer to read a proper printed paper.'

She smiled inwardly, wondering whether it was accurate to describe the local rag as a *proper paper*.

'I'm pleased to hear it,' Will said. 'I could do with more customers like you – 'cos when I say everything's going online, I include grocery shopping in that. You should see the number of supermarket delivery vans that bomb up and down in front of my shop every day . . . really sticks in my craw, it does.'

Violet recognised an appeal for support when she heard one. It was worrying to think that Will's business might be struggling, and she made a mental note to buy more of her groceries from his shop in the future.

'That'll be £9.44, please,' Will said, when he'd finished scanning her items.

'You know what,' said Violet. 'I think I will have that bar of chocolate after all.'

At home, she kicked off her shoes and went to sit in the living room. Matthew had promised to pick up a Chinese takeaway for dinner that evening, but it would be at least an hour before he arrived.

She switched on the television to catch the tail end of *Pointless*, and began to read the paper. The front-page headline was a report of a two-vehicle crash at a local accident black spot. Local campaigners were once again calling for traffic lights to be installed near the busy road junction.

A cheer sounded from the television, as a pair of contestants scored a pointless answer. With one ear cocked for the next question, Violet opened the paper and began to skim-read the inside pages. An article on page five caught her eye, and she sat up straight to read it. As she absorbed the news story, her perception of some of the recent events in Merrywell began to slowly shift and alter.

Suspected cannabis grow discovered following local house fire

The emergency services were called to a fire raging from the roof of a house in Matlock on Sunday. Firefighters later found a number of cannabis plants being grown in the property. The blaze at the terraced house in Swinscoe Street began in the property's attic in the early hours of Sunday morning, and led to a full-scale emergency response. The fire spread to the roof, which was well alight by the time the emergency services arrived at the scene.

Firefighters from Derbyshire Fire and Rescue used an aerial ladder platform to tackle the blaze. In an update on Monday, detectives leading the investigation confirmed that police had found a number of suspected cannabis plants being cultivated at the property.

A spokesperson for Derbyshire Police said: 'No one was found to be inside the address at the time of the fire, and no one has reported suffering any injuries, but the house sustained substantial damage, as did a neighbouring property. At this stage in the investigation, it is believed the fire was caused by an electrical fault.'

The report concluded with a police appeal to anyone with information, or anyone who had noticed suspicious activity in the area in recent weeks.

Violet rested the newspaper on her knee and stared blankly at the television. She'd heard and read about these kinds of fires before. From her limited knowledge of cannabis growing, she knew it was commonly done in dark, hidden-away places such as the loft of a house, or an abandoned building. And if her train of thinking was on the right track, the plants could just as easily be grown in an old barn such as the one owned by Roy Geldard.

Had Simon set up his own mini cannabis farm in the barn? Could the cause of the fire have been a shorting of the electrics on a grow light, rather than a discarded cigarette?

Matthew arrived forty-five minutes later. As he placed the foil takeaway containers on the kitchen table, Violet told him about Roy Geldard's confession. Then, as she retrieved plates from the cupboard and chopsticks from the cutlery drawer, she launched into her theory regarding the cause of the barn fire.

'How sure are you about this?' Matthew said, when he'd heard her out. 'Just because Simon smokes the odd joint doesn't mean he's growing his own cannabis. And even if he is, how is that connected to Roy's confession?'

'I've haven't fully worked that out yet,' Violet said. 'But everyone keeps saying that Roy would do anything for Simon, so maybe he's confessed in order to cover for him.'

As always, Matthew was the voice of reason. 'That's a big assumption to make,' he said. 'Have you got anything to back up this arbitrary theory of yours?'

'I don't have any solid evidence, no, but when I think back to the day of the fire, I remember there was a distinct shift in Roy's attitude after he'd looked through the barn window. What if he peered in and saw a collection of cannabis plants? That kind of discovery would certainly explain his mounting anger, and his sudden insistence that Simon go home to "*sort out his mess*".'

'I'm sorry to pour cold water on the idea, but wouldn't Roy have known if Simon was growing marijuana? He could have gone into the barn any old time and worked out what was going on.'

'I don't think he goes down there very often,' Violet said. 'And anyway, the barn was padlocked. Roy said he didn't have a key and, at the time, I assumed he didn't have a key *with* him. But what if Simon fitted the lock to keep his grandad out of the barn? What if Roy didn't *have* a key?'

'He could have looked through the window.'

'Maybe Simon covered it up.'

'In that case, how did Roy manage to spot the plants on the day of the fire?'

'Maybe the covering . . . whatever it was . . . net, or paper or curtains, fell down during the fire.'

Matthew shook his head. 'Sorry, love, but that's a lot of "what ifs" and "maybes".'

Whenever Violet was in 'sleuthing' mode, Matthew was usually sporting enough to listen to her (often outlandish) theories, but this evening, she could tell his patience was wearing thin. It was obvious that he wanted nothing more than to unwind, relax and eat his Chinese food.

'I admire your tenacity,' he said, 'but you know, not everyone's as curious as you are. Some of us just want to get on and eat our dinner.'

Violet laughed. 'All right. Let's tuck in, before it gets cold.'

She sat down, piled Szechuan chicken and fried rice onto her plate, and changed the subject.

After their meal, they went into the living room and downloaded an old episode of *Morse*. As they watched the long-suffering Lewis jump from the passenger seat of Morse's Jaguar in hot pursuit of a suspect, their viewing was interrupted by another heavy rattling of the door-knocker.

'Who on earth's that at this time of night?' Violet said, as she paused the television programme.

'You stay there, and I'll go and find out,' said Matthew.

'Cheers, love. And unless it's an emergency, please tell whoever it is to come back tomorrow.'

She could hear Matthew having a conversation in the hallway – the other voice was male, but not one that was familiar to her.

After a minute, Matthew reappeared. Trailing behind him, looking agitated and upset, was Simon Geldard.

Chapter 30

Violet stood up and exchanged a look with Matthew – one that said *what-the-hell-is-he-doing-here?*

'Simon wants to talk to you about something,' Matthew said. 'I tried to persuade him to come back tomorrow, but he says it's important.'

If Violet had been home alone, she might have been unnerved by Simon's sudden appearance at Greengage Cottage – but with Matthew by her side, she felt perfectly safe.

'What is it you want to talk about, Simon?' she said.

'My grandad,' he replied, pushing his hands into his dark grey joggers.

Violet noticed that he'd removed his shoes before entering the living room. It was an unexpected courtesy – one that revealed a polite, respectful side to Simon that made her feel hopeful for his future.

'He's down at the police station,' Simon said. 'He's confessed to something he didn't do.'

Violet didn't know whether to act surprised, or admit that she already knew.

In the end, she did neither of those things. 'Do you mean he's admitted to assaulting Hilary Spenbeck?' she said instead.

'Yeah, that.' Simon tapped the carpet with the toe of his sock.

'Do you want to sit down?' she said, pointing to the settee by the window.

Simon looked ill at ease as he shuffled over and perched on the edge of the sofa, his arms resting on his knees.

'He didn't do it,' he said, joggling his leg as he continued to stare at the carpet.

'OK,' said Violet. 'But why are you telling *me* this? If you want to fight your grandad's corner, shouldn't you go to the police station?'

Simon scowled. 'The rozzers don't listen to people like me.'

'I'm sure that's not true, Simon,' Violet said.

He gave a disbelieving huff. 'I came here because you were nice to me the other day, and I thought you might help. I've heard you're good at stuff like this, and I don't know who else to talk to.'

Stuff like this. Violet wasn't sure whether he meant criminal investigations, or sticking her beak in where it wasn't wanted. Either way, it was yet another sign she had developed the wrong kind of reputation in the village.

'I'll help, if I can,' she said. 'But there's not a lot I can do unless you tell me why you're so convinced of your grandad's innocence.'

Simon lifted his head and stared at her, looking scared and reluctant and unsure of himself.

'Grandad's confessed because he thinks I killed Hilary. He said he was going to *fall on his sword* to protect me . . . whatever that means.'

'It means he's willing to take one for the team,' said Matthew, translating Roy Geldard's idiom into words Simon could relate to.

'But that's just it, I don't *want* him to,' Simon said, sounding exasperated. 'I wish he wouldn't interfere. Why can't he leave me be? I'm not a kid anymore. I don't need protecting.'

'You're his grandson,' Violet said. 'He'll always want to protect you, no matter how old you get.'

Simon sighed, and as he did so, all the fight seemed to leave his skinny body. 'I can look after myself,' he said.

If that was true, you wouldn't be here, appealing to me for help, Violet thought.

'Did your grandad tell you he was going to the police station?' she asked.

'Yeah . . . I tried to talk him out of it, but he wouldn't listen. I told him I didn't kill Mrs Spenbeck, but he wouldn't believe me.'

'Why not?' Matthew said. 'Are you in the habit of lying to him?'

Simon glared, clearly irritated by Matthew's lack of empathy.

To ease the growing tension in the room, Violet asked a different question. 'Why does your grandad think you killed Hilary?'

The only reply Simon gave was a shrug.

'You know, if you want my help, you need to tell me the whole story,' Violet said. 'Let's start by talking about last week's fire, shall we?'

'What do you want to talk about that for?'

'Because I think it's all part and parcel of why your grandad feels he has to protect you,' she said. 'Why don't you begin by telling me why the barn was padlocked, and more to the point, explain why your grandad didn't have a key?'

'He did have a key. He just didn't have it with him.'

It was obvious from Simon's lack of eye contact that he was lying.

'I don't believe you,' Violet said.

'Suit yourself. Doesn't bother me. I'm used to people not believing me.'

Matthew was standing next to the armchair – arms folded, feet apart.

'Maybe you should ask yourself why that is,' he said.

In a strop reminiscent of someone half his age, Simon threw himself against the back of the sofa.

'I'll ask you again,' Violet said, more firmly this time. 'Why didn't your grandad have a key?'

'He doesn't need one. He doesn't go near the place,' Simon

replied. 'The barn's my space. It's one of the places I hang out when I want to be on my own.'

'OK, but why all the security? On the day of the fire, when DS Winterton asked what was in the barn, you said there was nothing in there. Why would you padlock the door of an empty building? And why lock your grandad out of his own barn? My guess is, there was something in there . . . something you didn't want him to see.'

'No.' The sharp one-word denial was delivered belligerently. 'Grandad doesn't care what I do anyway.'

'I'd say he cares a great deal,' Violet said. 'He's proven that by confessing to a crime he didn't commit in order to protect you.'

'The only thing that proves is how barmy he is,' Simon said. 'He's wasting police time. I told him . . . I didn't kill Hilary Spenbeck. Why couldn't he believe me?'

'We'll come back to that in a minute,' Violet said. 'But first, let's finish talking about the barn. You see, I've been reading an article in the *Peak Times* . . .'

'You shouldn't believe everything you read in the papers, you know,' Simon said. 'That's what Grandad always says.'

'He's right about that,' said Violet. 'But it's not all fake news, and the report I read earlier definitely rang a few bells. It's made me rethink the fire in the barn, and question why you were so eager to put it out on your own.'

Simon lifted his chin and stuck out his bottom lip. Violet didn't know if the gesture was intended as a challenge, or whether he was genuinely interested in what she had to say.

'I suspect you were using the barn to grow cannabis,' she said. 'I don't know a lot about the process, but I do know the plants require heat and light and that the growing equipment sometimes causes electrical fires.'

Simon glared sullenly, brazening things out as best he could.

'You acted quickly last Thursday,' Violet said. 'When your grandad turned up, you were doing everything in your power to

187

put the fire out – but instead of being proud of your efforts, he seemed really, really angry. I think that's because he'd guessed you were responsible for starting the fire in the first place. Initially, I think he thought you'd discarded a cigarette – because he knew you smoked, didn't he? He may even have known that it wasn't just tobacco you were inhaling.'

Simon maintained a hostile silence.

'What I don't think he knew, was that you weren't just smoking cannabis – you were growing it.'

'What are you on about?' Simon said, curling his lip and trying to look nonchalant.

'Don't try and feign ignorance,' Violet said. 'You know what I'm talking about. I saw how agitated you were when Roy said he was going to look through the window to check on the fire. You tried to dissuade him, didn't you? You said it was dangerous, but he didn't listen, and because you were on the other side of the fence, there was nothing you could do to stop him. That must have been very frustrating.'

'What do you want me to say? Are you expecting me to fess up? Is that it?'

Violet waited, hoping her silence would prompt Simon to keep talking.

'You can't prove any of this,' he said. 'You're making it up as you go along. You're as daft as me grandad.'

Matthew unfolded his arms. 'Hey, you,' he said. 'Less of that. You're the one who came here, remember? If you want Violet's help, you'd better change your attitude, mate.'

'I came 'ere to get help for me grandad, not to be accused of all sorts by you pair.'

Matthew pointed towards the hallway. 'If you don't like it, you know where the door is.'

'Matthew's right,' Violet said. 'If you're not going to be honest, you may as well go. You obviously care about your grandad, otherwise you wouldn't have come here in the first place – but unless you're willing to cooperate, there's nothing I can do to help.'

'I am willing to cooperate,' Simon said. 'I just don't understand why you're banging on about the barn fire. What's that got to do with Grandad's confession?'

'Without knowing the facts, I can't be sure – but I imagine it's all of a piece. On the day of the fire, your grandad was angry from the moment he showed up – but after he looked through the window, he was fit to explode. He insisted that you go home and get . . . what was it he called it . . . your *mess* sorted out? You knew exactly what he meant. He'd found you out and he wanted you to clear the barn and dispose of the evidence before DS Winterton got wind of what you'd been up to.'

'No comment,' Simon said.

Violet sat down and folded her hands in her lap. 'You don't have to say *no comment* to me, Simon. I'm not the police. This is a private conversation. Whatever you say to me can't be used as evidence, so you may as well tell me the truth. You were growing cannabis, weren't you? Was it for your own consumption, or were you hoping to become a small-time dealer?'

Simon remained tight-lipped.

'Oh, for heaven's sake!' Violet jumped to her feet again and pointed to the door. 'Stop wasting my time and go home if you're not going to talk. I suspect you've got yourself into a mess, but unless you open up, there's nothing I can do for you *or* your grandad.'

Simon shuffled forward, but remained where he was, on the sofa. 'OK,' he said, mumbling self-consciously. 'You're right about the weed, but let's not get carried away. It wasn't a "grow" grow. It was a couple of plants for my own use. I wasn't gonna sell it, nothing like that – although I don't suppose you believe me . . . Grandad didn't.'

'Quite frankly, I'm not sure what to believe,' Violet said. 'Are you going to tell me what happened? Was there some kind of electrical fault? Is that how the fire started?'

Simon shook his head. 'It wasn't the electrics. There were a few bits of old hay in there, and I think the heat from the grow light must have caused some of it to smoulder. It was more smoke than fire. There was no major damage to the barn – but even so, Grandad let rip when I got home. He said Mum would have been ashamed of me, but I don't think she would. She'd have understood . . .'

'Are you sure about that?' said Matthew. 'From what I remember of your mum, she liked everything to be above board. If she was still around, I reckon she'd be telling you to get your act together.'

'Don't talk about my mum,' Simon said, leaping up from the sofa and stuffing his hands in his pockets again. 'I don't need a lecture from you. It was Violet I came here to see.'

'And my advice to you, Simon, is to go and tell DS Winterton the truth . . . whatever the "truth" is,' Violet said. 'I'll come with you, if you want me to.'

'There's no way I'm going to tell the coppers about the cannabis,' Simon said. 'Grandad made me get rid of everything . . . the plants, the grow light, the lot. It was a waste of good weed, but he didn't leave me much choice. If the police went into the barn now, they wouldn't find anything. And like I said, it was only a couple of plants – so they wouldn't be interested anyway. They've got more important things to worry about.'

'All right,' Violet said. 'Let's forget about the cannabis. Tell me why your grandad decided to make a false confession.'

Simon threw up his arms. 'Isn't it obvious?' he said. 'He thinks I had something to do with Hilary Spenbeck's death, so he's covering for me.'

'And is he right?' Violet said. 'Did you attack Hilary Spenbeck that morning at the garden centre?'

Simon jabbed an index finger in Violet's direction. 'Shut it,' he shouted. 'Just shut up, all right.'

Matthew stepped forward, placing himself between them. 'That's enough,' he said, pointing to the door. 'It's time you left.

Violet's been very kind and patient, and she's given you a genuine offer of help. If that's not good enough for you, you'd better go. I won't stand by and let you shout at her.'

He caught hold of Simon's arm and guided him to the door. Simon shook himself free, but stepped willingly into the hallway. As he bent down to put his shoes back on, he twisted his head and spoke to Violet over his shoulder.

'I thought you might be different, but you're just like all the rest. Nobody listens to me. Everybody assumes the worst.'

Matthew's patience was stretched to snapping point. 'You don't exactly make things easy for yourself, Simon,' he said. 'You're being very defensive, and in my opinion that can only mean you're hiding something. If you're serious about wanting to help your grandad, you need to speak to the police and tell the truth, even if that means getting into trouble yourself.'

'I'm out of here,' Simon said. 'I'm not gonna take advice from a couple of jumped-up do-gooders. You can shove your opinions, the pair of you. I don't need anyone's help. I'll sort things out on my own.'

Violet felt his reproachful eyes on her as he headed for the door. There was something else in his look too. Was it remorse? What had he done to feel remorseful about?

'Simon . . . wait—'

Ignoring Violet's plea, Simon let himself out of Greengage Cottage and slammed the door behind him.

'Well,' Matthew said, blowing air through his mouth. 'That wasn't how I was expecting the evening to end.'

'Me neither,' said Violet. 'I hope he's not going to do anything stupid.'

'Based on what he *didn't* say, I'm guessing he already has. That is one messed-up kid.'

'Which is why I wanted to try and help him,' Violet said. 'He's not had it easy, and I'm worried that if he goes too far down the wrong path, he won't be able to find his way back.'

'Do *you* think he attacked Hilary?'

Violet sighed. 'I don't know. Possibly. I just wish he'd tell us the truth. It's the only way we're going to be able to help him.'

'I'm not convinced he wants our help. What was it he called us? Jumped-up do-gooders? Cheeky sod.'

Violet smiled, but her stomach was churning. She hoped Simon wouldn't do anything rash, but given his mood when he left, anything was possible.

'Simon comes across as impetuous and abrasive,' she said, 'but actually, underneath all that, I think he's vulnerable. He's obviously in trouble, and I'd like to help him if I can.'

'How though?' Matthew said. 'Given his lack of cooperation, the only thing you can do now is get Charlie Winterton involved.'

'That's what I *should* do,' Violet said, 'but while ever there's a chance he'll go to the police himself, I'll hold off. Whatever trouble Simon's in, things will go much better for him if he speaks to them voluntarily and tells them what he knows.'

'Unfortunately, I don't think he's mature enough to understand that,' Matthew said. 'He's in panic mode, which makes him unpredictable.'

Violet sighed. 'I don't know what to do for the best. My head's telling me one thing, and my heart's telling me another.'

'And which one are you going to listen to?'

'For now, I'll follow my heart and do nothing. I'll reassess things in the morning and make a final decision then.'

Chapter 31

'Have you made up your mind about Simon?' Matthew said, as he and Violet entered the shopping village the next day.

'Yep, I'll call Charlie Winterton and tell him that Simon came to see me.'

'Are you going to let him know what he was using the barn for?'

'No, for now, I'll keep it brief. I'll tell him that Simon doesn't think Roy's guilty, and let Charlie draw his own conclusions from that. I've got a meeting to go to at ten o'clock, so I'll try and get hold of him before I set off.'

'OK. Try not to worry. You're doing the right thing.'

'Am I, though?'

'Trust your instincts, Violet . . . that's all you can do,' Matthew said. 'I'll ring you later to find out how you got on. In fact, it's your turn to buy lunch, so why don't we meet in the café later?'

She laughed. 'How could I possibly turn down such a gracious invitation?' she said. 'I'll call you when I'm on my way back from the meeting.'

She rang DS Winterton as soon as she got to the office. She felt nervous. The call was bound to get her into trouble – primarily with Charlie (who would accuse her of poking her nose in again), but also with the Geldards (neither of whom would thank her for interfering).

'Charlie, it's Violet,' she said, when he eventually picked up. 'I thought I'd better let you know that I had a visit from Simon Geldard last night.'

'Did you?' Charlie said. 'What did he want?'

'My help. Simon said his grandad has confessed to something he hasn't done, and he didn't know what to do about it.'

'Why was he asking you for help? He should have come and talked to me.'

'That's what I advised him to do. I even offered to go with him to the police station, but he didn't seem very keen on the idea.'

'Have you asked yourself why that might be?'

Violet sighed. 'I got the feeling he may have had a brush with the police in the past. Perhaps that experience has clouded his judgement.'

'If he's not willing to talk to *us*, how was he expecting you to help?' Charlie said.

'I'm not sure,' Violet said. 'I don't think he knew himself. Maybe he was hoping I'd act as an intermediary – but the only thing I was able to offer was unwanted advice.'

'I bet that went down like a lead balloon?'

'Yup,' Violet said. 'He took umbrage and stormed off. All I wanted him to do was tell you the truth . . . the whole truth, whatever that might be.'

She cringed, aware that in keeping the cannabis-growing a secret, she wasn't being totally honest herself.

'Did he say why he thought his grandad was innocent?'

'He thinks that Roy's confession is a misguided attempt to protect him. It sounds like Roy suspects Simon of being involved in Hilary Spenbeck's death – although Simon denies the charge, of course. He claims he's done nothing wrong, and doesn't need his grandad's protection.'

'And you believe him?'

'On balance, yes, but Simon seems troubled. I think he's hiding something.'

'I'll see if I can find out what that is,' DS Winterton said. 'How did Simon seem last night, in himself?'

'Angry and distressed,' Violet said. 'Agitated, I suppose. He's obviously got something on his mind. That's why I'm calling you now, so that you can have a word with him and work out what's going on.'

'It's a pity you didn't ring me last night.' Charlie gave a sigh. 'As it is, your call has come a few hours too late.'

'Why?' Violet said, as a horrible feeling of foreboding swept over her. 'What's happened?'

'We released Roy Geldard early this morning,' Charlie said. 'Initially, his confession seemed plausible. He told us he entered the garden centre through the rear gate, and he also described things that hadn't been made public – such as the owl, and the gash on Hilary Spenbeck's forehead. But there were gaps and discrepancies in his story . . . and when we pressed him for more information, we realised there were flaws in his confession.'

'What sort of flaws?'

'His story lacked detail for one thing. For instance, when we asked where he was when he assaulted Hilary, his answer was vague. "Somewhere in the middle of the garden centre", he said.'

'That's right, though, isn't it?'

'Yes, but when we asked him to be more specific, he couldn't give us a detailed description. When we asked about the scene of the crime, he told us there were plants nearby, but he couldn't remember what kind. He didn't mention the water features at all, and they were pretty hard to miss. When asked to describe what he was wearing, he said he couldn't remember. The more we questioned him, the cagier and more imprecise he became. We were obviously in no position to charge him, so he's been released, pending further investigation.'

'You think he's covering for Simon?'

'I'd stake my life on it,' DS Winterton replied. 'He didn't say as much, of course – in fact, he clammed up completely in the end and refused to say any more. We believe that Mr Geldard's confession was either a misguided attempt to protect someone who is, in fact, innocent, or a calculated attempt to pervert the course of justice by taking the blame for a crime he knows his grandson committed. The only way to ascertain the truth was to bring Simon in, to see what he had to say for himself.'

'Oh! So, you've already spoken to Simon?' Violet said, wondering why Charlie hadn't told her that straight away. 'What did he say?'

'He's not said anything yet, because we haven't managed to locate him. We went to his home last night, but he wasn't in. Officers have been checking the place every few hours, but there's no sign of him. Looks like he's done a runner.'

Violet's stomach was performing somersaults. Simon was a pain in the backside, but for some reason, she cared about the kid and wanted things to work out for him. Wherever he was, she hoped he was OK.

'Have you checked the barn?' she said. 'He told me that's where he goes when he wants to be alone.'

'Yes, we've searched the barn and all the other outbuildings, but Simon Geldard is nowhere to be seen. In my experience, when someone does a runner, it's because they're guilty of something. So, Violet, let me make myself clear: if Simon gets in touch with you again, you need to ring me. Straight away.'

Chapter 32

As Violet drove up to Highfield House for her ten o'clock meeting, she wondered whether Clayton Spenbeck had been updated on the latest developments. However, as the aim of the project they were about to discuss was to take his mind off Hilary's death, she decided not to mention the investigation unless he did.

Clayton led her through the dingy hallway into the dining room, which was dominated by a long mahogany table surrounded by eight spindle-backed chairs. Spread out at one end of the table were copious pieces of paper and notebooks, which she assumed related to the series of videos Clayton was hoping to film.

'This latest idea of mine has been a godsend,' he said, as he sat down and shuffled the notes into a semblance of order. 'For the first time in days, I've been able to think about something other than Hilary. I can't tell you what a relief that is.'

Violet pulled out a chair and joined him at the table.

'Good, because I'm sure Hilary wouldn't have wanted you to wallow,' she said, even though she was slightly surprised at how easily Clayton had managed to distract himself. 'Shall we start by putting together an outline for the first video? We'll also need to schedule in filming slots for the next twelve months, although you won't have to decide on the content for those until nearer the time.'

'I thought I'd begin with a segment on cottage gardening,' Clayton said. 'We sell loads of lupins, delphiniums, asters, echinacea et cetera at this time of year . . . but a lot of people don't know where to position them or how to look after them properly.'

Before starting on the outline, they talked through Bluebell Hill Garden Centre's best locations for filming, and discussed how long each of the segments should be (Violet recommended something short and to the point with a heavy emphasis on the visuals, whereas Clayton favoured a longer 'to camera' piece). In the end they compromised, settling on a three-minute video each month that would combine colourful and inspirational visuals with a short presentation or demonstration from Clayton. Violet used her phone to find a couple of comparable videos for Clayton to watch, and when they'd agreed on a style and tone, they created a rough storyboard for the first video and set a date for filming it.

By the time they had finished, it was almost midday.

'Have you heard about Roy Geldard?' Clayton said, surprising Violet with the question as she gathered her belongings, ready to leave. 'He went to the police station yesterday to confess.'

'Yes, I had heard. How did you feel about that?' she said, hedging to ascertain whether Clayton knew the confession had since been debunked.

'Surprised and dubious,' he replied. 'And as it turns out, my sense of disbelief was justified. First thing this morning, I had another phone call to say that Roy had been released without charge. Apparently, his confession was unsound. They don't believe he's telling the truth.'

Violet fastened her coat. 'I suppose you'll have to wait and see what happens next, then,' she said, hoping to bring the conversation to a close and avoid getting dragged in to any further speculation.

'They've promised to keep me updated,' Clayton said. 'But I have my suspicions now, about who killed Hilary.'

'You do?'

Clayton nodded. 'I reckon Roy's doing what he always does: looking out for family. It's fairly obvious to me that his grandson is the person the police should be talking to.'

'Do you really think Simon is capable of killing someone?'

'Given the right circumstances, yes . . . I think he is.'

'You didn't mention Simon the other day, when we were discussing possible suspects,' Violet said.

Clayton shrugged. 'It didn't occur to me at the time . . . my head was all over the place and I wasn't thinking straight . . . but now that I've had time to reflect, I'd say Simon's the obvious candidate. He viewed Hilary as "the enemy". She'd manoeuvred him into a job he didn't want in order to secure a piece of land Simon didn't want his grandad to sell. Theirs was always going to be a hostile relationship.'

'I'm aware that Simon gets a bad rap,' Violet said. 'People have gone out of their way to point out his faults – but the one thing no one *has* accused him of is being aggressive. Lazy, yes. Belligerent, tick. Brash and cheeky, double tick – I've experienced that first hand. He came to my house last night . . . He was angry and upset, and he fought his corner, but only verbally. At no stage did he show any signs of violence or aggression.'

'You'd be amazed what people are capable of when they're under pressure,' Clayton said, giving a sombre shake of his head. 'I do hope you're right though, and that Simon can prove his innocence . . . because the thought of a neighbour being responsible for my wife's death is beyond comprehension. I'll have to learn to live with it, if it's true, but for now, I must be careful to remember that Simon is innocent until proven guilty.'

As he finished speaking, the sitting-room door flew open and Anne Burridge strutted in, carrying a cake box and a shopping bag. She also had a folder, tucked under her arm. It was clear from her expression that she'd been expecting to find Clayton alone.

'I'm sorry if I'm interrupting,' she said, addressing her apology to Clayton, and all the while questioning Violet's presence with her eyes. 'I didn't realise you had company.'

'There's no need to apologise, Anne. Violet and I have been working on an idea for some videos, but we've finished our meeting, so you're not interrupting.'

'I thought you were supposed to be taking some time off,' Anne said. 'You told me you weren't going back to work until after the funeral.'

'This is just a little side project to take my mind off things,' Clayton said. 'Violet and I are still at the planning stage. We won't be starting properly until the funeral's over.'

'You do know there are things *I* need to talk to you about?' Anne said, sounding extremely miffed. 'Garden centre and tearoom business, I mean. For instance, the issue I mentioned to you the other day has been sorted, but I need to know what to do next. How do we get the customers back?'

'Sorry, but right now I'm not in the best frame of mind to help you with that,' Clayton said. 'You'll just have to muddle through without me.'

'I'm more than happy to keep things running on a day-to-day basis, Clay, but I do need *some* support,' Anne said.

Judging from Clayton's bored expression, Anne's appeal for help had fallen on unsympathetic ears.

'Perhaps that's something you could help us with, Violet,' he said, a hopeful look in his eyes.

'If you're talking about local marketing, I'd say word-of-mouth advertising is the best way to go. The fastest way to spread the latest news is to tell a few key people in the village and let the jungle telegraph do the rest.'

Anne gave a tight smile. 'Thank you, Violet. In that case, perhaps I should begin by telling you . . .'

Touché, thought Violet, wincing inwardly. The implication was clear. Anne considered her to be one of Merrywell's interfering busybodies.

Is she right? Violet wondered. *Have I become one of the local blabbermouths, incapable of keeping my 'trap' shut?* She sincerely hoped not, but if that was people's perception, she needed to work harder at developing more discretion.

'The truth is, Violet, we had a little problem earlier in the week,' Anne explained. 'One of our customers reported seeing a mouse in the tearoom, but I'm pleased to report that the situation has now been resolved, thanks to the efforts of a kindly volunteer. We've had the place checked over by a professional, and we are now – thankfully – mouse-free.'

'I'm pleased to hear it,' Violet said, assuming the 'kindly volunteer' Anne had mentioned was Lisa Wenham. 'Well done to you and whoever helped you out.'

'Thank you.' Again, that tight smile. 'I'd appreciate you spreading the word that everything has been sorted and *The Cuckoo's Boot* tearoom is back to business as usual.'

'I'll do what I can,' Violet said, as she swung her bag onto her shoulder. 'Now, if you'll both excuse me, I should be getting back to work.'

'Thanks again, Violet,' Clayton said. 'I'll see you in a few weeks for the first filming session. If you have any questions in the meantime, feel free to get in touch. You've got my number.'

Anne stood aside, clearing the way for Violet to make her exit. As she closed the door behind her, Violet heard the low, soft murmur of Anne's voice, followed by Clayton's reply. The only words she could make out were Clayton's.

'I really don't feel up to it, Anne,' he said. 'I'm sorry, but you're going to have to manage without me for a little while longer.'

Chapter 33

Violet emerged from Highfield House into bright sunlight. The lawn directly in front of the property looked neat, weed-free and freshly cut. Along the side of the house, close to where Violet had parked her car, was a colourful border filled with a variety of cottage garden flowers. At the back of the border, close to the wall, hollyhocks were coming into flower alongside bright blue delphiniums. At the front edge were clumps of late tulips, forget-me-nots, and sweet-scented wallflowers. Violet wondered whether Clayton could take credit for the upkeep of the garden, or whether it was a member of the garden centre team who tended to things.

As she pulled her car key from her pocket, she noticed a flash of movement in the thick bank of trees that lay further up Bluebell Hill, behind the house.

'Hello?' she shouted, wondering if she had perhaps discovered Simon's hiding place. 'Is someone there?'

The only response was the sound of footsteps retreating deeper into the wood.

'Who's out there?' Violet said. 'Is that you, Simon?'

Whoever it was clearly had no intention of showing themselves. Violet walked to the top of the garden and came to a standstill in front of a dry-stone wall, which ran alongside the woods and presumably marked the border between Highfield House and the Geldards' property.

She paused for a moment, listening. From somewhere in the distance came the drumming of a woodpecker, followed by the repetitive, eerie cawing of a rook from the top of a nearby tree.

Violet placed a hand on the lichen-covered wall, struck by its impressive construction. It looked robust, but would it come tumbling down if she tried to climb it?

The wall continued uphill on the left, skirting the edge of the wood. On the right, it dipped down, towards a section that appeared to be in need of repair. *Whose wall is this?* Violet wondered. *If it's owned and maintained by the Geldards, have they left it like this on purpose? Do they use this gap to cut across the Spenbecks' property, as a shortcut to the lane?*

She made her way into the dip and tested the fallen stones with her foot. Then, very carefully, she clambered over onto the other side. The rooks were cawing again, calling out what sounded like a warning, perhaps unsettled by the sight of a stranger invading their territory.

'Hello?' Violet shouted again. 'Are you in here, Simon?'

She stepped into the wood, which was carpeted with a dazzling expanse of delicately scented bluebells. Weaving between them, she followed a trail of disturbed bracken and snapped twigs. It felt cooler here, where the trees were blocking out the sun's warming light. From up ahead came the unmistakeable crack of someone treading on a dry, brittle branch. Violet stopped and scanned the gaps between the trees.

There was another flash of movement on the left, as a figure scurried away – someone wearing dark grey jogging bottoms and sporting a shock of blond hair.

'Simon, is that you?' Violet said, being careful to keep her tone friendly, even though she was shouting.

When no reply was forthcoming, she began to doubt herself. What was she doing here? What if it wasn't Simon who was lurking in the woods? And even if it was, wouldn't it be better to leave him to it and call DS Winterton?

With a jolt, Violet realised she was still holding the car key in her right hand, her fingers gripping it tightly. As a potential form of protection, it was less than useless. Better to drop her keys back into her bag and get in touch with Charlie, or Matthew.

Her fingers fumbled fruitlessly through her bag, searching every corner for her phone – but it wasn't there. And that's when she remembered. She'd passed it to Clayton so that he could watch one of the videos she'd found. He must have put it down amongst his paperwork when Anne Burridge arrived, and in her hurry to leave, Violet had left it behind.

'Stupid, stupid, stupid,' she said aloud. 'What is it with me and phones?'

Wandering through a wood without any means of communication was not a smart move. It was time she started taking more care of her possessions and her own safety.

She wondered what Matthew would say if she were able to call him. The answer came to her instantly. He'd tell her to get out of there. And he'd be absolutely right.

Struck by a sudden sense of urgency, she decided to do the sensible thing and beat a hasty retreat through the carpet of bluebells.

She turned around, back the way she'd come . . . and came face to face with Simon Geldard.

Chapter 34

'Simon!' Violet took two steps back, her heart racing. 'The police are looking for you.'

'I know. Why do you think I'm hiding in here?' he said.

He looked tired, and his hair was ruffled.

'Have you been out here all night?'

'Yeah. I needed some time on my own. To think.'

'They're bound to catch up with you eventually,' Violet said, her voice shaking. 'Why don't you make things easier for yourself and go and talk to them?'

'I'm not ready to do that,' Simon said. 'First, I need to work out what I'm going to say.'

Violet took another step back, giving herself more space in case she needed to make a run for it.

'You do know they've let your grandad go?'

He nodded. 'Yeah, I've been keeping an eye on the house. I saw them bring him back first thing this morning.'

'Have you talked to him? Does he know you're in here?'

'He'll have guessed where I am, but I haven't spoken to him. He can't call me because I've switched my phone off – I don't want the police using it to track me.'

'Is your grandad likely to come in here looking for you?'

'I doubt it,' Simon said, speaking through a massive yawn. 'He's not been too good on his pins lately. I don't think he'd be up for a trek through the woods these days.'

'From the look of you, I'm guessing you haven't slept,' Violet said.

Simon shrugged. 'I managed to get a couple of hours,' he said. 'There's a den, up there, through the trees. Grandad made it for me when I was little. I come here quite often, so he'll have worked out where I am and he'll know I'm safe.'

'Will he tell the police where to look for you?'

'Nah, Grandad wouldn't do that – and you'd better not grass on me either.'

Violet nodded her agreement. She was alone in a wood with a murder suspect. What else was she going to do, other than comply?

'I won't say anything,' she said, thinking on her feet. 'But you're going to have to talk to the police sooner or later. If you haven't worked out what you're going to say to them yet, maybe you could talk to me, to practise your story. I'm a good listener.'

'Story?' Simon said. 'You make it sound like I'm gonna be making stuff up. I'm not a liar, despite what everyone thinks.'

'Not everyone thinks that, Simon. I certainly don't. However, I don't think you've told me the whole truth. You're holding something back.'

Simon squinted, studying Violet's face as if assessing whether to trust her. As he leaned forward and pulled up his hood, Violet recalled DS Winterton's description of the person captured on the garden centre CCTV. Dark clothing and hooded jackets were the preferred attire of most young people, but Charlie had also mentioned a 'hunched posture'. The way Simon was standing right now – head down, shoulders stooped – matched that description exactly.

'Tell me if I'm wrong, but I think you were there, at the garden centre that morning,' Violet said, taking a chance. 'I also think you got into an argument with Hilary Spenbeck – but I'll never know what really happened unless you're willing to tell me about it.'

She smiled nervously, waiting for him to respond. Simon continued to glare.

'Of course, you don't have to confide in me,' she said, feeling intimidated by the intensity of his gaze. 'It's up to you. We can go and sit in your den and talk through what happened, or I can walk out of here, and go back to work. The choice is yours.'

'There's no way you'd keep your mouth shut if I let you walk away. As soon as you were out of earshot, you'd be on the phone to that detective mate of yours.'

'Actually, I don't have my phone with me,' she said. 'I had a meeting earlier with Clayton Spenbeck, and I left it at his house.'

Too late, Violet realised her error. She'd revealed too much. Coming into the woods had been a mistake – one that she'd now compounded by admitting she didn't have her phone. Foolishly, she'd exposed her vulnerability to someone she was still unsure about. Simon was what? Seventeen, eighteen years old? On the face of it, he was a skinny youth, brimming with unhappiness – but it was also possible that he had a propensity for violence. Could she trust him? Or should she run like the wind, back to her car and hope he didn't catch up with her?

Simon laughed. 'There's no need to look frit.'

'Frit?' Violet said.

'Sorry.' He smiled. 'I keep forgetting you're not from round 'ere. I mean you look frightened. Scared. Are you afraid of me?'

Was she? Did she really have anything to fear from him? The boy who'd been polite enough to remove his shoes before walking into her living room?

'No,' Violet said, making up her mind. 'I'm not afraid . . . frit.'

Simon gave a snort of amusement and shook his head. Was he laughing because she'd used a colloquialism, or because she'd completely underestimated the danger she was in?

'You *look* scared,' Simon said.

'Well, I'm not,' Violet said, trusting her instincts. 'Would I have suggested talking in your den if I thought you were going to hurt me?'

'All right, then. It's through there,' Simon said, pointing deeper into the woods. 'It's a sort of treehouse. Are you OK with climbing?'

'I'll give it a go,' Violet said, steadying her breathing to maintain a pretence of calm. 'As long as I don't have to go right to the top of the tree.'

Simon brushed past her and set off. Before following in his footsteps, Violet made one final assessment of the risk she was taking. Was Simon harmless, or was she putting herself in terrible danger by accompanying him into the woods?

He was striding away, forcing her to make a decision. She stepped forward, moving quickly to keep pace with him. Her pulse was racing, and her mouth felt dry. Somewhere above her head, a bird screeched loudly.

Was it her imagination, or were the trees thicker in this part of the wood? The undergrowth more tangled? Even the scent of the bluebells seemed cloyingly intense.

'It must be nice, having your own private wood,' she said, to ease the tension.

'It is,' Simon said, as he waited for her to catch up. 'I use the den as a hide, to watch birds. There are spotted woodpeckers, treecreepers, jays. There's even a pair of tawny owls. I come down here at night sometimes to watch them.'

Beneath his bluster, Simon had all the makings of an affable young man. Even so, Violet remained wary. She had no idea what he was about to tell her, but she had an inkling he was mixed up in the kind of trouble it wouldn't be easy to wriggle out of.

They waded through bracken, side-stepped bluebells and clambered over thorny stems of brambles until they reached a tiny clearing, with an ancient tree at its centre. Built some eight feet or so off the ground was a small treehouse. The platform it was built on looked strong and solid, but the treehouse itself was rundown and rickety.

When Simon had asked how she was with climbing, Violet had envisioned having to shinny up a rope or hoist herself into the tree using sheer muscle power – so it was a relief to discover that access to the treehouse was via a narrow wooden ladder. She let Simon go up first, and then, rather shakily, she followed – glad that she'd chosen to wear trainers that day. The top rung opened directly into the interior of the treehouse. Simon had already made himself at home, sitting, cross-legged on an old woollen rug.

'I've left the seat for you,' he said, in another display of unexpected good manners. 'I'd say "make yourself comfortable", but it's not the best seat ever.'

He gestured towards an old camping chair in the corner. Violet sat on it, grateful that it felt sturdy, which was more than could be said for the walls of the treehouse.

'Nice place you've got here.' She smiled, trying to lighten the mood and build a rapport. 'Minimalist and very . . . rustic.'

To her great relief, Simon laughed. She needed to connect with him if he was going to trust her with the truth.

'Come on then. Tell me what happened,' she said. 'Start wherever you want. Take your time.'

Simon bent his head and began to pull at a thread in the rug. For a moment, Violet wondered if he was going to clam up again – but then he cleared his throat and began to speak.

'I haven't lied to you,' he said. 'But you're right about me not telling you everything.'

'Go on.'

'It's true that Grandad was covering for me. He'd worked out I was there . . . at the garden centre on the morning Hilary died. I think he must have heard me letting myself into the house when I got back.'

Violet's heart was thumping. Wherever this was going, she had a bad feeling about it.

209

'When I finally admitted it, he made me tell him what happened. He asked loads and loads of questions. I realise now, he was getting the story straight in his head so he could go to the police and confess.'

'So, what did happen?' Violet said. 'Are you going to tell me?'

Simon gave a single, brief nod.

'While I was working in the tearoom on Sunday afternoon, I heard Clayton say he was going to leave the gate open for you. It was stupid of him, saying that in front of so many people, but that's Clayton for you. I could be polite and say he's naïve, but I've promised to tell the truth . . . and the truth is, Clayton Spenbeck is a dork. But what you also need to know is that, although he comes across as this nice, affable bloke, there's another side to him. A nasty side.'

'Has he been nasty to you?' Violet said.

Simon shrugged. 'He's made it pretty obvious he doesn't want me working for him. I've tried not to let it get to me, but he keeps picking on me and finding fault with everything I do.'

'Are you saying he bullies you?' Violet said, remembering the way Clayton had told Simon off about his shirt, reprimanding him in front of everyone in the tearoom.

'It's more like a sort of constant, petty nagging. It's like he goes out of his way to make life difficult for me.'

As if it hasn't been difficult enough, Violet thought, disappointed that Clayton couldn't be more sympathetic to Simon's circumstances.

'What about Hilary?' she said. 'How did she treat you?'

'Like something she'd trodden in,' Simon replied. 'I'm not daft – I know she only offered me the job to get Grandad onside. She was desperate to get her hands on the field and the barn – she must have been if she was willing to employ me.'

'Clayton said you're not happy about your grandad selling the land. Is that true?'

'Yeah. The price Hilary offered was nowhere near enough. She was ripping him off.'

'Are you sure that's your only reason for objecting? What about the small matter of using the barn to grow cannabis? You won't be able to do that if the barn's sold, will you?'

Simon frowned. 'I'm finished with all that now,' he said. 'And, anyway, the cannabis plants were a recent thing. I only put them in there after Grandad got rid of the horses.'

'I'm surprised you put them there at all,' Violet said. 'The fact that your grandad had emptied the barn must have alerted you to the fact that he was planning to sell it?'

'I don't think he was – not then. He'd found out he'd got Parkinson's, so giving the horses away was a sensible move – but even at that stage, he still wasn't keen on selling to Hilary. I wouldn't have put the plants in the barn if I'd thought there was any chance of him changing his mind.'

'But he did?'

'Yeah, and if I'm honest, it really peed me off. I've got a bit of money that my mum left me, and I'd used some of it to buy the cannabis plants and the grow light. I set up the plants, padlocked the barn, and I was waiting for the first crop – and then Grandad announced he was letting Hilary have the place after all. So annoying.'

'Did you try and get him to change his mind?'

'Yeah, course I did. I started out by trying to make him feel bad . . . I reminded him how much Mum had loved the barn. When that guilt-trip didn't work, I told him the barn was *my* space, and that I should be the one who got to decide whether to sell it.'

'I take it that didn't wash either?'

'Nah. He reckoned he wanted the money from the sale so he could give it to me. He's hoping I'll use it to set mesen up in business, or go to college and get some qualifications. It's kind of him, and I know he wants the best for me, but he doesn't understand how hard it would be for someone like me to do either of those things.'

'Nothing's easy unless you're willing to put in the effort,' Violet said. 'Studying . . . your own business . . . both of those options are open to you if you're ready to put in the work. Maybe selling the land was your grandad's way of forcing you to take positive action. Whatever his reasons, I'm sure he's got your best interests at heart.'

Simon rubbed the back of his head. 'I know,' he said. 'I just wish he wouldn't expect so much of me. I'll only let him down.'

'The only way you'll do that is if you're not willing to give it a try,' Violet said. 'You need to have more faith in yourself, Simon. Maybe it's not a case of your grandad's expectations being too high, but rather your own expectations being too low.'

He pulled a face. 'You can leave off with the lecture. The truth is, I don't *have* any expectations. I don't know what I want.'

'Perhaps it's time you found out then, and started making some plans.'

'Enough with the career advice,' he said, scowling crankily. 'I thought we were here to talk about what happened with Hilary.'

'Sorry,' Violet said. 'Carry on. Don't let me stop you.'

'On the morning it happened, there was a really strong wind . . . it had been howling round the house all night . . . so I got up early to come here and check on the treehouse. The way the gale was blowing, I thought I might find the whole structure scattered across the woods. Luckily – as you can see – it survived. Once I knew everything was OK here, I went across the field to check on the barn. It's a solid enough building, so I thought it'd be OK, but I wanted to be sure. Anyway, as I was walking alongside the wall between our land and the Spenbecks', I spotted Clayton and Hilary coming out of their house. Must have been about quarter past . . . maybe twenty past seven by then. I didn't want them to see me, so I squatted behind the wall and watched them walk down their driveway and up to the back gate. Once they'd gone inside, I went down to the barn. A few roof tiles had blown off and a drainpipe had been dislodged, but other than that, everything was fine.

'I was going to go home after that, to make myself a bacon cob, but as I came past the wood, I got to thinking. I knew Grandad was getting ready to sign off on the land sale, and the chances of stopping it were slim, but I wanted to have one last crack at Hilary . . . to try and talk her out of it. I climbed over the wall into the Spenbecks' garden – same way as you came over today, but in the opposite direction. When I got to the garden centre, I was banking on the gate being open, like Clayton had said it would be.'

'And it was,' said Violet.

'Yep. I let myself in and went looking for Hilary. When I found her, she was using a broom to sweep up some broken pieces of pottery. As I got closer, I could hear her cursing under her breath about the damage the storm had done. She nearly jumped out of her skin when she looked up and saw me standing next to her.'

'What did she say?'

'She wanted to know what I was doing there,' Simon said. 'I told her I'd come to ask whether she'd consider pulling out of the deal to buy the land. I tried to explain that the barn meant something to me, and that I didn't want my grandad to sell it – but she just laughed in my face. She told me she knew exactly why I wanted to hang on to the barn.'

'What did she mean by that? Do you think she knew about the cannabis plants?'

'Yeah, I reckon she must have found out somehow. She'd probably been over there, snooping around. Either that, or she'd made a lucky guess.'

'Or maybe someone else told her about the cannabis,' Violet said. 'If she was buying the barn, I'm guessing she must have had a survey done. Could the surveyor have seen your plants?'

'No, Hilary sorted the survey out yonks ago, long before I put the plants in there. A few months back, Grandad found out she'd snuck some architect friend of hers into the field so he could look at the barn. She didn't ask Grandad's permission, of course . . . typical Hilary . . . but I s'pose she wanted to make sure the building was sound before she put in an offer.'

'And she refused to consider your request to withdraw that offer?'

Simon nodded. 'She said there wasn't a cat in hell's chance. She told me to clear off . . . said if I didn't, she'd tell my grandad and the police what I'd got in the barn. I told her she had a bad attitude. I was angry, really angry, so I laid into her – but only verbally. Nothing physical.'

'What did you say to her?'

'I said she was horrible and selfish and domineering . . . that she was a jumped-up nobody and that everybody in the village thought she was making a fool out of Clayton. She flipped at that last remark. She flew at me . . . started thrashing me with the broom handle. She was really going for it, saying Clayton didn't need her help to make a fool of himself.'

'So she was the one who hit you? Did you fight back?'

Simon shrugged. 'Not at first,' he said. 'I put my arms up to protect my face and told her to calm down, but she'd lost it. *Really* lost it.'

Violet remembered the bruises she'd seen on Simon's arms, and felt guilty for assuming Roy had been the one who'd inflicted them.

'She had me backed up against a display stand,' Simon said. 'She could see I didn't want to hit her back, so she was really letting rip, venting her frustrations. The last thing I wanted to do was hurt her, but I couldn't just stand there and take it. There was a bunch of garden ornaments on the stand behind me, so I felt around and grabbed the first thing I could lay my hand on. It felt heavy, and I knew it could do some real damage if I swung it too hard, so I told myself to be careful.'

'Were you wearing gloves?' said Violet.

Simon shook his head.

'My prints will be on it, I know they will,' he said. 'But I promise you, I didn't hit her hard. It was only a sideways blow to fend her off, but there must have been something sharp sticking out of it, because it cut her. It wasn't a serious cut, nothing like that. It was a tiny nick, but it startled her. She stumbled and lost her footing, and landed flat on her back. That's when I made my escape. I got out of there, while I still could.'

'The post-mortem showed that she hit her head as she fell,' Violet said.

'Oh, God.' Simon groaned. 'I assumed she was OK. I left her lying there, but I thought she was just winded.'

'The more likely scenario is that she knocked herself out,' Violet said.

Simon buried his face in his hands. 'So it was my fault she died. You've got to believe me, I wouldn't have left her like that if I'd known.'

'Actually, the fact that she fell over might not have been your fault, Simon. The post-mortem mentioned that Hilary had the beginnings of an ear infection that could have been affecting her balance. Maybe that's why she stumbled – it might also have been the reason she fell in the tearoom the previous day.'

'Are you just saying that to try and make me feel better?'

'No, honestly, I'm not,' Violet said. 'I really don't think it was your fault. Think carefully, Simon, because this is important. Was Hilary alive when you left her?'

'I thought she was,' he replied, looking suddenly tearful. 'But now, after what you've just told me, I'm not sure. The truth is, I didn't stick around to check. I should have done – I know that now – but all I could think about at the time was getting away from there. From *her*.'

'If you've told me the truth—'

'I have,' Simon said.

'Well then, it sounds to me like you acted in self-defence – although you shouldn't have fled the scene. You should have stayed to make sure Hilary was OK and called for help if she needed it.'

'I know. I'm sorry, OK? I panicked.'

'What I don't quite understand, is why you took such great care to avoid the CCTV cameras? Why bother, if you thought Hilary was still alive?'

'I wasn't aware I had dodged the cameras,' Simon said, looking genuinely baffled. 'I didn't even think about the CCTV.'

'Even so, the police might view it as a calculated move on your part to avoid detection. They may even accuse you of running away because you knew Hilary was seriously injured.'

'Well then, they'd be wrong.' Simon uncrossed his legs. 'When I left, I had no idea Hilary was badly hurt. You asked me to tell the truth, and I have done – but even now, you don't believe me, do you?'

'*I* believe you, but what you need to understand is that the police or a jury might view things differently.'

'Look, I haven't got a Scooby where the CCTV cameras are at the garden centre.' Simon pulled up his knees and rested his chin on them. 'I wait tables in the tearoom . . . Why would I need to know about security? If I avoided the cameras, it was pure luck. To be honest, I was more concerned about Clayton seeing me as I ran out.'

'Clayton?'

'Yeah,' Simon said. 'When I pelted round the side of the retail building, I knocked over some pots. It made a right racket.'

Violet remembered the overturned plants she had restored to an upright position as she'd entered the garden centre that morning.

'The plants that you knocked over,' Violet said. 'Was that a palm . . . and some yuccas?'

'I dunno what sort they were, and I certainly wasn't going to stick around to pick 'em up. The wind had already knocked loads of pots over, so I didn't think anyone would notice a few more.'

Violet was about to ask what time Simon had left the garden centre – but she stopped herself, realising she already knew the answer to that question. The CCTV camera had recorded him crossing the front of the retail building at 07.44.

As she paused to reflect on Simon's version of events, Violet felt her pulse quicken. All of a sudden, it was as if various switches were clicking into place in her mind.

Simon had said that Hilary *landed flat on her back.*

Not face down.

'Can we go back to something you said a minute ago,' she said, feeling slightly breathless. 'You mentioned that when you left her, Hilary was lying on her back in the water feature.'

'She was on her back, yeah,' he said. 'But not in the water feature. She was sprawled out on the floor, on the concrete. She was lying *next* to the water features, but not in amongst them.'

Violet took a shuddering breath, recalling the scene that morning – Clayton Spenbeck's red-rimmed eyes as he'd looked up at her. *I was on my way to meet you and I found her here*, he'd said. *She was lying face down in the fountain.*

What if Hilary *wasn't* lying in the fountain when Clayton found her?

What if it was Clayton who'd been lying . . . *through his teeth*?

Chapter 35

Violet stared at Simon's desperate, angst-ridden face. It was clear from his expression that he still thought himself responsible for Hilary's death. Assaulting her had probably been the last thing on his mind when he'd set out to see her that day – but he obviously believed she had died as a result of his actions.

Violet was a lot less sure.

'Simon, I need you to clarify something else you just said.'

She leaned forward on the camping chair and stared deep into his eyes. She needed him to look at her as he replied. It was the only way she would know for certain whether he was telling the truth.

'When you knocked over the pots, you said you were afraid Clayton might have heard you? What made you think that?'

'Because I saw him, coming up from the bottom end of the garden centre. He was a way away, but he was walking pretty fast and I was worried he was gonna spot me – so I shot round the corner of the retail building, out of sight. That's when I collided with the pots.'

There was something blatantly honest about Simon's demeanour – his tone of voice, his body language, his whole aura. He was definitely telling the truth – which could only mean one thing: Clayton Spenbeck had been lying.

The first words he'd said to her on the phone that fateful morning had been a lie, and Violet suspected he'd been lying to her ever since.

She recalled his breathlessness when he'd said: *I'm down at the lower end of the garden centre at the moment.* At the time, she'd assumed the raggedness of his breathing had been brought on by his exertions sorting out the fruit trees. But what if he was breathing heavily because he'd just killed his wife?

Violet had arrived at the garden centre a few minutes before eight o'clock. When she rang Clayton, he'd claimed he was returning from the 'lower end', heading up towards the middle of the garden centre. But Simon had seen him doing exactly that at 07.44.

'You're absolutely sure it was him?' Violet said. 'This is crucially important, Simon. The person you saw, was it definitely Clayton?'

'Yeah. Let's be honest, he's quite a distinctive-looking guy, isn't he? You can spot that white streak in his hair a mile off. I only got a brief glimpse, but it was definitely him. Even if I hadn't seen his hair, I'd have known him from his walk. I'm good at recognising people from the way they move.'

'OK,' Violet said, as she began to formulate a plan. 'In that case, I need you to listen carefully and do exactly as I say. You have to trust me on this. The fact is, I'm fairly certain you didn't kill Hilary Spenbeck. The injuries to her head were superficial. The glancing blow you gave her wasn't what caused her death.'

Relief smoothed away the anguish on Simon's face, but she could tell he was still on edge.

'I appreciate you having faith in me,' he said, 'but I'm not sure the police will agree with you.'

'You have to go and talk to them,' Violet said. 'That has to be your priority now. Tell them everything you've told me. Once you've presented them with the facts, they'll have no choice but to believe you.'

'Are you kidding? What makes you think they'll listen to me? They didn't believe anything Grandad told them, did they?'

'That's because your grandad made a false confession. He pumped you for information so that he could make himself sound credible.' Violet said. 'Thankfully, he didn't pump hard enough and his plan backfired. When the police asked about specific details, your grandad was unable to provide them, and his story fell to pieces. Roy must have repeated what you'd told him about leaving Hilary lying on her back – whereas the police knew she'd drowned in a water fountain.'

'Drowned?' Simon said. 'Are you serious?'

'Yes. What I don't know yet is whether she came round, got up and accidentally fell over again, into the water fountain, or whether someone found her unconscious, dragged her over to the water feature and placed her face down in the water.'

Simon's jaw had dropped open. 'When you say "someone", do you mean Clayton?'

'That's what I intend to find out,' Violet said. 'I'm going to go back to Highfield House.'

Simon winced, sucking air through his teeth. 'Are you sure that's a good idea?'

'Possibly not, but I'm working on the assumption that Anne Burridge will still be there. She was with Clayton when I left.'

'Want me to come with you?'

'No, thanks for offering, but you need to go home, talk to your grandad and ask him to take you straight down to the police station. Tell the truth and shame the devil, Simon.'

'I'll be dropping myself right in it if I do. Up to my neck.'

'You need to make it clear that Hilary was the one who attacked *you*,' Violet reminded him. 'Show them the bruises on your arms. OK, so you did end up hitting her, but only the once and only in self-defence. Now, you need to defend yourself again. Go and speak up, and let the police know you're not a bad person.'

He nodded. 'All right. I'll do it. And I suppose the sooner I get it over with, the better.'

Violet gave him a thumbs-up. 'Let's get going, shall we?'

They descended the ladder and retraced their steps through the wood. Walking in single file, they weaved through the bluebells and bracken, until they were back at the dry-stone wall.

'My house is up this way,' Simon said, pointing beyond the trees towards the top of Bluebell Hill.

'Good luck,' Violet said, wishing she could give him a hug. 'I'm going to climb over the wall and go back to Highfield House.'

'It's really not a good idea, you know,' Simon said. 'If you're determined to do it, I ought to come with you. If Clayton did kill his wife, you shouldn't be on your own with him.'

'If Anne's there, I won't be on my own,' Violet said. 'Besides, I have to go back anyway, to get my phone. As soon as I've retrieved it, I'll call someone to let them know where I am.'

'OK. If you're sure, but be careful.'

Violet watched him walk away, following the path along the wall. After a few yards, he stopped and looked over his shoulder, flashing her a quick smile.

'By the way,' he said. 'Thanks. For believing in me.'

'You're welcome,' she replied. 'All you need to do now, is start to believe in yourself.'

Chapter 36

When Violet returned to Highfield House, it was Anne Burridge who opened the door.

'Hello, Violet,' she said, sounding less than pleased to see her again. 'Back already?'

Violet gave a warm smile, hoping to melt away some of the frostiness. 'Actually, I never left. I've been for a walk in the woods, and on my way back to the car, I realised I'd left my phone in Clayton's dining room.'

'The woods?' Anne said. 'Do you mean the spinney on the other side of the wall?'

'Yes, the woodland on Roy Geldard's land.'

'You want to be careful. If Roy catches you trespassing, he's likely to chase you off with a shotgun.'

'I was only in there briefly, and as you can see, I emerged unscathed.' Violet challenged her with a smile. 'Is it possible for me to have a word with Clayton? I won't keep him long.'

Anne stepped to one side. 'You'd better come in,' she said, opening the door properly. 'We're in the kitchen, having lunch.'

'I'm sorry if I'm interrupting.'

'Don't worry, it's only a few sandwiches,' Anne said, with a dismissive flick of her hand. 'I brought them over from the tearoom. If it wasn't for me, I don't think Clayton would be eating anything at the moment.'

Violet wondered if the regular provision of food was all part of Anne's attempt to . . . how had Joyce put it? *Make herself indispensable.*

'Violet! Hello, again,' Clayton said, as she followed Anne into a large kitchen fitted with old-fashioned olive-green units and a breakfast bar. 'Did you forget something?'

'My phone,' she replied. 'I think I must have left it in the dining room.'

'Feel free to go and get it,' Clayton said. 'If for some reason you can't find it, let me know and I'll ring the number. That's often the easiest way to locate a missing phone.'

Violet slipped back into the hallway and through into the dining room. There was no sign of her mobile on the tabletop, so she checked under Clayton's scattered papers, in case it was hidden amongst them. There was no phone, but as she lifted one of the notebooks, a scrap of paper fluttered to the floor. As she bent down to pick it up, she spotted the phone lying face down on the carpet, next to the chair in which Clayton had been sitting. She crouched under the table and pushed her hand through the gap between the chair legs to retrieve it.

When she stood up, she realised she was still clutching the folded piece of paper. As she dropped it back onto the tabletop, it fell open and she noticed the words that were written on it: *You are useless. Don't bother me again unless it's an emergency.*

The writing was unfamiliar, but the loops and flourishes suggested it had been written by a female hand. Hilary's, maybe?

The spiteful tone of the note made her shudder. Without knowing why, she picked it up again and pushed it into her pocket. The air in the dining room felt suddenly stuffy, and instead of feeling quaint, the dark, outdated furniture, flowery patterned carpet and swagged curtains felt oppressive. Violet had an overwhelming urge to get out of there, but before she did, she needed to ring Charlie Winterton.

The call went straight to voicemail, leaving her no option but to leave a message.

'Charlie, it's Violet,' she said, keeping her voice low. 'I've spoken to Simon Geldard and he's on his way to the police station to make a statement. Please listen to what he has to say before making any snap judgements. Once you've heard his story, I think you'll want to talk to Clayton Spenbeck. I'm at Clayton's house now, and Anne Burridge is here too. I suspect all is not what it seems with those two.'

She ended the call and, with a growing sense of trepidation, returned to the kitchen.

'I found it,' she said, brandishing her iPhone above her head. As she slipped it into her pocket, her hand brushed against the note she'd picked up from under the table. Why hadn't she left it in the dining room? Should she hand it over to Clayton and see how he reacted, or keep it in her pocket and throw it away when she got home?

Violet took a deep breath and made up her mind.

'The phone was on the floor,' she said, 'along with this.'

She slid the piece of paper across the breakfast bar, to where Clayton was sitting. 'I'm not sure if it's important, but I thought I'd give it to you anyway.'

'It'll have fallen out of my notes,' he said. 'There's all sorts of accumulated rubbish in those folders.'

He flipped open the piece of paper, glanced at it briefly, and then looked up at Violet. 'Did you read it?' he asked.

'Yes . . . I'm sorry. It fell open and I couldn't help but see what it said. I wasn't sure whether to give it to you or not.'

Anne pulled the note from between Clayton's fingers.

'What is this?' she said, looking genuinely puzzled. 'This is Hilary's handwriting.'

'It is,' Clayton said, clearing his throat. 'Some wives leave love notes around the house for their husbands to find, but Hilary preferred to leave those kind of messages. It saved her having to speak to me.'

'That's horrendous,' Anne said, dropping the piece of paper as if it was on fire and about to burn her fingers. 'I know from bitter experience that Hilary could be cruel, but I never imagined she would stoop to this . . . It's awful, Clay. A form of bullying.'

Clayton screwed up the note and stood up.

'It's really no big deal,' he said, as he tossed the crumpled paper in the bin. 'I'm used to Hilary's little foibles.'

'Foibles?' Anne wrinkled her nose. 'That note isn't a foible, Clayton. It's pure nastiness.'

'That's enough, Anne,' he said, holding up his hand. 'I don't wish to discuss the matter. Besides, I won't be coming across any more vicious notes from Hilary, will I? All of that's in the past now.'

'Well, thank heavens for small mercies,' Anne said. 'For goodness' sake, Clay, you were her husband – and a very kind one at that. Why would she behave like that?'

Clayton picked up his empty plate and took it over to the kitchen sink. 'I've already told you, I don't want to discuss it.'

'That's your prerogative,' Anne said. 'But it might do you good to talk, rather than keeping your emotions bottled up. I'm always here for you, Clayton. You do know that?'

'Yes. Thank you, and I appreciate your kindness, but let's talk about something else, shall we? I'm sure Violet doesn't want to hear about my marital woes.'

Anne looked momentarily startled, as if she'd forgotten Violet was there. 'No. No, of course not,' she said, when she'd collected herself. 'I'll show you out, Violet. I'm sure you have things to do and places to be.'

She lifted a hand to guide Violet towards the door, but Violet folded her arms and stayed where she was.

Chapter 37

Clayton had turned towards the kitchen window and was staring out into the garden.

'Before I go,' Violet said, addressing the back of his head, 'there's something I'd like to know. About you and Hilary.'

He spun around, the half-smile on his face signifying a willingness to talk – but it seemed Anne Burridge had other ideas.

'Really, Violet,' she said, her voice laced with disapproval. 'The last thing poor Clayton needs is you prying into his private life. Have you no sympathy? The man's grieving, for pity's sake.'

'Is he?' Violet said. 'I'm not so sure about that.'

Clayton's eyebrows twitched, and he stared at her with eyes filled with . . . what? Fear? Rage? The realisation that he was about to be exposed?

'You told DS Winterton that you had a happy marriage,' Violet said, jumping in before she lost her nerve. 'Now you're saying that Hilary was in the habit of sending you spiteful notes. That doesn't sound like the behaviour of someone in a healthy, loving relationship.'

Clayton smiled nervously. 'Hilary was never completely happy with anything,' he said. 'In fact, she was perpetually dissatisfied and discontented, especially with the business. She always wanted it to be bigger and better, and over the years, I'm afraid that same attitude permeated into the fabric of our marriage.'

He leaned back against the kitchen sink and folded his arms. 'Not that the state of my marriage is any of your business. Would you care to tell me why you're asking about it?'

'I'm trying to work out how you really feel about Hilary's death,' Violet replied.

'Are you indeed? And to what end? Do I take it you're planning to accuse me of something?'

'Don't engage with her, Clay,' Anne said. 'She's an interfering busybody; everyone knows that. You don't have to answer her questions.'

Despite the vigorous way Anne was defending him, Clayton seemed exasperated by her presence. 'You're contradicting yourself, Anne,' he told her, scowling dismissively. 'A minute ago you were saying how much better I'd feel if I talked – now you're telling me to keep quiet. Do make up your mind.'

'I meant talk to *me*, not to her.'

'I don't need to talk to you about how things were between me and Hilary. You've been monitoring our marriage since the wedding day.'

Anne opened her mouth to formulate a response – but, unable to think of one, she pressed her lips together into a thin, angry line.

Clayton unfolded his arms and gripped the edge of the sink. 'Within a few years of marrying Hilary, it became clear that she and I wanted different things,' he said, turning away from Anne to address Violet directly. 'She didn't think I was ambitious enough. I have to admit, she was probably right about that. The truth is, I irritated her and she irritated me, and we argued on an almost daily basis. She took great pleasure in riling me, and sending those little notes to remind me of my failures. However, both of us understood that no marriage is perfect – and so we continued to muddle through. We even had occasional moments of happiness . . . our good times.'

'So, what changed?' Violet said, asking the question to test her theory. 'At what stage did you reach breaking point?'

'Breaking point?' Clayton laughed. 'My goodness, Violet. What are you talking about?'

'I'm talking about the point at which you realised you couldn't go on,' she replied, jumping in with both feet. 'Did that feeling creep up on you gradually, or did it only hit you on Monday morning when you found Hilary lying unconscious? Is that when you decided to seize the moment and change your life forever?'

'What is she blethering on about, Clayton?' said Anne. 'What does she mean?'

'She's talking nonsense,' Clayton said, through a watery smile. 'Complete baloney. What is it you're hoping to achieve here, Violet? Is this wild story intended to catch me out? Is that it?'

'I'm trying to get to the truth,' she replied. 'You see, I spoke to Simon Geldard a few minutes ago. He's admitted to hitting Hilary, but he says he did it in self-defence.'

'He said what?' Clayton pushed himself away from the sink and stood up straight. 'Why didn't you say something before, woman? Have you told the police about this?'

'No, Simon's going to talk to them himself.'

Clayton threw back his head and scoffed. 'He told you that, did he? And you believed him? Really, Violet, I thought you were smarter than that. The boy's a weasel; you can't trust a word that comes out of his mouth. You should have called DS Winterton immediately.'

'I couldn't do that, because I didn't have my phone,' Violet said. 'Besides, Simon has assured me he's going to speak to the police, and I believe him.'

'I agree with Clayton,' Anne said. 'You're a fool. The boy can't be trusted.'

Clayton was pacing around the kitchen with his hands on his cheeks. 'I had a feeling Simon Geldard might be mixed up in all of this,' he said. 'Roy's confession was obviously a botched attempt to take the blame for his grandson's crime.'

'Shall I ring the police, Clay?' Anne said, rifling through her handbag for her phone.

'Please do,' he replied. 'The sooner Simon Geldard is apprehended, the better.'

'By all means go ahead and call them if you want to,' Violet said. 'But I'm not sure it's necessary. I suspect the police are already on their way.'

'On their way?' said Clayton. 'On their way to where?'

'Here,' Violet replied.

'I expect they'll be coming to tell you about Simon's arrest,' Anne said.

'Actually,' Violet said, 'I think it's more likely they're coming here to arrest *you*, Clayton.'

'What are you talking about?' Anne said, her hackles up. 'What is wrong with you, Violet? How dare you? Why would they want to arrest Clayton? What are you accusing him of?'

Violet hesitated only briefly.

'Murder,' she said, crossing her fingers and hoping she hadn't jumped to the wrong conclusion.

Chapter 38

'It's time for you to leave,' Anne said. 'Please go. *Now*. Before I lose my temper.'

'Hang on a minute,' Clayton said, holding up a finger. 'Let's not be hasty. I'd like to hear what Violet has to say for herself. As accusations go, this is up there with the wildest of them, but I can't help being intrigued.'

Anne stamped her foot. 'Why are you encouraging her, Clay? Don't just stand there and let her slander you – throw her out.'

'All in good time, Anne. First, I want to know why she thinks I killed Hilary. Come on, Violet. Tell me. How can you justify making such a preposterous claim?'

Violet knew she would never recover from this if she was wrong, no matter how many apologies she made – but she'd already said too much to back down now.

'During my conversation with Simon, I got to thinking about timing,' she said, reluctant to reveal the only piece of truly incriminating evidence against Clayton.

'Timing?' Clayton laughed. 'That's it, is it? That's all you've got?'

'Simon turned up at the garden centre and argued with Hilary,' Violet said. 'She lashed out at him, and in order to defend himself, he struck her across the forehead. She fell backwards and passed out, presumably having bumped the back of her skull as she hit the ground. Simon fled the scene immediately, but he believes Hilary was alive when he left.'

'He would say that, wouldn't he? And I suppose if Simon said put your hands in the air, you'd do it?' Clayton laughed again, but it sounded forced this time. 'You really are surprisingly gullible, Violet.'

'If I've been taken in by anyone, I'd say it was you,' she replied. 'I believed your account of discovering Hilary's body, and I was convinced by your show of grief – but it's hard to argue with facts.'

'Facts?' said Anne. 'What facts? This sounds more like a fairy story to me.'

Violet shrugged. 'You're the one hoping for a happy-ever-after, Anne, not me. You're right, though. It's not my place to accuse or question Clayton. That's DS Winterton's job. He'll be here soon enough, so perhaps I'd better do as you've asked, and leave.'

'Oh no you don't,' Clayton said, taking a step towards her. 'You can't just come in here, drop a bombshell, and then clear off. I thought you and I were friends, Violet? Don't I deserve an explanation of some kind?'

'I'm sure you'll get what you deserve,' Violet said. 'But that doesn't necessarily include an explanation from me.'

'Oh, I think it does,' Clayton said, going over to the door and standing in front of it. 'I insist. You're not walking out of here until you've substantiated your outrageous claim. Come on, tell me . . . what makes you think I killed Hilary?'

'For what it's worth, I don't believe it was premeditated,' she said, feeling increasingly confident now that Clayton was so obviously on the back foot. 'I suspect it was a split-second decision. You stumbled across an opportunity . . . a moment in time in which you were able to visualise a different future for yourself, a *better* future – one without Hilary, the wife you no longer loved or even liked.'

Clayton huffed. 'My relationship with Hilary was complex. I

231

admit there were days when we barely spoke, but we put up with each other. It's true we were no longer in love – if indeed we ever were – but we had things in common, and we had a business to run – together. Why would I put all that we've worked for in jeopardy?'

'Because your heart was no longer in it. You'd stopped caring about the marriage and the business. I'm guessing you work here at the garden centre because that was what your father expected you to do – but I don't think you've ever shared his passion for horticulture.'

'You're in no position to make such a sweeping statement,' Clayton said. 'You barely know me.'

'No, but I've spoken to plenty of people who do, and I gather you would have preferred to pursue a different career altogether.'

Clayton shrugged. 'We don't always get what we want in life.'

'That's true,' said Violet. 'And I imagine that's the reason you were happy to occupy a back seat in the business and let Hilary take the reins.'

'Why wouldn't I? She was always so much better at running the garden centre than I was.'

Anne placed her arms across her chest. 'None of this explains why you're accusing Clayton of murder,' she said, in the same snarky tone that Hilary might have used. 'If you're going to make that kind of outrageous claim, the least you can do is provide irrefutable evidence.'

Violet was already having second thoughts about saying anything at all. She would have been better off retreating to the safety of the shopping village and leaving everything in the capable hands of Charlie Winterton.

'Anne's absolutely right,' Clayton said. 'So, come on, Violet. What have you got to say for yourself?'

'I know you lied to me,' she said, patently aware that he wouldn't let her leave until she'd justified her claim. 'I rang you as soon as I arrived at the garden centre, and you told me you were down at the far end of the site, near the fruit trees.'

'I was,' Clayton said.

'I dispute that. I think you were already with Hilary by then. When I arrived at the water fountain, you said you'd found her there, but that's not true, is it?'

Clayton clenched his fists, his knuckles showing white beneath the skin. Violet wasn't sure how accurate her version of events was, but she was obviously close enough to the truth to unsettle him.

'I think you found Hilary several minutes before I arrived,' she continued. 'She'd hit her head . . . she was probably unconscious . . . but her injuries weren't life-threatening. You must have assumed she'd had an accident and taken a tumble. Or maybe you knew she'd been assaulted. Did you spot Simon running away as you walked through the garden centre?'

'As I've already told the police, I didn't see anyone that morning, other than you,' Clayton said. 'But you're right – when I discovered Hilary's body, I thought she'd had an accident, or collapsed.'

'But it wasn't Hilary's *body* you discovered, was it? She was still alive when you found her. She was lying on the ground, unconscious, having sustained a minor concussion – and the situation presented you with a huge dilemma. You had a choice to make: call for an ambulance, or manipulate the scenario to your advantage and rid yourself of Hilary once and for all. You opted for the latter.'

'You're talking rubbish,' Clayton said. 'This is pure speculation. A complete fantasy. Where's your proof, Violet? Do you have any? Any at all?'

He was right. The only thing Violet could confront him with were observations. She had no real evidence to back up her claims, but that didn't mean she wasn't right.

'You dragged Hilary's unconscious body over to the nearby water feature,' she said, determined to see this excruciating conversation through to its conclusion. 'One of her shoes came off as you moved her. I noticed it lying there when I arrived, although

I didn't realise its significance at the time.'

'It probably came off when she fell,' Clayton said. 'A discarded shoe doesn't prove anything.'

'What about your jacket?' Violet said. 'When I touched your arm, I noticed the sleeves were wet. That must have happened when you placed Hilary face down in the water.'

'Or when I pulled her *out* of the water.'

'Maybe, but I noticed you took your jacket off before you spoke to the police. Were you afraid they'd spot the wet sleeves and ask about them? You were obviously hoping everything would be cut and dried . . . that Hilary's death would be ruled an accident, and that you would finally be free and clear of her.'

'This is a very entertaining tale, Violet, but it's a work of pure fiction, and you can't possibly expect me to comment,' Clayton said. 'You're well out of order – and the last thing I'm going to do is condone your interrogation by defending myself. I'd like you to leave, please. As for our latest filming project, I think we can forget about that, don't you?'

'Absolutely,' Violet said. 'Because if my suspicions are correct, you'll be in no position to give out gardening advice – unless it's from behind bars.'

Clayton snorted, feigning indifference. 'Can you show Violet out please, Anne?' he said. 'I think we've heard enough from her, don't you?'

When Anne didn't immediately jump to his bidding, Clayton's face flushed an angry red.

'Be honest with me, Clay,' Anne said. 'Is there any truth to this, or is it just a product of Violet's overactive imagination?'

Clayton placed a hand on the back of his head and flounced over to the window. It was a dramatic, over-the-top gesture, more befitting of an amateur actor in a French farce.

'*Et tu*, Brute?' he said, playing the loyalty card. 'I expected better of you, Anne. Why are you turning on me?'

'I'm not,' she said, rushing over to him and gripping his arm.

234

'But please, I need to know the truth. Is Violet right? Did you kill Hilary? Did you do it so that we could be together? Is that it?'

'Don't flatter yourself,' Clayton said, snatching his arm from her grasp. 'It's time you stopped hanging on to my coat tails, woman. For goodness' sake, get a life!'

Anne stepped back as if he'd slapped her.

'And don't look at me like that,' Clayton said, his face burning with rage. 'Have you any idea how tiresome it is to have someone constantly trailing after you, pining for something that never was, and never will be? If I'd wanted to be with you, Anne, I'd have made it happen years ago when I was still single.

'You want the truth? Then listen up. I didn't want you then, and I don't want you now. What I *want*, what I yearn for, is freedom – freedom to do whatever I please, whenever I please, without having to seek permission from anyone else. Hilary was a control freak, and I was tired of letting her have her own way. She never cared about me. It was the garden centre she fell in love with. She saw me as a money-making opportunity – that's the only reason she married me. She'd had a poverty-stricken childhood, and she was determined to improve her lot as an adult.

'My father saw Hilary for what she was – as a matter of fact, I think he rather admired her ruthlessness – but he warned me about her, even before we set a date for the wedding. He told me what I'd be letting myself in for, but at the time, I didn't care.'

'So it *was* you?' Anne said. 'You killed her?'

Violet held her breath and waited, aware that Anne was succeeding where she had failed. At last, the truth was coming out.

Clayton let out a long, slow breath. 'I regretted it almost immediately,' he said. 'It was a moment of madness . . . a crazy decision, made in the blink of an eye. I saw an opportunity to end my unhappiness, and I grabbed it. I swear I knew nothing about Simon Geldard's involvement. When I came across Hilary, she was lying on her back, out cold. She'd been complaining of feeling nauseous, and I assumed she'd fallen over and hit her head.

When I saw her lying there, my first thought was that the situation could have been so much worse. *Imagine if she'd fallen into the fountain*, I thought . . . and that's when the idea came to me.

'Before I knew it, I was pulling her towards the water features. I turned her over and placed her face down in one of the fountains. I must have sat with her for at least ten minutes. The next thing I knew Violet was calling me – and it was as if the sound of my phone snapped me out of a deep trance and brought me to my senses. It was only then that I realised . . . *truly* realised the enormity of what I'd done. I was disgusted with myself. Horrified. The tears I was shedding when you found me, Violet, were tears of remorse.'

'And yet you weren't remorseful enough to confess,' Violet said. 'I remember you were breathless when I spoke to you on the phone, but I assumed it was because you'd been sorting out the trees and exerting yourself physically. I realise now you were in shock – although not shocked enough to prevent you from fabricating a web of lies and assuming the persona of a grieving husband.'

All at once, Clayton seemed to crumple. 'I'm sorry,' he said. 'I shouldn't have done what I did. It was idiotic and selfish – a catastrophic bid for freedom. If I had my time again, I'd do things differently. I definitely wouldn't have acted as I did if I'd known Simon Geldard was there that morning. I've got no time for the lad, but I wouldn't knowingly have implicated him or anyone else in Hilary's death.'

'I'm sorry, but I think that's exactly what you've been trying to do,' Violet said. 'I'm sure you'd have been more than willing to sit back and let Simon take the blame.'

'I didn't think there'd be any need to blame anyone,' he replied. 'I assumed Hilary's death would be ruled an accident, which just goes to show how naïve I am. Hilary always said I was gullible. Perhaps she was right.'

Anne was weeping softly. Her face was pale and she was leaning forward, arms across her chest, as if something inside her had broken.

Clayton placed a hand on her shoulder. 'There's no need to look quite so devastated, Anne,' he said. 'You've spent years hankering after something that was never meant to be. From now on, you need to start living the life you were meant to have. Enjoy it. Make the most of it. You're the one person who stands to benefit from this whole debacle. It doesn't look as though I'm going to get my freedom, but at least you will.'

'Shall I ring DS Winterton?' Violet said. 'Are you ready to hand yourself in to the police?'

Clayton's shoulders sagged. 'Do I have a choice?' he said.

'There's always a choice,' Violet replied. 'This time, I hope you'll make the right one.'

Chapter 39

Three weeks later

The news of Clayton Spenbeck's confession had sent shockwaves through the village and it was several days before life in Merrywell returned to its usual, tranquil pace.

Thankfully, preparations for the upcoming village fete provided a much-needed distraction for the local residents. Vegetables were watered and coddled, ready for the produce display; cake recipes were perfected for the baking competition; and bric-a-brac was gathered for the annual jumble sale. Weather apps were checked regularly in the run-up to the event, and to everyone's relief, the day of the fete dawned fine and sunny.

The activities began with a parade of decorated floats, starting at St Luke's church. People of all ages joined the procession as it wound its way through the main village street. Among the crowd were Violet and Matthew, who tagged along as the floats headed down Brook Lane towards the village hall and the school.

As the procession entered the playing field, a brass band struck up a lively rendition of *Congratulations*, and the stall holders took that as their cue to open for business. Dotted around the field were half a dozen fairground rides, a tombola stall that was raising funds to repair the church roof, a Mr Whippy ice-cream van, and a hot dog stand. At the far end of the field was a temporary stage, on which a local band from Bakewell would perform a country music set later on. There was also a show ring, which was gearing up for its first event – a canine contest in which Molly's Jack Russell, Alfie, was competing.

Hand in hand, Violet and Matthew checked out each of the stalls in turn. The sun was warm, and the air was filled with the smell of crushed grass, mixed with occasional wafts of fried onions from the hot dog stand. Friends and neighbours exchanged news, children ran around excitedly, and cheers of delight rang out from the splat-the-rat stall.

'It's on days like this that I remember why I moved to the countryside,' Violet said, as she paid for the Denby Pottery vase she'd selected from the bric-a-brac stall. 'Village fetes are such a quintessentially British thing to do, aren't they?'

'The fete's been a tradition in Merrywell for as long as I can remember,' Matthew said. 'These events are never hugely successful in terms of fund-raising, but they do lift community spirits. And let's face it, after what happened with the Spenbecks, we Merrywellians need something to cheer us up.'

Following the dramatic events at Bluebell Hill Garden Centre, there had been a last-minute change of sponsor for the fete. Judith Talbot had stepped in to officiate the opening ceremony, and the event was now being funded by the shopping village's Traders Association.

The garden centre was temporarily closed, and its future remained uncertain. Clayton had pleaded guilty, and was in prison awaiting a date for his sentencing hearing. Hilary's funeral had been a low-key affair in the end, despite the presence of the local press and a TV camera. There had been no wake afterwards, and neither Clayton nor Anne Burridge had attended the service – in fact, Anne hadn't been seen in Merrywell since the day of Clayton's reluctant confession. There was a rumour circulating that she was considering leaving the area altogether, to make a fresh start. Violet thought that would be a wise move.

'Look at Judith,' Matthew said. 'She's in her element.'

The council leader was clambering onto the stage, accompanied by the brass band's version of 'The Floral Dance'. Today, Judith had ditched her usual sombre clothing and was instead wearing a colourful, flowery dress and a flamboyant hat that would have been more appropriate at a wedding.

'I think she thinks she's the mayoress,' said Eric, who had sidled up to them as they waited for Judith's speech to begin.

'Hi Eric,' Violet said. 'Is Fiona not with you?'

'She'll be along in a minute. She's over at the coffee van at the mo, checking there are no teething problems. Sophie's more than capable of running it on her own, but you know what Fiona's like.'

A couple of weeks earlier, the Nashes had invested in a vintage mobile coffee truck, which they planned to take out to local events and food fairs, as a way to generate extra income and spread the word about *Books, Bakes and Cakes*. In theory, Sophie had been given full responsibility for arranging bookings and managing the truck, but it was still early days, and Fiona was staying close at hand in case she was needed.

As Judith reached centre stage, she gave a 'royal wave' to the crowd and waited for someone to adjust the height of the mike, so that she could deliver her speech without craning her neck.

Fiona arrived in the nick of time.

'Sorry I'm late,' she whispered, sounding slightly out of puff. 'Problems with the steam wand, but it's all sorted now.'

Violet smiled, hoping that the 'steam wand' was something to do with the coffee machine and not a euphemism.

'Also,' Fiona said, 'I was waylaid by Roy Geldard on my way over here. He's given me an update on Simon, but I'll wait until Judith's finished before I tell you about it. She'll shoot daggers at me if she catches me talking during her big moment.'

Judith gave a fractionally too-long, but nevertheless excellent speech, and when it was over, Violet, Matthew, Fiona and Eric wandered over to the splat-the-rat stall.

'Roy told me that Simon's received an official warning from the police,' Fiona said, as Matthew and Eric attempted to splat the beanbag rats as they were dropped down a makeshift drainpipe. 'However, he won't be charged for assaulting Hilary, because he was acting in self-defence. I'm afraid Roy didn't get off quite so lightly. After his false confession, he's been fined for wasting police time, or perverting the course of justice . . . something like that. Serves him right, I suppose.'

'I'm guessing he won't be able to sell his land and barn either, now that the garden centre's closed,' Violet said.

'Actually, I've got some news about that as well,' Fiona said. 'The garden centre's been put on the market and they've already had a lot of interest. A guy from Sheffield's been to see it, and he called in at the BBC after his visit. He's thinking about putting in a bid and, if he's successful, he wants me to supply the tearoom with bread and cakes.'

'That's brilliant news,' Violet said.

'Yes, all being well, I'll be one of the tearoom's suppliers, rather than its competitor,' Fiona said. 'You're right about the Geldards' land and barn though – the sale's fallen through – although it sounds like the Geldards are hoping to turn that to their advantage.'

'How so?'

'Simon's keen to go ahead with some of the things that Hilary was planning to do. He's spent the last week ploughing one of the fields, ready to plant pumpkins, and if everything goes well, they'll be holding a pumpkin picking event for Halloween. Plus, Simon wants to use some of the money his mum left him to renovate the barn and turn it into a venue for events.'

Violet thought that would be a much more sensible way for Simon to spend his inheritance.

'Hilary's vision will come to fruition after all then?' she said.

'Do you think Simon will get his act together . . . now that he has a project of his own to look after? I do hope so – for his sake, and for Roy's.'

'Me too,' Fiona said. 'Simon needs to realise how lucky he is. It's not everyone who gets a second chance.'

'Very true,' said Violet. 'Only a fool would pass up the opportunity to make a fresh start.'

Matthew had splatted so successfully he had won a prize.

'In these situations, I believe it's traditional to present the spoils of victory to your sweetheart,' he said, as – with an exaggerated flourish – he handed his prize to Violet. 'There you go; don't say I never give you anything.'

Violet gave a snort of laughter. 'How romantic! A toy rat. Just what I've always wanted. I hope you won't be offended if I give it to the cat?'

'I'll forgive you, providing you buy me a 99 from the ice-cream van.'

'We're going to head off,' Eric said, pointing in the opposite direction. 'Fiona wants to go and check on Sophie again, see if she needs any help. We'll see you later.'

As the Nashes marched towards the coffee truck, Violet and Matthew wandered over to the Mr Whippy van. As they passed the show ring, they spotted Molly. She was shouting to them, jumping up and down excitedly and waving something in the air.

'Alfie won a rosette,' she said.

'Really?' Violet knew that Molly had entered Alfie in the obedience competition, but she hadn't expected the mischievous Jack Russell to win anything.

'Yes,' Molly replied, sounding immensely proud of her pet. 'Cutest dog category. First prize.'

Violet laughed and gave a thumbs-up.

'Are you happy?' Matthew asked, as they joined the queue for ice-creams.

'Yes,' she said. 'Are you?'

'I always am, when I'm with you.'

Over on the other side of the playing field, Violet caught a glimpse of Simon Geldard. His arm was draped across the shoulders of a girl she didn't recognise, and he was laughing. Violet hoped he would be OK, and that he would make the most of his second chance, just as she intended to make the most of hers.

Murder in Merrywell

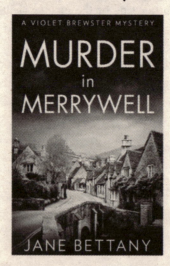

Welcome to Merrywell. Population: small. Secrets: aplenty.

Ex-journalist **Violet Brewster** is keen to make a good first impression in her new community, having just moved to the small village of Merrywell. When Violet hears about the mystery of Helen Slingsby, who disappeared from the village forty years earlier, she decides to help uncover what happened. But despite Violet's best efforts, she can find no trace of the missing woman.

As Violet talks to the other residents, it becomes apparent that something sinister is lurking beneath the village's idyllic exterior.

When a villager is found dead in their home, Violet becomes convinced that the murder is connected to Helen. Did Helen ever really leave Merrywell? Who in the village is hiding something? And can Violet finally solve this forty-year-old mystery before someone else gets hurt?

Murder at the Book Festival

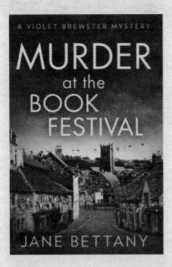

When a body is found at the Merrywell Book Festival, amateur sleuth **Violet Brewster** must leave no page unturned to solve the mystery . . .

The small and idyllic village of Merrywell is getting ready to host its first ever book festival, and Violet Brewster is delighted when she is asked to interview the star author.

Leonie Stanwick, now a bestselling romance author, is the featured guest of the festival. She was born in Merrywell, but abruptly left when she was 18 years old and never came back.

But the festival takes a dark turn when Leonie is found murdered; her return to the village had clearly shaken someone up. When a shocking secret about Leonie's past is revealed, Violet's suspicions must turn to her own neighbours. Who in the village was intent on making sure Leonie could never leave the village again?

Murder at Maple Grange

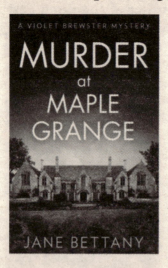

Maple Grange is the perfect place to retire for the residents of Merrywell. But when a murder investigation unfolds on its grounds, **Violet Brewster** must dust off her sleuthing skills once again!

Violet Brewster has just finished a project at local retirement village Maple Grange, when she learns that one of the residents, Phyllis Gibson, has passed away suddenly.

Violet is surprised that Phyllis left her a beautiful jewellery box in her will. When she goes to collect it, Maureen Bond, Phyllis's best friend, tells Violet that Phyllis had become paranoid during her last days, and was convinced that someone was trying to kill her.

When Maureen is pushed off her balcony, it becomes clear that something ominous is happening at Maple Grange. Violet is certain that the clues lie within the jewellery box. As the dangerous occurrences continue, can Violet unlock its contents and uncover the killer, before someone else gets hurt?

Don't miss the third book in the Violet Brewster Mystery series, perfect for fans of Clare Chase and Fiona Leitch! These books can be read as part of a series or as standalones.

Acknowledgements

Huge thanks to everyone involved in editing, book production and sales at HQ Publishing, especially my wonderful editor, Sophia Allistone – whose perceptive feedback and ideas have been invaluable. Thanks, Sophia. I am truly grateful for all of your hard work and support.

I am also enormously grateful to those of you who continue to read and review my books. You are the people I keep in mind as I write, and I hope this latest novel meets with your approval.

The ongoing support and encouragement of friends, family and fellow authors means a lot to me and is much appreciated. Special love and thanks go to my sister, Dawn, who continues to champion my books at every opportunity.

I've had great fun writing a murder mystery set in a garden centre. I love shopping for flowers and plants almost as much as I enjoy visiting tearooms (although I'm not a fan of stale scones or mice, so I'll probably give *The Cuckoo's Boot* a miss!). Whenever we visit a garden centre, my husband heads off to find what he calls 'the dead and dying section' – by which he means the scraggly, moribund plants that someone has forgotten to water. They are usually tucked away in a corner somewhere, and heavily reduced in price. Howard loves a bargain, but the main reason he buys these plants is to give them a second chance. He takes them home, waters them, and pots them on – and is rewarded handsomely for his efforts. Thank you for being such a kind, nurturing person, Howard. I love being married to someone who can make things bloom!

Thank you again for reading *Murder on Bluebell Hill* and reconnecting with Violet Brewster.

If you'd like to know what the future has in store for Violet, be sure to follow me on social media or visit my website for updates.

Website: janebettany.co.uk
Facebook: facebook.com/JaneBettanyAuthor
Instagram: Instagram.com/bettanyjane
Threads: threads.net/@bettanyjane

Dear Reader,

We hope you enjoyed reading this book. If you did, we'd be so appreciative if you left a review. It really helps us and the author to bring more books like this to you.

Here at HQ Digital we are dedicated to publishing fiction that will keep you turning the pages into the early hours. Don't want to miss a thing? To find out more about our books, promotions, discover exclusive content and enter competitions you can keep in touch in the following ways:

JOIN OUR COMMUNITY:

Sign up to our new email newsletter: http://smarturl.it/SignUpHQ

Read our new blog www.hqstories.co.uk

𝕏 https://twitter.com/HQStories

𝕗 www.facebook.com/HQStories

BUDDING WRITER?

We're also looking for authors to join the HQ Digital family!
Find out more here:

https://www.hqstories.co.uk/want-to-write-for-us/

Thanks for reading, from the HQ Digital team